THE B[...]

by

FAITH EDEN

CHIMERA

The Bridle Path first published in 2000 by
Chimera Publishing Ltd
PO Box 152
Waterlooville
Hants
PO8 9FS

Printed and bound in Great Britain by
Omnia Books Limited,
Glasgow

THE BRIDLE PATH

Faith Eden

This novel is fiction – in real life practice safe sex

By the same author:

INNOCENT CORINNA

One

The caravan was small: three wagons, ten pack horses and four outriders, all of whom seemed disinterested in either road or surrounding hillsides, their world confined by the cloud of thick dust that accompanied the short procession's laboured progress. To the two watchers, hidden amidst the rare outcrop of trees atop the ridge, their lack of alertness could mean only one thing.

'Probably salt,' said Jorkan of Karli, a sparse framed, heavily bearded fellow, whose rough breeches and thick leather tabard betrayed all the signs of many weeks upon the road. His companion, younger and fairer of skin, nodded.

'They have come from the right direction,' he agreed. He turned to face west and raised one hand, shading his eyes from the steadily dipping sun. 'They will only just make the river crossing by nightfall,' he calculated, 'so they will have to camp again this night.' The older man grunted and wiped the back of his hand across his dry mouth.

'As they have camped these many nights, Paulis,' he said. 'Such caravanners have no spare silver for lodgings, believe me.'

'Then perhaps—'

'Perhaps nothing, my young friend,' Jorkan snapped. 'Look closer down there and tell me what it is you see. Three wagons, each with two wagoneers, four horsemen also, as many men as you have toes and we are but two thumbs to oppose them. Do you seriously think it is worth such odds in order to steal a few sacks of salt?'

'But they must have other goods in those wagons,' Paulis

protested. 'Some silks, maybe, or perhaps still a few slave women.' Jorkan snorted again and wheeled his mount around.

'Slave women?' he echoed. 'I somehow think not. The day is late and the horses will be tired. If they had slaves in those wagons, by now they would be walking, saving the strength of the horses until they make camp. Besides,' he added, spurring his horse into a walk, 'what would you do with slave women, beyond the obvious?

'The laws of Illeum, even here near the borders, are strict on such matters. Without the correct bills of sale and pedigree, anyone found attempting to sell slaves is liable to arrest on the spot. The punishment for such an offence is also harsh beyond the possible rewards for the risks involved, unless, that is, you fancy yourself as a lifetime slave, perhaps even as a eunuch in the house of some fat merchant?'

Captain Niti Ingrim surveyed the thirty or so blue and gold clad bodies that his men had lined up alongside the trail and allowed himself a small smile of satisfaction. The ambush had been perfectly timed and staged, the small detachment of Illeum soldiers not expecting any trouble this far from the border. Ingrim's force had fallen upon them and slain more than half their number with arrows before they had time to react, and the outcome had never been in any doubt.

Even more pleasing, from Ingrim's point of view, was that there had been no casualties among his men, a better result than he could have dared forecast. He looked across to where his second-in-command, Sergeant Orfal, was supervising the clearing up operation, and raised his arm. Orfal, seeing the summons, left what he was doing and came dutifully trotting at the double.

'How many uniforms?' Ingrim demanded. Orfal hesitated, tallying on his fingers.

'Fourteen unmarked, sir,' he said, at last, 'plus six or seven more that can be sewn or patched. The remaining half dozen are too badly bloodstained, I'm afraid.'

'That will do,' Ingrim said. 'There are the four counterfeit tabards that the decoys wore and another six in our wagon. Have you checked their carts yet? I expect you will find spare clothing there, too.'

'I'll see to it immediately, sir,' Orfal barked. 'And the bodies?'

'Have a detail take them deep into the woods and bury them well,' Ingrim ordered. 'Tell them to use all the lime. We don't want some hunter's dog scrabbling about until we are well away from here.'

'No sir,' Orfal agreed. 'I'll see to it personally. And do we start changing into the uniforms now?' Orfal, like Ingrim and the rest of their party, was dressed in the clothing of a civilian traveller, only his bearing and language betraying his military status.

'Not yet, sergeant,' he replied. 'We are still too far west and could easily come across one of the local garrison squadrons. This relief detachment, especially the officers, could well be known to the local troops, so it would be safer to wait. When you have seen to the burial party, come back and bring your map with you.

'My plan is for us to split up into several smaller parties and rendezvous a few miles from the castle itself. Varragol is so far removed from the rest of Illeum that they won't know whom to expect. The uniforms will be all they worry about and even some of your lads' accents won't trouble them. So many of the outlying garrisons are recruited from outside Illeum itself – why should one more small detachment be any different?'

'Aye, captain,' Orfal grinned. 'We'll be in among 'em before they have time to realise their mistake.'

Ingrim smiled back. 'All in good time, sergeant,' he replied.

'But make sure that none of these cut-throats moves before I give the word. We may have to bide our time there for a day or two, just until we have the lie of the land. If our man turns out not to be there, that this is some kind of hoax after all, then bloodshed would be pointless. All we should do then is to alert the area to our presence.'

'Aye, sir,' Orfal said. 'I'll make sure they all know the situation.'

'They'd better,' Ingrim snapped. 'I'll personally disembowel the first man who fucks up and castrate you into the bargain, understood?' Orfal, his weathered features inscrutable, raised his right arm to his shoulder in salute.

'Understood, sir.'

The girl was barely out of her teens, though her body was developed to a ripe maturity, shoulders and thighs nicely muscled and with a slender, flat waist. The ropes that bound her wrists and held them upstretched to the two iron rings near the ceiling forced her onto tiptoe, further enhancing the length of her lower limbs, though the continued discomfort of her position did little to improve the shape of her features, which remained twisted in pain, eyes hollow with fear.

Silently, she stared back at her captors, knowing that any pleas for clemency would be wasted and that any sounds that demonstrated either her fear or her agony would serve only to add to their evident enjoyment of her helplessness and their power over her.

The two men were as chalk and cheese: the older silver-haired, fat, swathed in voluminous silken robes that seemed to mirror the rolls of fat about his jowls and eyes, whilst the younger fellow was black-haired, muscular, fit and, if the circumstances had been different, even handsome, with the swarthy looks of a native of Colrasia, that southern continent that remained largely the source of myth and mystery, save for those few travellers and traders that periodically appeared in the northern, civilised world.

His garb was that of either a hunter or, in his particular case, that of the typical overseer: leather breeches and jerkin, woollen shirt, high boots with heavy soles and with heavy, studded bands about wrists and neck, such that offered protection against teeth, thorns, horns, or even knives. His dark eyes were expressionless, but ever alert, and the girl could see that he missed nothing, as he had not missed her hiding place among the riverside bushes the previous evening.

The third member of the trio was female, not quite as tall as the younger man, but tall nonetheless for a woman, and made even taller by the elevated heels of her long boots. In age she was somewhere between the two men – perhaps forty, the girl guessed – but no less fit looking than the hunter fellow and possibly as strong, for her shoulders, upper arms and thighs were the equal in girth of his and, but for the burgeoning breasts and flaring hips, could have leant her a masculine look that her cropped red hair did little to ameliorate.

Her name, as the girl had discovered upon her original arrival in this house, was Bextra, and she was the penultimate arbiter regarding the fate of the slaves of Daskot Mennim, the fat, pig-eyed obscenity who now viewed Demila's – for that was the hanging girl's name – predicament. The same Daskot who had taken her to his bed upon her arrival here and performed such obscenities upon her young and innocent body.

'You have done well, Master Pecon,' Daskot smirked. The bounty hunter nodded, saying nothing, a man of few words. 'As ever, you have wasted little time in earning your fee. Five silver telts, I believe?'

'Ten,' Pecon said, unblinking. Daskot's liquid features oozed into an obsequious smile.

'Ten for the slave's return,' he said, 'less five for the

enjoyment of such delicious woman flesh, unless you would have me believe that you made no use of her last night?'

'Ten,' Pecon repeated. He half turned, regarding the merchant out of the corner of one eye. 'Whether she was used, or not, is of no weight in this matter. She is, and was, no virgin.'

'And if you've left the slut with child?' Daskot snapped. 'What then, my friend, eh? Who will bear that cost?'

Pecon raised one eyebrow slightly. 'I venture not you, milord,' he retorted. 'Not unless it is possible to rear a child from infancy to adulthood for less than the five telts you seek to charge me as insurance against such an event. More likely you would have the brat drowned at birth, if I am any judge.'

'You go too far, Pecon!' Daskot shrilled. 'Have a care with that pagan tongue—'

The younger man whirled upon him and, before the fat merchant could move, seized him about the throat, callused fingers embedding themselves amidst the folds of fat and cutting off Daskot's air supply with brutal efficiency. The older man squealed, his mouth flapping open, as his feet were all but lifted clear of the stone floor.

'I would rather have a pagan tongue in my head than no tongue at all,' Pecon growled. His free hand now held a wickedly curved knife, that had appeared in its grasp as if by sorcery. Daskot's eyes rolled, his tongue lolling between his lips. 'Pay me my ten telts, you wobbling heap of thievery, else I'll give you the chance to test the accuracy of my judgement!'

He relaxed his grip and let the merchant drop back, staggering until Daskot came up against a side wall, where he stood, gasping to restore air to lungs that struggled at the best of times. The blade in Pecon's hand twirled, glinting in the lantern light, and slid back into the scabbard at his belt, but the point had been well made.

10

'Here,' Daskot panted, reaching within the skirt of draperies within which he perpetually dwelled, pulling out a small leather purse. He held it out at arm's length, his other hand exploring his neck, as if unable to believe that the bones and blood vessels there were still intact. 'Here,' he repeated, 'take your money and be gone.'

A hand shot out and the purse was snatched away, but the bounty hunter made no move to leave. Instead, as he tucked the purse within the larger pouch that hung from the opposite side of his belt to that from which he had drawn the knife, he simply turned back to look once more at Demila.

'I shall count this before I do go,' he said, 'but meantime, I have a fancy to study Mistress Bextra at work. I presume the girl is to be treated in the usual fashion reserved for runaways in these parts?'

Bextra, who had made no move to interfere and protect her employer, now looked towards him for guidance. Daskot hesitated, the fear in his eyes now given way to anger, but it was clear he had no wish for another demonstration of Pecon's power. Sullenly, he nodded and turned towards the door that led up into the main house above.

The dust of the summer evening smelled sweet-sour on the gentle breeze, reaching into the innermost nasal passages with a touch that lulled the senses and spoke of promises of balmy mornings and weeks of dry weather to come. Lady Corinna of Illeum, seated behind the gauze curtain that screened her from potentially prying eyes in the market arena below the small private gallery, sniffed gently, wiped her top lip discreetly with the back of one slender hand, and turned to her tanned male companion.

'Barbaric,' she said, softly, nodding downwards in the direction of the coffle of female slaves who currently occupied the centre of the sand-strewn oval. 'The entire process is simply barbaric.'

The Lord Savatch half turned, eyes narrowing, the ghost of a smile playing across his thin lips. 'Do I sense just the slightest tinge of something in those words, my pet?' he ventured. Corinna stiffened, flicking back her blonde tresses, and exhaled a tempered snort.

'No,' she said, simply, 'not in the least. And only a male could possibly not understand the difference of feelings in this that I say. Look at the poor creatures down there, for the sake of all that is sacred.' She jabbed a finger in the direction of the tableau below their vantage point.

'Who are they?' she demanded. 'What are they? Where have they come from and what have they done in this life to deserve *that*? Unless you have been where they are now, how could you possibly hope to understand?' She drew in a deep breath and the sigh that followed was pregnant with exasperation.

'The difference to which I refer, my beloved *master*,' she continued, at length, 'is that as between rock and water. To play-act a ritual, even a ritual based upon reality, is something far removed from the reality itself.' She pursed her lips, considering her next words with care.

'There is,' she said, 'a chasm between the wish to surrender and the demand to surrender, a gulf between what one desires and can achieve and that which is totally beyond one's ability to control, as there is a lifetime of difference between the lash applied lovingly, knowingly, and the whip brandished simply as a means of control by one barbarian over an alleged other.'

Savatch turned back, affecting an interest in the proceedings beneath them, considering his young wife's remarks. For a full minute there was a silence between them and, when he finally spoke, it was with carefully weighed words.

'I think,' he said, 'that my beloved princess has perhaps

12

lost sight of certain elements. This world is far from perfect, as I, of all people, know only too well, yet 'tis the only world we have. Castes, classes – we make them not, for the bounds were set long before we first walked this earth, but they are there and each has its rules, its boundaries, its benefits and its pitfalls.'

'So, the rules were not made by us,' Corinna snapped, 'but should that mean we ought not to seek to rewrite them?'

'Should we seek to rewrite history, then?'

'History is that which is already written.' Corinna shook her head, the trace of a smile flitting across her taut lips. 'It is the future to which we should look, my beloved lord.' She stood, turning away from the scene, sweeping her flowing robe about her long legs, her fingers clutching at the silky fabric. 'The past,' she said, her voice little more than a whisper, 'cannot be changed, but it should be remembered and put to good use, for the present is but the history of the future.

'The chains, the whips, the slave hoods, all those will I remember until my dying breath, as also I shall remember those moments when I gladly surrendered to the instincts that they – and you – unearthed. But also shall I never forget those other, those most awful hours, those hours when…' Her voice tailed off and she stood silent, staring at the blank wall that formed the back of the small observation box. Savatch took two paces towards her, reaching out a hand that caressed her bare shoulder.

'I know,' he said, sombrely. 'And I think I understand.'

'Maybe,' Corinna said. 'And then again, maybe not.' She took his hand and drew it around in front of her, placing the wide palm beneath her full breast. 'Maybe if you had but a single week bearing such as these,' she said quietly, 'then might you just begin a voyage of comprehension.

'Were it not for my own birthright, I might even now be as those poor creatures are below,' she continued. 'Whilst men rule, and rule as their forefathers have done before them, little will change. A few women may still tear themselves a fragmented corner of humanity and a few more, such as myself, may be spared man's worst excesses in the name of nobility, but for most of my sisters there is little in this world for which to be grateful.'

'Then we should, perhaps, be grateful for what there is,' Savatch suggested. His free hand had inched about Corinna's hip, the fingers now pressing against the inside of her thigh through the flimsy fabric of her gown. Automatically, Corinna pressed backwards, feeling the swelling of his groin as it pressed against her soft buttocks.

'You are sometimes little more than the animal I first thought you,' she muttered, but made no move to resist as his hand probed deeper between her thighs.

'An animal that I think you would never seek to tame,' Savatch whispered, his mouth nuzzling against her ear. 'Rather, I think, you still yearn for this animal to bring out and tame the animal within you.'

'Your skill with the whip is unsurpassed, my lord,' Corinna snickered, her eyelids drooping, the slaves in the courtyard below now forgotten. 'And bettered,' she added, dreamily, 'only by your skill with your rod!'

Paulis prised a fragment of stone from the hard baked earth and, without rising from his sitting position, sent it skimming across the yellowing grass slope. The rough pebble bounced three, four times and clattered into the projecting rock that had been its intended target. However, far from triumphant at this hit, Paulis remained sour-faced.

'How much longer are we just going to sit around here?' he complained. 'This is nearly two days now and all we have seen are salt caravans. Apart from those two fat merchants this morning,' he added, accusingly. 'They would have been

14

easy pickings, for sure.'

'Quite probably,' Jorkan conceded, 'though they may have had more beneath their robes than you suspect, my young friend. The addition of meat to the bones does not always mean that the bones themselves are any the weaker.'

'A swift arrow or two would soon have settled their flab, no matter what bones it hung on,' Paulis persisted. Jorkan sighed and climbed down from the flat stone on which he had been sitting.

'Save your arrows, Paulis,' he said. 'And we shall soon be away from this forsaken road. I promised you rich pickings and rich pickings we shall have, but not from common robbery. If it's rich victims we sought, then the northern road would have been far more fruitful. This route is seldom travelled by much other than the salters, as you have seen for yourself.'

'Then why do we remain here?' Paulis complained. 'I have sat here and watched sun and dust and when we were presented with an opportunity, you had us spurn it.'

Jorkan moved down behind Paulis and laid a hand on the younger man's shoulder. 'We wait here for the chance of a far greater opportunity, lad,' he said. 'And our prize itself is not to be found on this road, merely the pointer to where it is to be found.'

'You speak in riddles, you old fox,' Paulis muttered. 'Perhaps you should explain in words that this poor simpleton might comprehend, for I am convinced there is much you have yet to tell me. I have put my trust in you, uncle, so should I expect less than that you should place yours in me?'

Jorkan settled himself onto the rough grass and sighed. 'Indeed not,' he said. 'You are right and you have the right to know.' He pursed his lips, his right eye twitching and pointed east, to where the road disappeared among the nearest foothills.

'We await a messenger, Paulis,' he said, quietly. 'This

messenger will bring instructions for a quest, which, if we undertake and complete, will pay far better than any couple of fat merchants we might find in these forsaken parts.'

'And do you know the nature of this quest?'

Jorkan nodded. 'Some of it,' he said. 'I know only that a certain party is prepared to pay handsomely for the death of another certain party and more, still, if we could place another certain party into their hands.'

'And the identity of these "certain parties", uncle?'

'That is why we wait here,' Jorkan replied. 'I was told nothing more than that which I have told you now, other than that we would be met on this road and given the information we require. I suspect that our would-be patron, whoever he might be, would wish to lay a crooked trail between us and himself.'

'It sounds, also, as if this might not be the first time you have undertaken such work,' Paulis said. He looked across, fixing Jorkan with a strange glare. 'The tales you brought back of your exploits along the caravan trails were maybe not as our family was always led to believe, I think?'

Jorkan smiled ruefully and nodded. 'Aye, lad,' he grunted. 'But then, there are certain matters that are better left untold. A common bandit draws little attention in most parts, as you know.'

'Whereas, a paid assassin…'

'Is best left unsung,' Jorkan finished. 'Those that would pay for my services pay for more than a swift arrow and a sharp-edged blade. Still tongues are essential and loose tongues would soon be stilled if their wagging draft stirred the wrong ears.'

'The man we are to kill,' Paulis said, 'will travel this road?'

'Maybe,' Jorkan said, 'but then again, I doubt it. As I said, I do not know the details yet, any more than you do, but I suspect that he will not only not travel this road, but that he will be found many miles from it. Not for nothing have we been sent out here to meet with our herald. Our real work will take place in a far different setting, I think.'

It had been a long and painful afternoon for Demila. Bextra was an established mistress of her profession, typical of those women who sought employment as slave handlers in the houses of the wealthy. Not only the equal of most men in strength, but more than their equal when it came to showing little or no compassion to their charges, treating them as if they were little more than livestock on a country farm, animals to be used, disciplined and reared only for their value to their owners.

As a recaptured runaway, Demila knew well enough that the treatment she had received originally at the woman's hands would pale into insignificance now, for she had heard the stories from those girls with whom she had shared the cages at the market and seen, too, the two former escapees that had been offered for resale on the day Daskot had purchased her.

Now, as the expressionless Pecon looked on, the woman set about her work with a relish that was all too evident. She began with Demila's waist-length black hair, seizing and twisting it into a long tail with one hand and shearing it off close to her scalp with the other, leaving only a ragged stubble, which in turn was quickly lathered and shaved.

'You'll need no hair where you're going,' she snarled, as Demila whimpered in fear of the flashing razor. 'You'll be sold on as a field hand, or maybe a stable girl, and the less hair to matte with mud and dung, the better. We'll have these off, too,' she added, jabbing a finger at one of Demila's eyebrows.

The trader who had bought Demila from the men responsible for her original abduction from her home village in Erisvaal had previously shaven what had been a thick bush of pubic hair, and the few wisps that had since re-grown now also fell prey to Bextra's ministrations, so that when she finally dropped the razor back into the earthenware bowl, not a single hair was left on Demila's body, save for her eyelashes.

'I always think there is something quite pleasing about them when they are reduced to this, don't you?' Bextra laughed. Pecon said nothing still, but the corners of his thin mouth twitched upwards slightly. 'Perhaps you would care for another sample of her?' she added. 'Once I have finished with her, that is. Or maybe you would like to stripe her back and arse, as compensation for my master's apparent lack of appreciation?'

'I always think it a pity to mar unblemished flesh,' Pecon said. 'There are other punishments without reverting to the lash, or is your homeland of Mesarium still locked in the dark ages?'

'Indeed not!' Bextra snapped, her eyes flashing. 'I could find a hundred penances for this stupid girl, but my master has given me his instructions and I must carry them out.'

'Even though you would rather find a far more subtle use for such a dark peach, eh?' Pecon said. Bextra drew back her shoulders and lifted her chin in defiance.

'My master's observations concerning your tongue are well made,' she retorted. 'The art of diplomacy must be little considered in *your* homeland.'

Pecon's mouth curved into a full smile, though the expression fell short of reaching his eyes. 'My father,' he said slowly, 'taught me it were best to say what was in one's mind than to piggle with fine words that mean nothing and you, lady, are no better and no worse than many others in your trade. Tell me now that you have never taken any of your soft-titted charges to your own bed and I will take you at your word, if'n you swear it on the Wind Goddess that your people hold in such reverence. If not, then hold your own

18

tongue and pierce this wench's, along with the rest of her.'

Bextra bridled still, but, as she regarded the tall bounty hunter, she quickly recovered her usual detachment and returned his smile, revealing two rows of even white teeth, even save for the two long incisors that seemed more pointed and pronounced than would be considered normal.

'It would seem that you have read me better than I supposed,' she said, deliberately lightening her tone, 'but, in my country, the love of one woman for another is considered to be more pure than that of woman for man. Besides,' she added, patting her flat and strongly muscled stomach, 'there is then no chance of getting a belly full of small limbs.'

'So, you have never known a man, eh?' Pecon said.

Bextra's smiled contracted to a wicked grin. 'I never said as much, sir,' she said, looking and sounding almost coy now.

'But you have your preference,' Pecon suggested.

The grin on her face remained. 'On cold days I prefer soup,' she said, 'whereas, on hot days I might prefer iced wine.'

Pecon studied her, approving her statuesque physique and the brief garments that did little to conceal it. 'And what would today be?' he smirked. 'Do the winds blow hot, or cold?'

'That, sir,' Bextra reposted, 'is yet to be determined. First things first and this thing,' she added, nodding towards the limp form hanging from the wall, 'is first, or I am falling down in my duties.'

'Indeed,' Pecon agreed. 'One must earn one's silver, before one can spend it. But forget the lash for this one. Ring her teats and her clit, plus her nose, and then hood and cuff her.'

'But Master Daskot—'

'Is a greedy, fat, lazy old bastard,' Pecon interrupted her. 'And if I offer him thirty silver telts for this wench, he'll take it gladly. He'll do well if she makes that much at market and it'll cost him three of those pieces for the auctioneer's book.'

'Thirty telts for *this*?' Bextra echoed in astonishment. 'The market price for field women is only twenty-five this summer, surely you would know that?'

'The market price for a field hand, back scarred and welted, cunnie stitched and clit cut, yes,' Pecon agreed. 'Such a creature has then only one use and I think we would both agree that would be a waste here.'

'Then why not offer Daskot the bare twenty-five telts?'

'Because I choose not to,' Pecon said. He took a step closer to Demila, who was now watching him carefully through half closed eyes. 'And because, if I did, he would take great delight in refusing my offer anyway, as his way of repaying me for earlier. Whereas, the prospect of the extra five telts will be irresistible to someone who would seek to risk his own hide in order to cheat me of that very sum.

'And, if that thought sits uncomfortably with you, lady,' he added, 'then you can simply forget to account to me for the slave hood and cuffs you will supply with her. The two telts they would fetch can be yours instead. Call it your own commission, if you like.'

'Perhaps,' Bextra said slyly, one hand resting lightly across her lower stomach, 'I would prefer to take my commission by other means.'

'Then take it that way too,' Pecon laughed. 'I am sure you are worth easily double whatever that fat charlatan pays you.'

'Easily,' Bextra said, and turned to pick up the tray on which her piercing needles and the small brass rings lay waiting.

The Lady Dorothea carefully closed the heavy ledger and lifted it onto the lower shelf of the three that sat in the alcove alongside the wide fireplace.

'It has been a very profitable year, Agana,' she said. Dorothea herself was tall, but her black-skinned companion was almost a head taller, her high boots and erect posture adding further to the impression of height and power, the coiled whip that hung from the broad belt about her waist simply a badge of her authority at most times, for her mere presence was enough to cow even the most rebellious slave.

'Indeed, lady,' she murmured, her brown eyes flicking about the room. 'By my own count, I make it that we have shipped on more than ten score girl slaves and four score boys.'

'And you disapprove of my keeping the dozen or so of each that I have selected from our traffic, eh?' Dorothea rejoined. 'No, don't deny it, Agana, for I know you too well.'

'It is only that it means extra mouths to feed, lady,' Agana said, 'and the household already has what many would consider a sufficiency of pleasure slaves. Some extra field hands, maybe, but...'

'You make a good point,' Dorothea replied. 'Give instructions to the regular traders that they can bring us back a few sturdy specimens on their return trips. Tell them I shall offer one pleasure girl for every two suitable for field work, even if they be former runaways. I presume you will have no trouble ensuring that their spirits remain broken?'

'None at all,' Agana said. 'But why bother with runaways? The trader Halik had six perfectly suitable slaves in his last caravan and his prices are lower than any you could expect to pay for anything coming back from the cities.'

'But they were all males, Agana,' Dorothea pointed out, 'and I have always felt it is a mistake to use the sort of male slaves who are suitable for field work. I have forty or more guards here in this castle and we are some days away from their nearest source of pleasure, so why reduce their options here, eh?

'A few sturdy field women will make them good sport and maybe keep them from impregnating the girls within the household. How many have needed the doctor's attentions this past year, eh? Not to mention how many of my pretty boy slaves have spent half their days unable to sit down

21

comfortably.

'No, Agana, I think a few cheap runaways will help our situation in more than one way. You can tell Halik that we will still be in the market for fresh field slaves from the east, but not males.'

Agana nodded. 'As you wish, lady,' she assented.

'And now,' Dorothea continued, signifying that the discussion was at an end, 'how is our special slave progressing?'

'Snow in summer – how this reminds me of home.' The speaker, Vala Valkyr Kirislanna Friggitsdottir, more usually known as Alanna, turned in her saddle and smiled back at her companion, the now red-haired Jekka, who rode a half-length to her right and rear. Jekka, like Alanna, was naturally white blonde, but when the need to disguise her Yslandic pedigree had led her to dye her hair the previous year – despite the fact that, in common with most of the females of her race she was considerably taller than six feet – the young warrior decided the change of colour was to her liking and had continued with it ever since.

Curiously, although the flame colour contrasted well against her pale skin, it was certainly no indication to her character, for Jekka's temperament was generally as placid and detached as it was possible to be. She even killed with an air of remoteness, preferably with one of her steadily growing collection of lethal gadgets, although in hand-to-hand combat she was as deadly as Alanna and any other of their warlike race.

'You know what reminds me of home?' she replied. 'No people, that's what. And why are there no people? I'll tell you why,' she went on. 'There are no people, because all there is is snow. Snow, snow and more snow. I never can understand why any of you get so nostalgic about snow when we are further south. Give me green hills and running streams every time.'

'Warm nights have much to be said for them,' Alanna agreed, 'but the cities of the south are too full of the people you seem to yearn for, and not the sort of people I care to spend too much time in such proximity with.'

'You prefer these wastelands?'

'At times, yes.' Alanna sat back in her saddle, her gaze travelling across the entire horizon. 'Unspoiled by the hand of man,' she sighed. 'True virginity.'

'On which subject you're suddenly the great expert, heh?' Jekka grinned.

Alanna ignored the quip. 'This is a little used trail,' she said, changing the subject. 'This snow has lain since the last fall, three days since, yet there are no tracks.'

Jekka shrugged and pointed ahead to the approaching line of peaks. 'Even from here it is obvious that there are only two passes,' she said, 'and the last snows probably blocked them. Had you thought of that, princess? What stops horses in one direction will stop them in the other. Or are we to sprout wings and fly over that range?'

'The two passes are seldom open,' Alanna said. 'We are so far north that the snows remain for most of the year, which is why this trail is so deserted and why I chose it as our route. The main route into the interior of the Snow Kingdoms lies forty leagues to the south, but this is a safer journey for us. Fewer eyes upon us, Jekka, and few tongues to wag.'

'I couldn't fault your reasoning on that score,' Jekka retorted, 'but that still doesn't answer my question. It's all very well travelling unobserved, but there is little point to any journey unless it can be completed.'

Alanna did not answer immediately. Instead, she reached inside her fur robe and withdrew a small cylinder of horn. Reining in her mount, she passed the container to her companion.

'Look inside,' she instructed. 'It is a chart copied from an original that few people have ever seen.'

Removing her mittens, Jekka inserted two slender fingers inside the cylinder and withdrew the roll of vellum it contained, spreading it across the neck of her mount and peering at the lines and symbols. Once or twice she raised her head to look along the tooth-like row of peaks that dominated the skyline ahead.

'It seems to be accurate enough,' she grunted, 'but then there is very little here to confuse a scribe. Snow, snow, mountains, snow – oh, and a river.' She jabbed a long fingernail at the dark line. 'That would be the great lump of ice we keep crossing, yes?'

'It would,' Alanna agreed. 'I am told that river is a river only for one tenth of the year. But look again, Jekka. See where it crosses the mountains ahead of us? See also where the scribe has marked the trails?'

Jekka pored over the little map once more.

'If the scale is accurate,' she said, 'then it crosses yonder peaks some four or five leagues to the south of this trail, yet I see no pass marked here, nor do I see one in reality.'

'Because there is no pass,' Alanna explained. 'The river, when it is a river, flows through a system of underground caverns. For most of the year, however, it is frozen, both before it goes underground and again when it emerges on this side. You may have noticed that the level of the ice we have crossed is far below the banks that contain it.

'Beneath the mountains themselves, there will be no level at all, neither water nor ice. Just a dry bed, along which we can ride with ease.' She raised her right arm and pointed ahead and a little to the right. 'When we next encounter the ice river, we simply follow its course.'

'And when we come out on the other side, what then? We

could spend a lifetime riding this wilderness in search of our quarry.'

'We could,' Alanna said, 'but there will be no need. Our quarry knows of this route, too. It is how they are able to ride and raid and flee back to safety without the Illeum patrols ever catching up with them, for the soldiers naturally patrol the borders by the southern trails.'

'But if the authorities in Illeum now know the truth, why not just move their patrols north and look here instead?'

'That would be far too simple for politicians,' Alanna laughed. 'Yet I can see their reasoning. Illeum soldiers moving deep into the Snow Kingdoms would be a breach of the treaties and these bandits would quickly use that to their advantage. Besides, once they have made use of the underground pass, they have a choice of many miles of border where they might cross. It would require three or four regiments of soldiers to have any chance of catching them.

'Which is why we are here, my dear Jekka. Two women, even Yslandic warrior women, can slip into the interior unnoticed, take care of this leader fellow and his chief cohorts and slip out again. And if we are detected and caught, then Illeum will deny all knowledge of us, naturally.'

'Naturally,' Jekka echoed, but her eyes twinkled humorously. 'Two renegade bitches out to steal themselves a few krones, eh?' She rolled the map, slid it back into its cylinder and returned it to Alanna. 'Well,' she said, pulling on her mittens once more, 'at least now I know where it is we're supposed to be going.'

'It doesn't usually bother you,' Alanna said. 'Only what we have to do once we get there.'

'Precisely,' Jekka said, 'so let's get there as quickly as possible. The sooner we get there, the sooner we can come back. Damned snow,' she muttered, spurring her horse forward again.

Agana M'gnaz regarded the figure of Fulgrim, the former Lord Fulgrim of the Vorsan States, and smiled the same grim smile of satisfaction and distaste that she had smiled every one of the previous three hundred and seventy-eight days since he had been given into her charge.

The fact that they had once been nominally allies – given that her mistress, Lady Dorothea, had been part of Fulgrim's original clandestine allegiance with Lord Willum, the Protector's stepbrother – no longer mattered to Agana. She had seen the horrors that this beast had inflicted, not only upon his captives, but eventually upon Dorothea and Agana too, and Agana had used the ensuing year to extract a horrific revenge.

Never again would Fulgrim fill an unsuspecting and reluctant womb with his seed, for Agana had long since removed his testicles. He could still achieve an erection, given sufficient stimulus, but there was little to drive where once there had been an insatiable lust, and such stimuli as he now received were calculated to arouse other sensations indeed.

Agana kept him in the dungeons almost without respite, allowing him exercise in the fresh air only once every ten days or so. In the meantime, collared, hobbled, nipples pierced and ringed like those of a common slave girl, his world was one of perpetual darkness, broken only by the lamplight that signified the return of Agana to exact her regular daily tribute. And the scars on his back, buttocks, thighs and shoulders bore testament to her methods of ensuring his compliance.

Today she had brought with her four of Dorothea's house slaves – two near emasculated pageboys and two maids, all clad in the identical pastel toga shifts and ornate sandals that were the household uniform preferred by Dorothea, and all with their faces and nails painted and powdered as their mistress decreed. Nearly all the prettified boys, like Fulgrim, no longer had testicles, but they, unlike the prisoner, were frequently encouraged to enjoy and exploit the natural urges that still beset them.

The maids needed even less urging, despite the ever ready supply of male members that would not risk an unwanted swollen belly before the year was out, for Agana, at Dorothea's behest, saw to it that there was always a great spirit of competition between the household girls.

On this particular morning, those slaves considered by Agana to have performed all their duties the most satisfactorily were to be given the reward that the black amazon had been offering for many months now. Fulgrim, the once mighty and spiteful warlord, now a quivering, pale-skinned slave with shaven head and heavy chains, would be made to perform a service for each of the four slaves in turn.

Usually, Agana forced him to employ mouth – lips and tongue – bringing each of her charges to orgasm in turn, though occasionally a more spirited girl would seek permission to bring him to a state whereby she might mount him. So successful had Agana's tactics been that she was even now considering the possibilities of extending these rituals, wondering how much encouragement from her whip would be needed in order for him to satisfy every one of Dorothea's thirty plus house girls, whilst perhaps in turn being used by each of the twenty house boys, most of whom now needed no second bidding, regardless of the orifice on offer or the sex of its owner.

However, on this occasion the black overseer had a new twist to introduce, for one of the female slaves she had brought with her was not chosen for the quality of her work, but rather for a perceived lack of total effort. And so she was to be punished, and in a way that Agana hoped would add even further to Fulgrim's frustration and misery. First, though, she decided to proceed with the usual round of spoils – she might not be able to use these stupid creatures to drain Fulgrim's balls, but she could certainly see to it that they drained much of whatever stamina was left to him…

Lady Dorothea of Varragol lay back among the thick pillows, stretching languidly, one hand idly tousling the curly head that was buried between her open thighs.

'Ah, Moxie my sweet,' she cooed, 'your little tongue grows more cunning by the day, I swear it. Oh!' She shivered, her fingers knotting into the buxom little maid's tresses. 'You little vixen,' she laughed, relaxing again, 'I should spank that rosy bottom for you.'

Moxie's face suddenly appeared above the thick bush of pubic hair. She was flushed, but her eyes sparkled and her full lips were curled into a smile. 'Does my rosy bottom displease my mistress that much?' she quipped.

Dorothea smiled back at her. 'Come up here, my little peach,' she said, patting the pillows beside her. 'Come let me suckle on those beautiful teats, for I would sleep now and those big bubbies are such a comfort.'

Moxie wriggled up the bed, her heavy breasts swaying as she moved, and Dorothea could hardly wait to take them in her hands. Already the nipples were wet with milk, the daily medication she received from Dorothea's personal physician ensuring the impressive melons lactated permanently. It made them tender to the touch and sometimes painful, but Moxie's comfort was secondary in her mistress's scheme of things. As long as there was a constant supply of the sweet nourishment, Dorothea was content and, so long as Dorothea was content, Moxie was happy.

The young maid, in reality a slave, sold to Dorothea by her innkeeper father, was well aware of the alternative lives available to the majority of young women. Even her former life, serving in her father's rundown tavern, had been nothing compared to the deprivations suffered by such as field workers, brothel slaves and worse. The castle palace at Varragol was a haven in comparison.

At least, she reflected, as Dorothea took her right nipple into her mouth and began suckling on it, it was a haven to those who remained in the mistress's favour. For some here, their existence could scarcely have been worse had they already been consigned to the seven halls of infinite purgatory.

Three centuries earlier, the first castle of Garassotta had been built as a bastion against the barbarous hordes that had then spread west and south from the lands known as the Snow Kingdoms, coming via an area of Illeum's northern neighbour, Sorabund, where mountains, thick forest and treacherous marshland meant a sparse population and an easy route for raiders.

The original keep and its eastern wall was now largely a ruin, but generations of the castle's owners had added the fortified palace, a formidable outer curtain, complete with high watchtowers and a deep moat fed by underground springs, little of which had been of any real relevance since long before Corinna's birth, for her father, Lord Lundt and his father before him, both hereditary Protectors of Illeum, had mounted punitive expeditions deep into the interior of the Snow Kingdoms, inflicting terrible casualties among the warrior tribes there.

Finally, the mountain chieftains had begged an armistice and the then young Lundt had personally negotiated a peace that had lasted now for more than a quarter of a century. By its terms, the hunter warriors of the eight known Kingdoms had received favoured trading status for the beautiful and often rare pelts that were now used in the making of the exquisite winter robes of all the noble and wealthy in Illeum, and few people under the age of thirty could now recall the last real trouble in the border regions.

A few renegade minor chieftains still ventured through the passes during the months of spring and summer, but these were merely minor sorties. The small castle garrison, together with whichever regiment was garrisoned in the nearby army town, were more than a match for the ill-equipped and under strength marauders, their regular patrols assuring that only a handful of sheep and cattle were ever taken, the raiding parties so anxious to avoid any direct confrontation that they kept well away from even the remote farmstead buildings. As a result, the only human casualty in two and a half decades had been an elderly shepherd, and rumour had it that his death had actually been caused when he tumbled into a ravine in the middle of the night, the cracked and empty wine flagon found near his broken body suggesting that he might well have become lost and fallen even if he had not been fleeing from the raiders who had decimated his then untended flock.

The Stewardship of Garassotta had therefore come to be seen as little more than a sinecure, a fact that had not escaped Lord Lundt's stepbrother, Willum, when the title had been bestowed upon him. His already twisted mind had seen this posting as a final humiliation and he had thus been more than ready when the scheming Vorsan noble, Fulgrim, had suggested that together they might oust Lord Lundt and install Willum in his stead.

Their initial scheme had involved the abduction of Corinna, though she remained unclear as to the part she had ultimately been expected to play in their overall strategy. The Lady Dorothea of Varragol, another distant relative, had also been involved originally. But she, too, had been betrayed by the infamous plotters and suffered so greatly herself at Fulgrim's hand that Corinna and Savatch had not sought further retribution after the death of Willum and the eventual overthrow and capture of Fulgrim.

Lord Lundt, ignorant of Savatch's initial culpability in

Corinna's kidnapping, had agreed to accept Dorothea's fresh oath of allegiance, realising that stories of strife among the ruling family would not benefit the security and continued stability of the state. The truth, he decided, should be available only to those with whom it could be trusted, and so a complex story had been constructed to explain away both Corinna's temporary disappearance, Willum's death, and the madness of Willum's wife, Benita, whose mind had actually snapped under the torture inflicted upon her by her vicious husband.

Corinna's then new husband, Prince Lazlo Haas of the small coastal kingdom of Haafland, had guessed there was more than was being publicly admitted, for the changes her experiences had wrought in the once innocent Corinna were all too obvious, and the appointment of Savatch as her personal captain had confirmed the suspicions that formed in even his wine-addled head. His marriage to Lord Lundt's daughter had been one of political expediency, and Corinna viewed him with disgust and contempt from the beginning.

If Lazlo had ever harboured thoughts that his new bride might one day become more disposed towards him, the arrival of Savatch quickly dispelled them and, never one to put up much of a fight in any cause, he had bowed to the inevitable. Although nominally still married to Corinna, he accepted Lundt's offer of a generous pension and returned to his homeland under the pretext of pressures of state business and, with his own father now aging and consumptive, it was unlikely he would ever return.

In the male dominated society and politics of Illeum women, once out of sight, were generally quickly out of mind, and Lord Lundt was rapidly persuaded by his daughter that the castle at Garassotta was sufficiently beyond the immediate eyesight of the court at Illeum City to provide a sanctuary for her and her new love. The idea that a woman – a girl, moreover – should be appointed to the Stewardship of Garassotta was initially met with some misgivings. But when the story was put about that the young Lady Corinna had become ill with the tubular disease and that the clear fresh air in that north eastern outpost had been prescribed by her physicians, resistance quickly subsided.

Besides, as Lundt was quick to point out, Garassotta had remained untroubled for so long that her title meant little, if anything, and the inner circle of advisers and officials, aware that something had gone awry in her marriage to the heir of one of Illeum's oldest allies, could not fail to concede that she would be better off as far away from the glare of big city life as possible.

The year since she had come to Garassotta had been pleasant enough, Corinna had to admit. But now, as she sat in her high tower bedroom, looking out over the rolling treetops towards the nearer peaks of the Bund ranges, she knew that she had expected more from her life here.

True, as nominal head of this small province and a good week's journey from the capital city, she was no longer quite so subject to the rigorous protocols that governed the palace and court life. She could ride, hunt, fish and move among what there was of the local population with a refreshing freedom, but...

But there had to be more, and even her life with Savatch was no more than a parody, a pale copy of those weeks in which a combination of he and his whip had stirred the demons within her.

'Damnation to all men!' she cried, pounding the stone window-sill with her fist. The wind about the tower sucked her voice out through the open window, where it dissipated and died among raucous cries of the flock of ravens that were circling the battlements just above. 'And damn you, too, my Lord Savatch,' she muttered, turning back into the room.

Moving slowly, Corinna crossed to the large ornate bed

that dominated the semi-circular chamber and knelt beside it, reaching underneath until her fingers closed on the handle of the low chest. With an effort, she managed to slide the heavy timbered box out into the open and then reached beneath the mattress for the small key she kept hidden there. A moment later, the lock turned with a well-oiled click and she lifted the lid, laying it back against the bed.

The leather of the slave hood was as supple as the day it had first been crafted, the metal hooks and buckles gleaming from the regular polishing they received. Gently, Corinna lifted the soft hide in her hands, raising it to her nose and inhaling the warm aroma of the hide, remembering that first time she had worn it and the terror of the darkness and silence it had enforced as Savatch's wagon rattled and bumped out of the gates of Illeum City, one more naked slave girl in the back arousing no more than the expected carnal interest among the unsuspecting sentries.

Reverently, Corinna laid the hood on the edge of the bed and reached down again to scoop up the wide slave belt with its attached cuffs. She had worn this, too, for that fateful journey, and had retrieved it, together with the hood and the ankle fetters, from Savatch's saddlebags before they had finally left Dorothea's castle mansion. He had seen her take the items, but said nothing, yet they had remained in the chest ever since their arrival at Garassotta, despite their regular private charades in the meantime.

'Maybe now,' Corinna whispered to the empty room. 'Maybe now is the time.' She fingered the ankle cuffs, staring past them to the simple slave sandals that were the final contents of the chest, and a curious smile began to spread across her delicate features.

Pecon sat just within the circle of firelight, well away from the wagon, playing idly with the small pile of coins that lay on the chamois spread between his feet. He had separated them into piles: fifteen gold krones, six piles each of ten silver telts, and a large handful of copper and bronze pennies, a total value of just over twenty krones.

Inside the wagon lay four bundles of silks and three casks of spirits; together with the four handcrafted swords he had acquired from the smithy in Falstrad, they represented another ten krones, and with the girl likely to fetch at least two krones more, if and when he decided to sell her on, he could be well satisfied with his year's labours.

Chasing runaway slaves had long since ceased to offer any real satisfaction, but at least it had proved a lucrative employment since Pecon had resigned from the Vorsan Guard corps and provided him with what was now a sizeable stake for his next venture. Between here and his intended destination there would be more slaves, no doubt, but whether he decided to track them or buy them depended upon the individuals.

The girl, Demila, was a perfect specimen for the latter purpose. Tallish, young, muscled thighs and buttocks, with the potential for even better development given the appropriate training. Another eight or ten similar girls would ensure Pecon a warm welcome when he eventually found the trader from Erisvaal, whom he had met up with in Illeum City the previous summer. Ten like Demila, plus Pecon's own singular talents and the extra money he could offer, would be worth a half share in the fellow's enterprise, of that Pecon had no doubt.

Wrapping the coins carefully in the chamois, he slipped them back inside the pouch that usually hung from his belt and, with a grunt, rose on stiffening legs, turning to where the girl sat with her back to the wagon wheel to which he had tethered her.

Sightless within the slave hood she had worn without a break for the past two days, she started at his approach, her breathing quickening as he knelt beside her to unlock the chain that ran from her collar to one of the stout spokes.

'Come to the fire,' he said, tugging on the short leash. 'You are cold.' He should, he realised, have given her a fur, or brought her to the warmth of the fire earlier. Naked, but for her slave belt and the halter that supported and lifted her breasts, the damp night air had brought her shivering flesh up in tiny bumps, though she had not dared to complain.

Sitting her down by the fireside, Pecon quickly unbuckled the blindfold section of her hood, revealing her dark eyes in the flickering light. Wordlessly, she stared up at him, her uncertainty reflected in the twin dark pools.

'Can you cook?' he demanded gruffly. Uncertainly, Demila nodded. Pecon pointed to the wagon. 'When you have warmed yourself,' he said, 'you will find salted meat and some vegetables in a sack. There are pots, too. Prepare us both a meal and bring the ale jug, also.' He took up the bow and quiver he had lain aside earlier.

'With luck,' he said, straightening up, 'I shall find us a fat rabbit for the pot, too.' He stared down at her. 'I shall not be gone long, so I suggest that if you have any ideas of escaping you forget them. I found you once and I shall find you just as easily again, especially now your ankles are hobbled.'

'Yes, master,' Demila whispered. 'I shall be here and the food will be ready, as you order.'

'Good.' Pecon stood for a moment or two, studying her in silence. 'Have some of the ale yourself,' he instructed at last. 'It will help keep out the night air.'

'Thank you, master,' she replied meekly, lowering her eyes.

'And wash yourself whilst I am gone,' he said. 'I don't want the trail dust in my bed this night, nor the smells of the day on you. You will find some spiced water in the wagon. Douche yourself well with it and make sure you don't miss anything. You may be a whore slave, but you don't have to stink like a midden.'

'I see our little friend is quite perky this morning, my lord,' Agana laughed, flicking at Fulgrim's upright member with the short switch she habitually carried. Fulgrim, lashed face up over the heavy sawhorse style frame, grimaced, but said nothing. The young page who stood between his splayed thighs flinched in sympathy, but did not break his rhythm, for he was close to what he considered a climax now. The irony of this was not lost on Agana.

'A pity that our other young friend here hasn't the balls for the job either,' she sneered, 'but then I'm told that at least two of the new guard relief might not be averse to making use of your services.'

'Bitch!' Fulgrim hissed through clenched teeth, trying desperately to will his rampant rod into submission, hating the way in which it now responded of its own will to even the most hideous of the humiliations this awesome woman subjected him to. 'May your soul rot in the lowest of the seven halls of hell,' he wheezed, straining against the bonds that held him, even though he knew it was a futile waste of his strength.

'If my soul goes to the seventh hall,' Agana laughed, flicking at the head of his bulbous erection once again, 'then surely we have been told false, for there must be an eighth for such souls as yours!' She tapped the page smartly across his naked shoulder.

'Come, Pester!' she urged. 'Finish yourself in the noble lord's hole and stop making such a pig's meal out of the thing. Imagine you're rodding your beloved little Moxie and that he has teats to compare with hers, though I should not let her ladyship become a party to such thoughts, let alone the making of them into actions. The thought of any male despoiling her beloved bitch maid would be more than enough to have her order the skin stripped from your back!'

With a final tremor the page finished and withdrew, panting

heavily, and Agana lost no time in moving to the next stage of Fulgrim's ordeal. Expertly, she released him from the trestle without ever leaving him the full use of his arms and legs, ensuring that, even if he did presume to test what remained of his strength against her awesome muscles, there would only ever be one outcome.

Very soon, wrists strapped behind his back, he knelt in the centre of the stone floor, as the first maid stripped off her flimsy shift and stepped towards him.

The hapless noble knew only too well what was expected of him, as he knew the punishment for failing to comply. Wearily, he lifted his face and the lithe girl moved her feet apart, thrusting her crotch to his face. Fulgrim opened his mouth, tasting her sweet musk as her lips met his, probing inside them with his tongue, eager to bring her to a peak as rapidly as possible and earn the eventual respite that would come only when he had settled all of Agana's daily choice.

The first maid, young even by the youthful standards of Dorothea's household 'pets', was evidently also very inexperienced, though nonetheless willing for that fact, and quickly peaked, her slender fingers gripping Fulgrim's shining pate as support for her buckling knees. She was quickly replaced by the second page, already erect from the ministrations of the older maid, and Fulgrim gagged as the lad's thick shaft was forced between his lips.

Fighting against his immediate urge to snap his jaws shut about the vulnerable flesh – Agana had made it very clear what he could expect if ever he assuaged such a reaction – Fulgrim closed his eyes and tried to shut out what was happening. At least, he thought sourly, these lads were no more capable of an ejaculation than he was himself, but the degradation he suffered was in no way lessened by this fact.

The second page was finished far quicker than his fellow earlier, but now came Agana's final enactment. Exhausted and shamed, Fulgrim continued to make no resistance as she thrust him up against the square timber frame that filled one end of the narrow chamber, securing his ankles to the struts, so that he was forced to stand with his legs spread uncomfortably wide. Only when she had immobilised his lower limbs did she release his wrists and strap them high above his head.

'Now, my lord,' she rasped, holding up the peculiar shaped gag for him to see, 'let us arrange a little dance, shall we?' She prised Fulgrim's jaws apart and thrust one end of the stubby phallus between them, buckling the strap tightly about his head to prevent him ejecting it. The shorter end filled his mouth completely, while the longer end projected crudely from his face. Agana turned to the second maid, who had removed her shift, though with obvious reluctance.

'You will keep your hands by your sides, slut,' she instructed. 'If you move them I shall double your punishment, understood?' The girl nodded. Agana gave her a critical look, particularly her small, pert breasts.

'Not much of a cushion to put between you,' she remarked acidly, 'but then you can't all hope to compete with Moxie, can you?' She tucked the switch into her belt, grasped the girl beneath her armpits and lifted her bodily, swinging her towards Fulgrim. The maid, knowing what was expected of her, obediently opened her legs as Agana positioned her gaping sex above Fulgrim's still erect organ.

Slowly, Agana lowered the hapless girl, turning to nod at the first maid, who quickly stepped forward to guide the waiting shaft into the yawning warmth. The descending girl groaned as she was penetrated, for despite his lack of testicles, Fulgrim was well made in what remained of his manhood, and a small cry of surprise tore from the back of her throat as his full length was sheathed within her.

Now, leaning forward, she opened her mouth, taking the

free end of the penis gag deep into her throat, closing her teeth about it, for this was now her only means of steadying herself, her feet remaining an inch or so clear of the floor.

'And so,' Agana said, turning away to select a long crop from the rack at her side, 'we shall begin our little mating dance.' She flexed the braided whip once, flicked it twice through the air between them and then, with no further ceremony, brought it around in a hissing arc, a vivid line springing across the hanging maid's defenceless buttocks to the accompaniment of a sharp report.

The youthful body jerked and bucked, a whimper forcing its way past the gag to which the girl clung and, at the same time, a muffled grunt came from Fulgrim.

'She is to receive twenty more, my lord,' Agana chuckled, pleased at the initial results of her ingenuity. 'Twenty more, at half minute intervals. I doubt she'll come as happily as these others, but I venture she'll come nonetheless, and she'll stay there till she does, or take another dozen. You, on the other hand, dare not lose the firmness upon which she now rides, for if her feet once touch the floor, then you will spend the next day hanging by your toes from the ramparts above.'

The crop whistled through the air once more and again the girl jumped, her eyes screwing tightly closed as she ground her teeth into the hard leather phallus. Behind Agana the second maid stood transfixed, one hand between her thighs, a single finger toying with the swollen clitoris that had forced its way between her outer lips, but she seemed unconscious of the fact that her companions could see exactly what she was doing. Agana, however, missed nothing.

'Get your hands away from yourself!' she snapped. 'Put them to some better use. You two!' she ordered, turning to the pages. The youths, startled, were not slow to understand and sprang forward to stand, one on either side of the miscreant.

'On your knees, slut,' Agana commanded. 'And keep them both nice and hard until I am finished with this whore!'

The girl dropped to her knees, her hands reaching to take the semi-flaccid organs of the two pages. Immediately, the one on the left began to swell and stiffen, though the other was slower to respond. Eventually, however, the girl had them both at attention and Agana, grinning evilly, turned back to her main task.

The vicious leather scythed the air again, a third welt appearing in the space between the first two. This time only a hiss of escaping breath came from the girl, but the violent bucking brought a tortured cry from behind Fulgrim's half of the gag. Agana stepped away again.

'A pretty dance,' she murmured. 'Perhaps next time I should bring some musicians down here to provide a soothing accompaniment, eh?'

'Your hair!' Savatch stood in the doorway of Corinna's bedchamber, his mouth open wide with astonishment. Naked, save for the scrap of silk that was wound about her hips, Corinna smiled back at him, eyes twinkling.

'You like it, my lord and master?' she asked. Savatch took a step forward, shaking his head, for with her blonde tresses died a dark brown, Corinna was almost unrecognisable.

'But why?' he demanded. Corinna's smile grew mysterious and she nodded towards the chest that stood at the foot of the bed. Savatch's eyes followed her direction and for a few moments he stood mystified. Then, as he recognised the box for what it was, the light of realisation began to dawn in his eyes.

'Ah,' he said slowly. 'I think I begin to understand. The little trip away of which you spoke last evening, eh?' Corinna nodded. 'A trip that maybe could have an element of discomfort?' Again the nod. Savatch moved further into the room and stood, one foot raised up and resting on the corner of the trunk.

'One master and slave among many,' he said thoughtfully. 'One poor, dark-haired wench in bondage, rather than a golden-haired princess in her tower, eh? But why not a golden-haired slave?'

'Too many eyes, my lord,' Corinna replied simply. 'Too many eyes.'

'And what of the ears?'

'Ears hear what they hear,' Corinna said. 'I shall simply tell my maids that we wish to spend a few days in our own company and that we shall leave by night in order to attract less attention. A mild sleeping draught in their evening wine will assure that they do not stir to be witnesses, and the guards on the gate will not challenge their captain, surely?'

'But they will surely wonder at the sudden appearance of a slave girl,' Savatch pointed out.

Corinna grinned, impishly, her green eyes flashing. 'Who says her appearance will be sudden?' She turned, gliding across the floor to stand immediately in front of him, reaching up to encircle his neck, pressing her full breasts, with their heavily ringed nipples, against his chest.

'The Lady Corinna has negotiated the purchase of a girl slave from the village of Slacht, beyond the garrison town. I have dispatched Commander Pohl to collect the wench and I shall give my ladies orders that she is to be kept in these chambers during our absence. Only the gate men will see "her" departure with you and they will also assume that I am inside the wagon, asleep after a trying day at my duties.'

'And what is to become of this slave wench when I take her from here?' Savatch asked, his own eyes now reflecting amusement.

Corinna shrugged. 'That would be for her master to decide,' she said. 'After all, a slave can have no will of her own, surely?'

'Not even the most wilful slave,' Savatch agreed.

Melina's initial horror and fear had long since given way to near total exhaustion and a feeling of desperation that this journey would never end. The band of men, drinking as they rode, seemed oblivious to the plight of their captive, staggering along in the wake of the last horseman, the leash from her bound wrists tied to the pommel of his saddle threatening to drag her through the knee-deep snow if she failed to keep her feet.

It had been like this for more than two days now, ever since the raiding party had descended upon her uncle's remote farmstead. Her uncle, his three sons, his wife and her elder sister, had all been slaughtered amidst the burning buildings, horribly butchered as they tried to flee. Melina had initially hidden in a ditch, soaked and mud covered, emerging only when she thought the murderous bandits had gone. But two of the men had remained behind, perhaps suspecting that there were survivors still in hiding, and had ridden her down as she ran across the grain fields.

She had cowered between their horses, covering her head, waiting for their swords to dispatch her as they had dispatched the rest of the family, but instead of killing her, they dismounted, stripped her and took her in turn, twice each. The two fur-clad, blond-haired ruffians then tied her wrists and taunted her, using their short whips, cracking them about her ankles to make her dance.

At last, tiring of the game, the elder of the two had taken a leather hood from his saddlebag and drawn it over her head, leaving only two narrow slits through which she could see. The hood was attached to a stiff leather collar and there was a lock to secure this about her neck. Melina understood the significance of this immediately, for she had seen women in such hoods brought to the marketplace in the nearest town.

Death was not to be her fate, at least not immediately. The hood declared otherwise – it declared her now a slave.

When the two riders had finally caught up with the rest of their band, with Melina slung across the saddle of the younger fellow, their leader, whose name was Mielgaard, removed the hood long enough to examine her features and nodded, apparently satisfied.

'Nice and young,' he growled, scratching at his tawny beard with dirt encrusted fingernails. 'A wide arse and firm tits. When we finally get around to selling her in the Erisvaal markets, she'll fetch a decent price. Meantime, she'll make a good bed warmer.'

On that first night, when the men had made camp, Melina found herself being passed around the entire band in turn. Over and over again she was taken and in every conceivable way until finally, as the men began to tire and the drink to take effect, they left her huddled under a fur, only to be kicked rudely awake at dawn.

One of the men produced a pair of knee length boots for her and another wrapped a short fur cloak about her shoulders, but she realised these were not acts of kindness. As they moved north and east and the snows began, they were simply protecting her as an investment, for dead of the cold she would be worthless to them.

By the second nightfall, despite the footwear and cloak, Melina was chilled to the bone, for they offered her no other clothing or protection. Her teeth chattered and her hands and buttocks felt numb, so that it was almost a relief when the first brigand threw her down onto his furs and climbed on top of her. At least the action that followed stirred the blood in her veins and his body, though coarse, hairy and foul smelling, was warm against her.

The younger of her two original captors, whom his fellows

43

called Sprig, had been the last to take advantage of her this night and had allowed her to remain next to him, beneath his thick furs, until it was time to break camp again the following morning. By the pale dawn light, Melina studied his face for the first time and saw that, despite the stubbly beard and thick eyebrows and the skin made dark by the snow glare and the wind, he was, in reality, little more than a boy. A rather large and powerfully built boy, it was true, but a boy nonetheless, and probably younger even than Melina herself.

As the party prepared to move out, it seemed that Sprig had now appointed himself as Melina's temporary master. He carefully rebound her wrists in front of her, looped the free end of the leash to his saddle and then, after considering for a few moments, opened one of his saddlebags and took out a length of woollen cloth, which he wrapped about her waist to form a skirt. Melina tried to smile her thanks at this perceived kindness, but Sprig ignored her efforts to establish anything more between them.

'You just fuck extra well tonight,' he snapped. He jabbed a grubby finger against her lips. 'Nice and soft,' he observed. 'You learn to use them well and I maybe ask Mielgaard if I can take you as my share of this expedition. You will look good in my hut, I think. The women of our village will then know that I am a real man.'

Melina's heart sank. If she had been expected any further consideration from this young monster, his words dashed any such hope, for it was clear he saw her only as some sort of trophy. He would make sure that she did not freeze to death, but that was all. Apart from that, he regarded her merely as something on which to slake his lust.

They entered the underground system midway through that third day. The cavern system was dank and eerie, a faint illumination coming from patches of glowing moss that clung to the rocky walls. But at least the air was now above freezing point, if not by much, and the silt soil beneath her feet made walking a lot easier than pushing through the snow outside.

Sprig scarcely gave Melina a backward glance during all this time, apart from when the party made periodic rest stops. During these short breaks he offered her water and dried meat and pushed her to one side for her to empty her bladder, but he did not speak. Neither did he remove the slave hood, leaving it in place as if to emphasise her new status the more.

Eventually, several hours after entering the caves, they arrived at a place where the basic tunnel opened up into a wide chamber, the roof disappearing up into the darkness, a wide flat shelf of rock projecting over the embankment to one side, that would be above the water level when the river was actually flowing. Dismounting, the brigands led their horses up a steep and uneven slope and Melina realised that this was where they intended to make camp for the night.

The little plateau, Melina saw, was littered with the debris of previous camps, including a rough circle of rocks, soot blackened from earlier fires, a few stumps of charcoal crumbling at its centre. Immediately, Mielgaard ordered Sprig to begin collecting wood for a new fire, and the young giant began untying Melina's wrists. For the first time in many hours, he spoke to her.

'You will help,' he said curtly. 'And do not be foolish, for there is nowhere to run.' He led the way back down to the riverbed and the pair of them worked their way back and forth, prising pieces of dried branch and twigs from the soft soil, flotsam carried down on the current when there had been one. In a surprisingly short time they had accumulated a considerable stack of kindling, which Sprig began to ferry up to the camp, leaving Melina to continue scavenging for more.

As she paused to draw breath, peering into the gloom all about her, Melina had never felt so miserable and forlorn in all her young life. Sprig, she knew, had been right: there was no point in trying to run off, no point at all. Even assuming that they did not ride her down almost immediately, beyond the caves at either end lay nothing but snow and ice. She was poorly clothed and had no food and no means of starting a fire for herself. Without these murderers she would be dead in a day at the most.

Sighing deeply, she bent to her work once more, blinking away the tears that blurred her vision and stung her cheeks.

'How old are you, slave?' Pecon looked at Demila, who was crouched at his feet, where she had remained for perhaps half an hour, unmoving, unspeaking, but watching his every move. The sudden breaking of the silence seemed to catch her unawares and her eyes, flickering behind the leather slave mask, looked wary.

'I – I don't know, master,' she replied, her voice little more than a whisper. 'They think about twenty summers, but no one is sure.' Pecon picked idly at his teeth and considered this.

'You have been a slave for most of that time?' he said, eventually.

Demila nodded. 'For a long time, yes master,' she demurred. 'I cannot remember much of before that time.'

'But you were not always in Daskot's household?'

She shook her head again. 'No, master,' she said. 'For many years I was owned by a farmer – in a place they call the Vaal, which is the land where I was born, so I was told. He bought me from another when I was but a child, but I remember little of that.'

'You were a field worker?'

'No, master, not as such,' Demila replied, her voice now steadier as she appeared to grow in confidence. 'When I was still little, I worked in the kitchens on the great farm and then I was trained to the bridle.'

'To the bridle?' Pecon echoed. He sat up straighter, his eyes narrowing. 'Explain further, slave.' Demila's eyes showed confusion, but, after a brief hesitation, she continued.

'My master – my master then,' she corrected, 'trained and used slaves to act as horses, or ponies. We pulled carts and carriages, taking the surplus crops to market and also conveying the overseers about the estate. The bigger, stronger slaves were also raced against each other and against the pony slaves from other estates.'

'I see,' Pecon mused. His mouth twitched slightly, but his face remained a mask of inscrutability. 'Tell me more,' he said. 'I have heard of these things, but I have never come across them personally.'

'There is not much more to tell, master,' Demila replied. 'I was trained as part of a team of four girls, all of about my age, but I was too slight and did not develop sufficiently as I grew older, which was why I was sold again.' Pecon studied her full breasts and flaring hips and now a smile did flicker across his face.

'Your development seems perfectly satisfactory to me,' he chuckled. Demila's eyes flickered again and her cheeks, beneath the rim of the mask, began to colour slightly.

'I was not tall enough, master,' she said blandly. 'Any girl who did not grow to a certain height was considered not worth training further. For the ordinary work there were always plenty of young slaves, so only the tallest and strongest were kept for racing and breeding. The rest of us were simply sold on, for other duties and purposes.'

'And Daskot, your last master, had purposes in mind that did not depend upon your height, eh?' Pecon grinned. Demila stared down at her feet. Pecon remained silent for several seconds, finally managing to loosen a piece of meat that had been annoying him for some while and spat it to one side.

'Stand up and remove your skirt,' he ordered, finally.

Demila, still without meeting his gaze, leapt dutifully to her feet, unclipped the metal fastening at her waist and let the brief leather garment fall away to dangle from one hand. Slowly, Pecon stood up himself, stepped forward and took it from her, tossing it away.

'Look up at me, slave girl,' he commanded quietly. Almost reluctantly, Demila raised her eyes. Pecon reached out and cupped her heavy breasts, one in each hand, drawing a small shudder from her.

'Tell me,' he whispered, 'do you prefer me as a master – to that fat pig, Daskot, that is?'

Demila swallowed and licked her lips. 'A slave is not permitted such opinions, master,' she replied hoarsely.

Pecon grunted. 'A slave is permitted whatever her master says she is permitted,' he said. 'Answer the question, or shall I take my whip to your pretty hide?'

Demila hesitated, swallowing hard again, but fear of another whipping quickly loosened her tongue. 'I am your slave, master,' she said, 'and I am loyal and obedient. My last master, as you say, was fat and smelled and almost crushed the breath from my body. You, master, are strong and handsome.' Her eyes downcast again, she seemed to be struggling for the right words.

'You are very handsome, master,' she said at last. 'A slave girl should be honoured to serve one such as you.'

'Then show me how you would serve me,' Pecon said gruffly. Without further ado, Demila dropped to her knees, her hands reaching out and up for the heavy buckle on Pecon's belt. Her deft fingers quickly loosened it and, a moment later, she was drawing his breeches down about his knees.

'Remove them completely, girl,' Pecon instructed. 'A master cannot be dignified with his pants about his ankles.' Obediently, Demila crouched lower, tugging each leg free over his heavy boots as he raised a foot in turn, placing the discarded garment to one side with a care that bordered upon reverence. But as she reached up again for the flaccid organ her actions had revealed, Pecon pushed her hands away.

'Use only your mouth,' he said. 'That is why the slave hood leaves the lower part of the face unencumbered, as you should know.'

'Yes, master,' she mumbled, and placed her hands behind her back, reaching out and stretching her neck, until her soft lips touched his already swelling organ. Skilfully, she encircled its head, drawing it into her mouth, her tongue already darting back and forth.

'Excellent,' Pecon sighed. His right hand moved to rest lightly on the leather-covered crown of her head, as it moved slowly back and forth between his thighs. 'Excellent,' he repeated, as his shaft began to approach a full erection. He closed his eyes, smiling contentedly.

'You, my little ex-pony,' he whispered, 'could well turn out to be the best bargain I have made in many a long year.'

The single lantern had been turned down as low as the wick could permit, its dim light falling far short of the shadows that reached out from the walls of the chamber. On the bed, naked now, Corinna lay, eyes open, staring up into the blackness below the ceiling, her breasts rising and falling in time with her slow, deep breathing.

From the open window the stillness of the night air was broken only by the occasional clink-chink of the sentries moving about on the walls below, and the plaintive hoot of the owl that had made the roof of the north tower its home. Within the castle itself all was now quiet, the two maids in the room immediately beneath Corinna's chamber sound asleep these past two hours, the drugged wine she had given them having done its work almost before she had left them.

Tentatively, she fingered the two heavy gold nipple rings

and then, in the semi-darkness, twisted them open and removed them, reaching out to place them on the table at the bedside. Gold rings, she reflected, were not suitable adornments for a slave wench, even one who had yet to be taken back into slavery, and she was certain her master would find acceptable substitutes.

Since entering the underground riverbed they had been leading their horses, though the silted and sandy bed of the dried out course was soft enough to muffle the sound of hooves. Alanna, however, did not believe in taking chances.

'This Mielgaard fellow apparently makes use of these caverns to camp overnight, out of the snow and ice,' she explained.

'Sounds sensible – for a man,' Jekka smiled. She stared up at the high vaulted ceiling of the cave. 'Not quite cozy,' she observed, 'but better than waking up under half a stand of snow.' They trudged on in silence for several minutes, before Jekka spoke again.

'How many men does this Mielgaard command?' she asked.

Alanna shook her head. 'It varies,' she said. 'Reports say he rides with as many as a score and as few as half a dozen. We'll have need of your shooting skills, without a doubt, but we'll still need to think of something to delay any survivors from pursuing us.'

'A few well aimed quarrels should dissuade them,' Jekka said dryly, 'but I may have a better idea, assuming we come upon them underground.' She stopped, drawing in the lead rein of her horse and moved around to one of the saddlebags.

'I saw this used once in Testagrat,' she said. 'Two Pendorsian warlords were battling for control of the city, but the city was none too keen on being ruled by any of them. The priests and students led an uprising and a young alchemist – some claim he was a wizard – came up with a clever little ruse.' She pulled open the flap of the saddlebag and withdrew a flattened flagon.

'I had another alchemist prepare this for me in Illeum City,' she said, uncorking the container and passing it to Alanna. Alanna raised it beneath her nostrils, sniffed and pulled a wry face.

'It smells like some sort of wine that has badly soured,' she said. 'What is it?'

'It's made from the green spirit that the Tamarinians are so fond of addling their brains with,' Jekka replied. 'Almost any spirit will do, but it needs be distilled over again.'

'Ye Gods!' Alanna coughed, having sniffed the vapour once more. 'What do you intend to do, offer these brigands a drink and blow the tops of their heads off?'

'In a manner of speaking,' Jekka grinned, 'though they don't get the pleasure of actually drinking it. What we do is this.' She took the flagon back and pointed to the neck. 'A piece of rag, soaked in a little of the spirit first, is stuffed into the opening and lit,' she explained. 'Once it is burning well, I simply throw the flagon towards our pursuers.

'When it lands, it breaks, and the burning rag ignites the rest of the spirit. The flash from it is quite impressive, believe me, and will be more so if we can use the thing somewhere where the roof is lower.'

'It will startle their horses, no doubt,' Alanna agreed, 'but that will only gain us a short respite.'

'As it stands, yes,' Jekka agreed, 'but there is more.' She reached into the saddlebag again and withdrew a small skin bag. 'Inside this,' she said, 'is ground sulphur and certain dried leaves that have also been reduced to form a powder. Together they burn to produce a thick black smoke.

'Just before lighting the bottle I place this inside, floating in the spirit. The heat from the flash will ignite the bag and its contents and, apart from startled horses, we leave behind a thick cloud through which no sane man would attempt to ride.'

'Very clever,' Alanna said, 'if it works.'

'It'll work,' Jekka replied confidently.

'And how many of these little toys do you have?' Alanna asked.

Jekka's grin reappeared. 'Just the one,' she said, placing bottle and bag back inside the saddlebag. 'Just the one.'

The door to the bedroom had opened noiselessly and the first indication that Corinna had of his presence was when a large hand clamped over her mouth and another grasped her waist, throwing her over onto her stomach. Face down into the pillows, even had she cried out her protests would have passed unheard, and the soft wad of fabric he then forced between her unresisting lips ensured that any sounds she made would remain safely within the confines of the thick walled bedchamber.

He worked as efficiently as she remembered from that first time. Swiftly, her wrists were chained at the small of her back, immobilising her arms temporarily while he moved to the next stage. He lifted her effortlessly clear of the mattress, sliding the slave belt beneath her stomach and lowered her onto it, wrapping the stout leather about her waist and drawing it together to secure it with the four individual buckles.

Corinna gasped as he tightened the band, sucking air in through her nostrils and grunting as he continued to reduce the circlet still further. Finally, when he was satisfied that he had made her waist as small as was practicable, he released the chain from her wrists and resecured them individually to the leather manacles riveted at either side of the belt for just that purpose.

Still unspeaking, he rolled her onto her back, from which position Corinna knew from experience, it would require either his assistance or a lot of effort on her own part, to either roll back or even sit up. However, neither alternative was an option as yet.

In the semi-darkness his form was little more than a silhouette as he bowed over her feet, first placing the slave sandals upon them and lacing them, criss-crossing the thongs up to her knees and then locking the heavy leather anklets into place, drawing her legs close enough together to accommodate the short chain that joined them.

He was ready for the slave hood now, and she had earlier drawn her long hair up into a high ponytail in order to facilitate its fitting. Twisting her long tresses into a temporary braid, he threaded them through the circlet at the crown, drawing the soft leather down and over the top half of her features, bringing the two side pieces over her cheeks and then passing the attached stiffer collar about her throat and joining it at the nape of her neck, where the small lock fastened.

Corinna peered out through the narrow eye slits, knowing he would soon buckle the blindfold over them, but not yet, for he wanted her to see his final preparations. He moved to the lamp, turning up the wick to increase the size and strength of the pool of light it provided, and crossed back to stand looking down at her.

'My most perfect slave,' he whispered, breaking the silence at last. He reached down, withdrawing the wadded gag from her mouth, one finger of his other hand raised to his lips, cautioning her against speaking. 'Stand, slave,' he ordered, taking her by the top of one arm to help her comply. She swung her legs slowly over the side of the bed, lowered her feet onto the thick rug, and awkwardly raised herself erect.

Now he held in his hand something metal, something that glinted, though dully, in the flickering lamplight. Corinna shivered delightedly as she recognised the simple iron inventory tags, the small rectangular pendants onto which every master or trader stamped the particulars of every slave.

They were attached to thick iron rings, thicker than the golden rings that had adorned Corinna's nipples this past year, and their girth stretched her piercings uncomfortably.

From the small bag he'd brought with him, Savatch now took a heavy pair of pincers, using them to crimp the rings, so that the hollow ends bit into the tongue ends, preventing them being removed without the aid of a similar tool. Corinna half closed her eyes, imagining herself a fully bonded slave, when these rings, the rings of the master who had finally purchased her, would be brazed closed in the smithy, removable then only by means of cutting or filing.

The tags felt heavy, pulling at her swollen teats, clinking slightly as she moved, but he was not through with her yet. Kneeling before her, he deftly detached the small gold rings that had remained through her outer labia since the previous summer, replacing them with thicker iron copies, one of which also bore a tag similar to the first pair, and then slipped a stubby lock between the two and snapped it shut.

'I see I shall not need my razor this time, princess,' he chuckled, running his fingers over her shaven pubis. Corinna felt the heat within rising, not just from the intimacy of his touch, but from the memories his words invoked, to that day, in another place and in another time that now seemed so far away and long ago, when a wide-eyed and frightened new bride had been forcibly shaved in her own bathtub.

'You mock your slave, master,' she said, lowering her eyes.

'That is a master's prerogative,' he said, 'and it is not the place of a slave to speak without permission. You have been too long without appreciating the privilege of speech, methinks.' He lifted the pear-shaped leather gag and she opened her mouth willingly to accept it, moving her mouth to adjust to its shape as he fastened the retaining straps to either side of her slave hood.

'And now,' he said, stepping back to take up the final item, 'we are ready to travel. Look upon your new master and remember the image until I restore the privilege of sight to you.' He stood for several seconds, unmoving, unspeaking, and Corinna stared back, already becoming lost in the forest of emotions and sensations. Finally, he held up the padded leather blindfold and, with an effort not to stumble, the Lady Corinna Oleanna, daughter of the Protector of Illeum and now a willing slave, stepped forward, head erect to receive it.

The two women took turns at leading the way through the seemingly unending cave system, going ahead on foot, whilst the other followed some distance behind, riding one horse and leading the other. It made for slow progress, but was safer, guarding against their approach being heard, or their stumbling across their quarry without warning. It was a trick both had learned at an early age and their caution proved well founded.

Jekka, using her mounted shifts to rest her eyes as well as her legs, was nevertheless instantly wide-awake at Alanna's return, even though the older girl moved with the silence of a mountain cat. Even before Alanna spoke, Jekka knew this was not just another change around.

'They've made camp,' Alanna said, speaking quietly. 'I smelt wood smoke long before I came upon them and was able to get up quite close.'

'Did you see our man among them?'

Alanna nodded. 'It's difficult to tell some of them apart,' she said, 'wrapped in their furs and all bearded as they are, but I identified one who seems to be giving all the orders. That must be friend Mielgaard, unless there are two bands of these fiends in the same area.'

'How many are they?'

'As we calculated from the tracks, about ten, and the mystery of the footprints is solved, too. They have a girl with them, probably taken from that last farm we saw, though she could have been with them longer.'

'Not one of their number, then?' Jekka said.

'Not unless they drag their own women around in slave hoods and collars, no.'

Jekka regarded her companion steadily. 'You think we should try to free her, don't you?' she said, accusingly. She sighed and swung herself out of the saddle. 'No,' she continued, 'you don't have to say anything – I just know you.'

'Would you have us leave her to these stinking vultures?' Alanna demanded.

Jekka shrugged. 'And what do we do with her then, even supposing we do manage to get her away from them? Gods of Mount Ignis, isn't this quest fraught enough as it is? I say let's just shoot this Mielgaard fellow and get our arses out of here in one piece.'

'And forget all about this poor wench?' Alanna made a sour face. 'I don't have to tell you the sort of life a slave girl can expect among the tribes of the Snow Kingdoms. First a shaman will use his knives and potions to ensure that she becomes barren, and then she'll be no more than a warm sheath for every fat cock in their mountains.

'Then, when she becomes older and no longer pleasing on the eye, they'll use her as a beast of burden and then, when her strength finally starts to leave her, she'll be cast into a ravine and her brains dashed among the rocks.'

'And non human vultures will pick her bones clean; yes, I know.' Jekka sighed irritably, but she knew it was pointless to argue further. 'All right, my princess and honoured leader, if we must, we must. And I assume you have thought as to how me might free this poor bitch without becoming vulture carrion ourselves?'

Sprig and Mielgaard had spent several minutes in animated discussion, both men gesturing with their hands. Melina, sitting cross-legged on the edge of Sprig's furs, strained her ears in an effort to catch what they were saying. But they spoke in low tones, despite the earnestness of their attitudes, and their dialect, more heavily accentuated when they spoke among themselves, was difficult to follow at the best of times.

Melina, however, knew full well the topic of their discourse; it was herself and her ultimate fate, for Sprig seemed determined now that he should own her and had approached Mielgaard in order to barter for this. The chieftain, however, did not seem well disposed to this proposition and appeared to be taunting his youngest follower.

The other men, though trying to appear disinterested in the argument, were plainly all following it closely. None ventured an opinion, none dared to interrupt, but there were several low guffaws of laughter, presumably each time their leader scored a particularly telling point.

At last, however, some sort of agreement seemed to have been reached, though the dark expression on Sprig's countenance as he returned to Melina suggested to her that it was not exactly to his liking. Standing over her, he stooped, grasped her wrists and hauled her to her feet.

'Come,' he said simply. Half dragging her, he strode back to the circle of light about the campfire and deposited Melina at Mielgaard's feet. Peering out through the narrow eye slits of the slave hood, she stared up at the chieftain's weathered and scarred face and her heart sank. Being Sprig's bed slut was bad enough, but now it seemed that Mielgaard had used his seniority to claim her as his own. However, when he finally addressed her, his words gave her some cause for hope.

'Hide face,' he grinned, baring a set of chipped and broken yellow fangs, 'it would seem our young puppy finds you pleasing. Do you find *him* pleasing?'

Melina looked from Mielgaard back to Sprig and nodded, slowly. 'Yes, master,' she whispered. The closing circle formed by the other brigands erupted into gales of raucous laughter at this. Mielgaard raised a huge hand to quieten them.

'At least the young slut has learned her place quickly,' he roared delightedly. 'She'll make a decent slave for any man. But is this young whelp man enough to deserve his own slave, that's the question, heh?' His gaze travelled around the arc of expectant faces.

'Get her over that big rock there!' he snapped. 'Tie her down tight and let's see how steady the whelp's hand is.'

Before Melina had time to react, several pairs of rough hands seized her, lifting her clear of the ground and bearing her across to where a particularly large rock stood near the edge of the plateau. They hoisted her over it, face down, and ropes were quickly snared about her wrists and ankles and drawn down its sides, spread-eagling her, legs wide apart, so that the only part of her body she could still move was her head.

Mielgaard strode up to her slowly. In his hand he held something orange, which he held out for Melina to see. It was a long thick carrot and she stared at it, uncomprehendingly. Seeing her confusion, he simply laughed the more.

'A wench has more than one use in the kitchen,' he chuckled, 'even a wench who can't cook. Now, some men like their carrots whole,' he continued. 'Me, I like them thinly sliced and my meat raw and bloody.' He moved around behind her, and Melina squealed in alarm when she realised what he intended. Her cries of protestation and feeble attempts at clenching her buttocks were of no avail, however, and the hard vegetable was quickly inserted into her.

'Let it drop,' Mielgaard warned her, stepping back, 'and I'll flay the skin off those pretty dugs of yours with a red hot knife, understand?' Melina, terrified even more than she was humiliated, nodded. She stared backwards and saw Sprig, a coiled whip hanging from his right hand, walking slowly towards her.

'Seven slices clean and the eighth with a sauce of blood,' Mielgaard said. 'One slice less, or more than one with her blood on it and you forfeit her to the rest of us, even your own share. Meet the test and she's yours.' He bent over, placing his bearded face close to Melina's.

'Best you try to keep that pretty arse still, hide face,' he sneered. 'The young whelp ain't as versed in the culinary arts as the rest of us and, just in case you haven't understood, he's going to have to use his whip to chop up the carrot you're holding so prettily. If he gives me seven clean slices and the eighth with just a little smear of your blood, you go to him.

'If not, well, bloody-arsed or not, you belong to the rest of us, and you've already had a taste of what that will mean.' He straightened and stepped away again, turning to address Sprig.

'Chop away, my young friend!' he roared. 'And don't forget, the pink bits are the girl, so don't start slicing her too quickly!'

Sprig took up an open-legged stance, shaking the whip out before him. He twitched his wrist a few times, snaking little loops along the length of the braid as it lay upon the rock, and measured his target carefully. Melina shuddered, screwed up her eyes and turned her head to face forward again.

She heard the whip hissing through the air like an arrow, the crack from its tip exploding to fill the air with a noise like a bough breaking from the top of a tree. Air hissed through her nostrils and she jumped, tensing for the jolt of pain. None came, but the assembled band let out a cry as one. Risking another look back, Melina saw one of their number step forward and bend to retrieve something from the rock behind her, holding it up in the manner of a trophy. It was a slice of carrot.

He passed it to Mielgaard, who examined it, turning it over and fingering the stub of greenery still attached to its domed end. He nodded grudgingly.

'Not bad for a whelp,' he said, and tossed the piece over his shoulder. 'Let's see if you can do that six more times, now, eh?'

Blindfolded, gagged, bound and hobbled, Corinna was completely at the mercy of the man who led her by the short chain he had clipped to the stiff collar of her slave hood. In the soft sandals she padded down stairs, along corridors, trusting to his guidance, the sound of her pulse echoing inside her head to the accompaniment of her laboured breathing, so that even her ears, part muffled by the soft hide that stretched over them, gave her little assistance.

After a few minutes they had reached the ground floor and Corinna's sense of direction and memory told her he was leading her along the wide corridor that ran almost the full length of the main building at this level, passing the great hall, the reception chambers, the antechambers and private rooms, and then on into that area which housed the small detachment of castle guards, the storerooms and the kitchens.

As she shuffled doggedly along, she occasionally fancied she heard the sounds of other people moving nearby, but after the first near encounter she put such thoughts out of her mind. After all, she reasoned, if any should be about at such an hour and see them, all they would see was a dark-haired slave girl being led away by the Stewardess's captain, and assume that the girl who had been brought into the castle earlier that day had failed to meet with the Lady Corinna's approval.

None would imagine that this was the lady herself, breasts and sex bared and ringed for public gaze, head bowed in its all-enveloping symbol of servitude, the hood of a slave now to be transported as just another piece of livestock, the hood and chains ensuring that she remained compliant and easy to handle.

Except that the hood and chains were having a totally different effect upon this particular slave and, as she continued to follow where the leash led her, the slave Corinna almost buckled at her knees as the first wave of orgasm threatened to betray her intended composure.

'They seem to have found a way of amusing themselves,' Alanna hissed, sliding back down to join Jekka, where the younger girl waited on the riverbed. 'They are playing the sort of game that only a man could find entertaining,' she added, and briefly described the scene she had just witnessed.

'In her arse?' Jekka echoed, wide-eyed. 'Some sort of stick, you say?'

'Something similar in shape, anyway,' Alanna said. 'I wasn't close enough to see properly. At a guess, I would say the fellow has to cut away as many pieces as possible before his whip finds her flesh, poor little bitch.'

Jekka picked up her regular crossbow, which was already cocked and loaded. 'Perhaps I should shoot the bastard now, before he gets too close,' she suggested, as another cheer echoed back along the tunnel.

Alanna held up a restraining hand. 'Not yet,' she said. 'Better the wench gets a bloody backside than we risk ourselves too soon. Let them play their game, for they are all drinking heavily as they look on. Before long they'll be falling asleep, or sluggish at best, and then we can move on them.

'Who knows, we may even be able to use the same trick we did at Varragol and reduce the odds a little to begin with. Judging from the smell, the small hollow just beyond that rock shelf is used as a midden, so in a while I think I shall go and hide myself nearby. A man with his drawers about his ankles is an easy mark.'

'My princess,' Jekka whispered, barely able to speak for laughing, 'I am beginning to wonder about you.'

The single sentry stood inside the doorway leading from the tower out onto the north rampart, almost invisible in the deep shadows. Above, thick clouds scudded across the night sky, obscuring moon and stars alike, so that the treetops of the forest that surrounded Castle Varragol on three sides became one black mass, devoid of feature or definition.

Ingrim leaned out over the wall and peered down at the inky thread of the moat and spat a ball of phlegm. Orfal, standing alongside him, kept his eyes firmly fixed on the inner courtyard, ears keened for any sounds that would indicate possible eavesdroppers below, though at this hour, apart from the night watch posted at strategic points about the battlements, the inmates of the castle palace would all be sleeping soundly.

'In the morning, then,' Ingrim said, straightening up and turning back to the veteran sergeant. 'As soon as the poison in the oats takes effect, any remaining Illeum guards on the walls are to be overpowered as quickly and silently as possible. After that, we can deal with whatever remains inside the palace itself, but we do not want to alert them to what is happening until it is too late for them to make any sort of stand.

'I don't want to have any more casualties among our men than is absolutely necessary, understand?'

Orfal remained stone-faced. 'Of course, captain,' he replied levelly. 'We'll go through them like a hurricane through a wheat field, only a lot quieter. What about the poison, though? If a whole watch starts rolling around holding their stomachs and groaning, someone's bound to get suspicious.'

'No need to worry about that,' Ingrim replied, smiling nastily. 'This stuff has been specially selected for the task. Ten minutes after swallowing it they'll just start feeling drowsy, which they'll probably pass off as tiredness or the effects of whatever they drank the night before. Another five minutes or so and they'll be fast asleep.

'The poison then starts to spread out and paralyse every part of the body, so within a further quarter hour they'll all be well beyond any hope of ever waking up again. No fits, no frothing at the mouth, no death agonies, just a nice, peaceful, tidy death. So make sure none of our lads touches anything from that pot, right?'

'Right,' Orfal agreed. He turned his gaze towards the shadowy sentry, though not from any fears of being overheard, for the guard was one of their own men. 'What about milady's little harem?' he asked. 'Only some of the lads were asking, if you know what I mean?'

'I know exactly what you mean,' Ingrim confirmed. 'As far as I'm concerned, once the guards have been accounted for they can share out the spoils in any way they want – including those soppy pageboys, for those who are that way inclined. But make sure they know that no one is to touch her ladyship and, apart from securing her, neither are they to interfere with the black bitch. The noble lord wants to keep that privilege for himself.'

'Yes, but I thought—'

Ingrim raised a hand, cutting Orfal short. 'Keep your thoughts to yourself, sergeant,' he warned. 'Lord Fulgrim will not thank anyone who reminds him of what these harpies have done to him and besides, I think you'll find he still retains the ability, if not all his previous drive, as it were.'

'I wouldn't want to be in that black cow's boots come tomorrow morning,' Orfal sneered.

Ingrim chuckled and turned away. 'Somehow, sergeant,' he said, 'I don't think they'd suit you anyway.'

Alanna plunged the blade of her knife in and out of the soft silt, wiping the blood from it, and bent to drag the second body away into the darkness, far enough so that the next man to come to empty his bowels would not see it. Not that he would be expecting to see anything, for the brigands were all now clearly and noisily drunk, those who had not already fallen asleep.

The presence of the girl was irksome, Alanna thought, as she laid the second corpse alongside the first. Without her to consider, it would have been a simple matter to remain hidden, ignoring Mielgaard's men and waiting for the chieftain himself. Even kings needed to relieve themselves eventually, and their contract had been to kill only this band's leader. That done, it would be an easy matter to slip away and they could have been back out into the snow covered open long before any of his men realised he was missing.

The official from the court who had approached the two Yslanders had not even asked for proof of their success; no head in a sack, not even a hank of hair and scalp. Alanna's integrity was beyond question, as was that of all the Yslandic warrior women. Her word that Mielgaard was dead would not be questioned, but it would never enter her head to claim this until it was so.

As events had transpired, assuming they both survived, she would indeed be able to take back the chieftain's head, but that moment was still a long way off. On the small plateau above at least eight men still lived, drunk or otherwise, and Alanna knew enough about these snow warriors to know that, once the first surprise had worn off, they could make even more dangerous adversaries in their present condition than if they were sober.

Sitting on the chest of the second corpse, she twirled her knife in her fingers and thought carefully. Two dead so far – how many more could she risk before one of them must surely become suspicious?

Away on the far side of the plateau Jekka now lay waiting among some broken rocks, her crossbow at the ready, her instructions, if the alarm should be raised, to take Mielgaard with her first shot. His death – and Alanna had no doubt that Jekka would indeed kill him, for her aim was the surest Alanna had ever seen – would hopefully cause enough initial confusion to allow the red-headed assassin to reload and shoot again. In addition, she had her miniature crossbow cocked and armed, less accurate than the larger bows at distance, it was true, but Jekka's position was easily within its range.

That would account for three of the men and Alanna's own crossbow would down another meantime. Four would remain then – two for each of them – but Jekka could reload that smaller bow with astonishing speed, so it was likely they would be facing three survivors against the two of them. Alanna nodded, satisfied. Those were good odds, she thought. Good odds indeed, and if she could take even one more out of the equation before the real fun started, it would all be almost too simple.

The guard on the gate at Garassotta Castle had been drinking, from what Corinna could hear of his speech, and on another night, she knew, Savatch would have made certain the man was severely disciplined for such a breach of regulations. Tonight, however, her 'captor' had other business on his mind and was eager to put as much distance between themselves and the castle in as short a time as possible.

However, Savatch being Savatch, he could not let the incident pass by completely un-noted. Through the muffling leather of her hood, Corinna heard the exchange quite clearly and could imagine the expression on the unfortunate sentry's face as he squirmed with embarrassment and no little dread as to the possible consequences.

'Tell me, soldier,' Savatch said casually, 'do I smell something in the air here, or is it just this damned head cold playing tricks with my nose?'

The man shuffled his feet, quite audibly. 'Er, perhaps it's

something in the moat, sir,' he ventured, just a little tremulously. Corinna heard Savatch give a little cough and then sniff again, quite deliberately.

'Ah, yes,' he said, with slow deliberation, 'it's definitely something rotten, something I most definitely shouldn't be smelling. Remind me upon my return, man, and you can spend a day down there skimming the surface and dredging for any animals that might have fallen in there and died, right?'

'Er, right... yessir,' the soldier acknowledged. 'Shall I organise a working party?'

'No, I don't think so,' Savatch drawled. 'One man should be more than sufficient. No need to waste the efforts of more than that.'

But for the gag distorting her mouth, Corinna would have smiled. The errant soldier might almost have preferred a week's stoppage of pay, or almost have opted for a short disciplinary flogging, rather than face the prospect of an entire day wading about in the murky waters that surrounded Garassotta Castle. For one never knew exactly what one might find down there, except that it would be guaranteed to be either dead, dying, or something that merited killing instantly anyway.

At this time of the year, when the springs that fed the moat were running particularly slowly, the low water level in the moat prevented it from draining and filling properly, and the warming effect of the sun produced in it an ideal environment for all manner of unspeakable growth. The apothecary spent many hours concocting solvents to pour into the glutinous mass, but these generally served only to mask the awful stench, rather than to deal with the actual cause of it.

The thin-soled slave sandals offered only a minimal barrier between Corinna's feet and the uneven track beyond the bridge. She had assumed that Savatch would have a wagon, or small cart in which to transport her, but it now seemed he was determined to put her through as harsh an ordeal as possible, for they proceeded on foot for what seemed an eternity.

At last, after what she guessed was a distance of at least two miles, he halted, drawing her close to him by the leash and pressing his chest hard against her quivering breasts. Corinna let out a stifled little moan and leaned into him, eagerly.

'Ah, a choice little slave, as ever was,' Savatch murmured. His powerful hands cupped her heavy globes, thumbs gently massaging her hard nipples. 'And such a wilfully shameless little slut, too,' he chuckled, teasingly. 'Such a show of public wantonness is totally unbecoming. Perhaps I shall find a village large enough to have itself a beadle and get him to give you a public flogging.'

Corinna shivered violently and shook her head, but the thought of being punished before a crowd of ogling rustics instilled other emotions, as well as fear, and she knew that Savatch was well capable of carrying out his threat. If he did, well, she thought, as he pushed her gently from him, it had been her idea. This charade and the agreement between them had been that she would receive nothing that any other slave might not expect from a strict master.

She felt his fingers parting her lower lips and fought to remain silent as one digit slid easily in and out of the lubricated tunnel, for this had quickly become a contest of wills and she knew precisely what was in his mind now. Here, somewhere in the small garrison town probably, standing helplessly at the roadside, Savatch was determined that the sometime Lady Corinna Oleanna, daughter of the Protector of Illeum, the single most powerful and respected man in the entire western continent, would come like the wanton little slave she so often yearned to be.

'It's a large old castle, uncle,' Paulis muttered, peering up at the towering walls of Garassotta from the cover of the thick undergrowth that marked the edge of the woods, 'and well guarded, too, from what we've seen so far. If our man is in there, it would be suicide to try to kill him.'

'To try to kill him inside the castle, yes,' Jorkan agreed, 'but we shan't try to do that, shall we? Our friend has duties that bring him outside those high walls and the information I was given was that he oft times rides out with just the lady for company and never with more than a couple of guards for appearances sake.

'In the morning, when the castle is awake and people are coming and going, we shall approach the gate, in the manner of any ordinary traveller and seek to buy provisions. They will probably send us on to the town, but it will give us a few moments in which to take our bearings.

'Then, in the town, we can find an alehouse. There is a garrison billeted there, so there should be no shortage of drinking holes, and soldiers love to talk, especially after a season or two stuck out in a place like this. And, when they drink and talk, soldiers like to brag, to show a couple of poor yokels like us just how important they are in the scheme of things.

'An hour or so of convivial company and I am confident we shall know a lot more about our friend's regular habits. We may have to wait a few days – several, even – but that is often the way of these things. Eventually, we shall corner our prey where there are no bolt-holes and no guards to protect him. And then—'

Jorkan made a gesture with his fingers across his throat and chuckled. Paulis shivered, for he had begun to realise there was a side to his uncle's character that none of the family or neighbours back home could even begin to suspect, let alone understand.

'Don't worry, boy,' Jorkan growled, keeping his eyes fixed firmly on the dark walls, 'you shan't need to cut any throats yourself, not this time. But if we take the lady as well, then you can have your fair share of her noble charms until we deliver her to our patrons.'

Mielgaard went down with Jekka's first shot, the iron bolt piercing his neck through, but he did not die quietly. His bellow of pain mixed with rage and surprise echoed around the cavern as he crumpled to his knees, fingers clawing at the shaft protruding from beneath the left side of his chin.

Jekka ignored him, hauling back the bowstring and thrusting a second quarrel into the waiting groove. The bandit chieftain was already a dead man, even if it might yet be a minute or two before the life finally ebbed from him, and if he succeeded in pulling the bolt free from his neck he would simply hasten his end, for the stream of blood that was now trickling from the wound would become a torrent.

Dropping to one knee, Jekka raised the bow again and drew the trigger back in a smooth motion. The string shot forward with a sharp twang and the projectile hissed across the thirty paces or so to the knot of confused figures. One of them whirled around, a shriek of agony dying on his lips, and pitched into the fire, sending a shower of sparks into the air.

A second, on the fringe of the group, threw up his arms, Alanna's first bolt taking him between the shoulder blades, its tip emerging like a red finger in the centre of his chest. Transferring her larger bow to her left hand, Jekka snatched up the smaller weapon. Usually she carried this strapped to her forearm, hidden within the sleeve of her robe, triggering it with the special device that curved around to fit into her fist, but for speedier loading she had decided to operate it in the more conventional fashion.

She took five paces towards the mêlée, aimed and fired,

already reloading even as her target fell, the short bolt embedded in his right eye. Such was the speed and surprise of the two-flanked attack that the bandits were still in utter confusion. Seeing their leader dead, or dying, they drew themselves into a small knot and, in doing so, forfeited any slender chance they might have had of any of them surviving.

Jekka's fourth quarrel found its mark in the heart of one man as a sixth jerked and toppled with Alanna's second in his thigh. The warrior princess, taking advantage of their opponents' slow reactions, had paused to reload and fire again, and now only two figures remained on their feet in the flickering firelight.

Unfortunately, one of them now had a knife at the throat of the other, and the smaller figure he held before him as a shield was the girl.

'Lower your weapons!' he snarled. 'Lower your weapons, or I'll slice her throat asunder.'

'Go ahead!' Alanna called back. With slow deliberation, she stepped forward, dropping her crossbow and drawing the gleaming sword from her belt. 'Kill her by all means,' she invited. 'Why should we worry about the death of one more slave girl? You'll be as dead as she soon after, anyway.'

The man's eyes darted wildly from Alanna to Jekka and back again. Slowly, he began to retreat, struggling to keep the terrified girl between himself and Jekka's bow, all the time not daring to take his eyes off Alanna's blade for more than a second or so at a time.

'If you want gold,' he said, his voice quavering, 'we have very little, but what there is is in the saddlebags nearest the fire. Take that, and there are some jewels there, too. They are not very fine, so I am told, but they will fetch a few telts in the nearest town.'

'So will this girl,' Alanna retorted. 'Let her go and drop your weapon and I'll spare your life. We've already got what we came for.' With her sword, she gestured towards the pile of corpses. 'One of those is the one they call Mielgaard, is that not so?'

The man nodded. Jekka laughed, raising the small bow she'd reloaded yet again.

'Kill the turd,' she said, simply. 'I can take his eye out from here before his hand can make a move.'

'No,' Alanna cautioned. 'Even in death he could inflict a mortal wound on the wench, and I see little point in spilling any more blood – even his. He's little more than a boy, can't you see?'

'Not with his trousers on,' Jekka laughed. 'It's hard to tell.' She lowered the bow again and stood easily, her eyes never blinking. 'Let the girl go and show us your little boy cock and maybe I won't kill you.'

'Why should I believe you?' Sprig retorted.

Alanna's eyes blazed. 'Because we are Yslanders,' she snapped back. 'Surely your eyes don't lie to you?'

'And what difference where you come from?' he sneered.

Alanna looked across at Jekka and shook her head. 'The boy's an imbecile,' she said. Turning back to him, she sighed.

'An Yslander's word is her bond, and the word of an Yslandic Princess is double bonded. Now, put down that pricking stick, go find your horse and get yourself out of my sight. I shan't ask again,' she added. 'My redheaded little friend over there is just itching to prove how good her aim is.'

Two

Lady Dorothea had kept her awake long into the depths of the night, but Moxie felt far from tired as the first fingers of the dawn began to creep over the distant hills. Leaving her mistress snoring heavily, she crept from the bedchamber and slipped up the winding staircase to her own, less ostentatious quarters.

Stripping out of the flimsy shift, she stood naked before the long mirror for a full minute, considering the possibilities. Dorothea, Moxie knew, would not expect anything further of her until nightfall, at least. However demanding she could be in some respects, she was sensible to the needs of her maid and bed companion and respected the younger woman's requirements in the matter of having time to herself and the freedom to enjoy it.

Initially, Moxie had been very wary about letting Dorothea have even the slightest inkling about her growing desire for intimate male company, fearing jealousy would bring about all sorts of retribution. But, provided that Moxie limited her liaisons to the youthful pages and kept the older, rougher guards at arms' length, her mistress was more than happy to turn a blind eye and, on occasions, actively encouraged her.

'Males should be put to good use,' she remarked, on more than one occasion. 'So long as we use them and not the other way around, that is how things should be.' She had even given permission for Moxie to instruct the household seamstresses in the making of an outfit that was modeled on Agana's favourite garb.

Moxie was terrified of the huge black woman, but there

was something almost regal about the way she strutted about the palace, whip at her belt, dark eyes ever on the alert for any misdemeanours among the pages and maids. And the first time Moxie laced herself into her own thigh high boots and tight corset belt, she began to understand why.

Now, slowly and savouring every moment of the ritual, Moxie began to dress herself. Boots, corset, the brief leather skirt beneath which only the thinnest scrap of chamois covered her shaven sex, and the leather bodice that almost managed to restrain her magnificent bosom, followed by the studded collar and the long, soft gloves.

Scooping up her hair, she tied it high with a short thong, adding the pin with its glittering bauble, and then turned for the door. She had yet to add the colouring about her eyes and on her lips, but such was not a task worthy of a powerful woman, not when there was always that fawning little idiot Pester ever willing to pander to her every whim.

Pester now slept in a small room by himself, a privilege Moxie had contrived some months since, and he showed no surprise at being roused at such an hour. Seeing Moxie regaled in all her leather glory, his eyes shone momentarily, but he knew better than to show too much enthusiasm. If he appeared too eager, Moxie was quite likely to send him to find another less willing participant in her intended charade, and the fearsome Agana would be around before long, rousting the youngsters from their beds to start the day's chores. To be deprived of the attentions of his beloved Moxie and left to the humdrum labours of the morning was too awful to contemplate.

There were two horses. Whether they had been arranged beforehand, or whether he had simply taken advantage of a situation, Corinna did not know for sure, though she was fairly certain that the former would be the case. Savatch believed in leaving little to chance, and even the most spontaneous seeming events had often proved to be the results of his careful preplanning.

The saddle on the horse into which he lifted her now most certainly could not have been there fortuitously and, as the thick dildo slipped into her yawning sex, Corinna let out a hiss of pure lust. She remembered a day when to have been mounted on such a device would have horrified her, and smiled to herself inside the secret security of her slave hood.

She was wicked, she knew that, and no doubt there was a god somewhere waiting to exact retribution for her shameless sins in some other world. But for now, as Savatch threaded a thong between her ankle cuffs, pulling it tight beneath the horse's belly, Corinna was past wondering about the afterlife and the possibility of unending purgatory. To leave her most base lusts unsated in this existence would be purgatory enough.

Moxie waited until they had arrived in the private stables before preparing Pester, not wanting to arouse the sort of comments that his appearance would be sure to provoke. From here, however, there was little chance of them being observed, except by the odd sentry on the walls high above, for there was a separate entrance to the outside, the keys to which were held by Dorothea, a duplicate passed discreetly to Moxie not long after her arrival here.

Without speaking, Moxie stripped the young page, wrapping a slave belt about his slender waist and cuffing his wrists to it at either side. A standard slave hood and collar quickly followed, a stubby, cock-shaped gag fastened between his jaws. The boots were her own special favourite, copying the design of the most feminine footwear, the tapering heels adding inches to his height and instability to his posture and gait. Forcing the pages to mince around in such impossible

74

footwear was a favourite pleasure of Moxie's and now she spoke for the first time, ordering Pester to parade up and down across the uneven flagstones, stifling giggles at his awkward progress.

'Enough,' she said at length. 'Come here and let's do something about that pathetic worm between your legs.'

Working with a deft expertise that would have amazed the patrons in her father's tavern, convinced to a man as they were that the buxom serving wench would never permit any man to have any really intimate contact with her, let alone have such contact with a male herself, Moxie quickly brought Pester's drooping shaft to attention and slipped the soft leather sheath over its length.

Tightening the laces, she wound the specially adapted strap about the base of his column, hampering the blood flow and ensuring that his ball-less manhood would remain erect until she required the use of it.

'Dirty little thing!' she said accusingly, and gave his organ a sharp flick with her gloved fingers. 'I think we should punish you for the unclean thoughts you so obviously harbour.'

Through the eye slits he watched as Moxie saddled the brown pony, Rollo, his unblinking stare never wavering from the slim shaft that arose from the middle of the polished leather seat. Satisfied that the girth strap was tight enough, she turned back to Pester and nodded.

Understanding exactly what was required of him, he shuffled his feet wider apart and bent over at the waist, waiting expectantly for the touch of her warm fingers and the cool oil they would apply to effect an easier entry for the waiting dildo. As he finally settled into the saddle the polished invader embedded to the hilt within him, its leather covered, flesh and blood engorged twin standing stiff before him, Pester would have been astonished if he could have seen the events taking place many miles from Varragol, and filled with sheer disbelief if he had known the true identity of that other slave who sat mounted in almost identical fashion.

Savatch had left the slave helmet in place, but removed the blindfold, allowing Corinna to see that they were now on the road to the north east of the garrison town. They road slowly, but the gentle swaying motion of her mount ensured that the saddle dildo kept up a constant, stimulating motion on her clitoris, so that several times Corinna was convulsed with minor orgasms and only the most supreme effort of willpower prevented her from exploding totally.

Riding just ahead of her, a lead rein attached to her horse's bridle, Savatch of course knew only too well the effect the tortuous journey was having on his captive lover, yet not once did he look back during at least two hours. In this time they met a scant assortment of travellers coming in the opposite direction: a farmer with what appeared to be his teenage son, riding on a wagon loaded with sacks, a lone man in his middle years, riding one horse and leading a pack beast behind him, and three women of varying years, travelling together on foot.

None gave Corinna more than a passing glance, save for the youngest of the three women, who seemed to study her intently, albeit with a deliberately sideways stare. The sight of a virtually naked slave girl being led by a master was too common to raise that much interest, let alone comment, but there was something in the girl's eyes that Corinna thought she recognised and understood, and she smiled impishly to herself once the women were behind her. She wondered, idly, how much different the girl's reaction might have been had she been able to see the true nature of her mounted position.

The sun was rising in the sky, though still some way short of its zenith, as they topped the brow above the small village. During the short journey down the gentle slope towards it, Corinna studied the few buildings. The village she recognised as Ar Fenook, named after a merchant farmer whose original house had been the first structure here and whose business, mostly in wool, had drawn the small population together. The founding father was long since dead, the once core estate now divided among several grandsons and great grandsons, but there remained a large mill, powered by the waters of a swift stream, a smithy, a general trading store, a small tavern and about twenty houses.

Away to their left, slightly detached from the main village, stood another cluster of perhaps half a dozen buildings, together with an assortment of outhouses and a larger structure, built on three storeys, now much dilapidated but once the home of Nedi Ar Fenook himself, but now abandoned as a dwelling.

As Savatch led the way into the circular grass clearing that formed the centre of the village, Corinna's eyes were drawn to the raised stone dais that dominated it. The platform was perhaps twenty feet long, half that wide and four feet high, with a set of roughly hewn timber steps leading up to it. At one end stood a high gibbet, beneath which a simple trestle was placed, upon which many a condemned felon had stood during his last moments of life, though, since Corinna's arrival at the castle it had not been used, the one execution confirmed during the past year having been concerned with an altogether different village and carried out, by her decree, using the more human gallows with its drop trap that Savatch had suggested was installed in the castle itself.

In the days of her step-uncle's stewardship, death had been the punishment for so many piddling little offences, and the local bailiffs had been given far too much authority and jurisdiction in the carrying out of sentences. In that view Corinna and Savatch were as one, and it had been one of the new Lady Steward's first actions to try to bring this backward region into line with the sort of thinking encouraged by her father in the more enlightened areas of Illeum. However, in Ar Fenook, as in so many other of the villages, the gibbets remained, a reminder, if one were needed, of those darker days only so recently passed. And here also, at the other end of the public scaffold, stood the pillory and its accompanying whipping post, these two structures still very much in regular use, though they were both stood empty this morning.

The appearance of Savatch brought the current bailiff, who was also head man, scurrying from the cottage he occupied at the side of the green, for the Lady Steward's captain's face was well known here, as in most of the other villages and hamlets. Corinna's features, too, were familiar to the local populace and she wondered what Melik Ar Fenook's reaction would have been had he known the true identity of the wretched creature he now appraised.

'A runaway, my lord?' he asked, curious. Savatch swung himself easily from his saddle, grinning at the bearded and neatly attired figure of the late Nedi's youngest grandson, now a man in his early forties.

'Not exactly, Melik,' he replied, affecting an air of disinterest. 'Just one stupid wench who hadn't the sense to learn how to please her mistress. You know how some of these barbarian girls refuse to accept their situation? This is just one that's a little more stubborn than usual, so her ladyship has instructed me to return her to the trader from whom she was purchased.'

'A stupid little slut she must be indeed,' Melik agreed. 'Rather the sort of life she could have expected at the castle than that she is now likely to get. If the Lady Corinna has washed her hands of her, the stigma will ensure her value is halved and all she can look forward to now will be the toil of a field slave, despite those fine tits.' He laughed harshly, his eyes never leaving Corinna, and she could imagine exactly what was going through his head.

'I might be interested in another field wench myself,' the bailiff continued, confirming Corinna's assumption, 'always provided the asking price were not too steep, of course.'

'Of course,' Savatch grinned, turning to lead both horses across to the nearer of the two public hitching rails, so that they might drink from the trough beneath it. 'However, her ladyship's instructions were most specific. I am to take the wench back to her former owner and, at my discretion, have her publicly flogged at every suitable stop on the way.' He turned and looked meaningfully towards the raised scaffold.

'This,' he said quietly, 'would seem one such suitable place and I know you are very practised in these matters.'

Melik's dark features creased into an ingratiating smile. 'You are too kind, my lord,' he said, 'but of course, I shall be only too happy to oblige. Would you like me to attend to it now?'

'Not immediately,' Savatch said. 'Put her in yon pillory for a spell and have some mud buckets placed handily for your villagers. She will give your women and children some sport whilst I take some refreshment at your excellent tavern. However,' he added, fixing Melik with a cold eye, 'make it well known that she is not to be touched in any other way, do I make myself clear? Not even you, Melik, so I'll see her belted and locked before I dine and I'll keep the key with me.'

'You want her fat little cunny plugged by other means?' Melik suggested. 'Only I see she has been given a filling seat already, as it were.'

Savatch nodded. 'Aye, I've a fat beast in my saddlebag that will fill her nicely,' he said, 'but I'll see to it myself. Now, away and fetch me a suitable belt for the wench.'

Agana fought desperately, killing one of the men, wounding a second and tearing the eye from the socket of another, but they were too many and the element of surprise had prevented her from reaching her sword. The short sharp dagger was no match for their clubs and field swords and she was quickly overpowered, bruised, bleeding and with a ring of four gleaming blade points pressing her back against the wall of her bedchamber.

'Traitors!' she hissed, staring up at them from the crouch of her defensive position. 'Infamous traitors. You will hang or burn for this treachery.'

'I think not, bitch.' The voice belonged to the man Ingrim, who pushed his way to the fore. Looking up into his face, Agana began to realise the truth. Ingrim had arrived at Varragol as the sergeant in charge of the relief guards, but now, as he stood above her, Agana could see that this was no sergeant and cursed herself for not having seen something before.

'Permit me to introduce myself,' Ingrim said, with a slight mocking bow. 'I am Captain Ingrim of the Vorsan Trachos Guard, and these are all my men. We now have total control of the palace and the castle and you, together with your employer, are our prisoner.

'All your own guards are dead, so further resistance is futile. I suggest, therefore, that you save yourself further trouble and injury and surrender without any more unnecessary stupidity.'

'I'd rather cut my own throat!' Agana hissed, the whites of her eyes brilliant against her dark skin. Ingrim choked back a raucous guffaw.

'I'll wager you would,' he said malevolently. 'I'll just wager you would!'

Pester dismounted with some difficulty and with great care, the shaft sliding from him only with reluctance, but Moxie made no move to help him. Instead, she stood back, tapping her riding crop impatiently against the side of her boot, chiding him on his laggardness. At last, he stood on the ground, teetering precariously on his stupid footwear, his eyes lowered and staring fixedly at his own rampant organ.

'Come here, boy,' Moxie ordered. Still unable to meet her gaze, Pester swayed across the few paces separating them, until she was able to reach out and grasp his throbbing shaft in its soft leather sheath. Tucking the crop into her belt, she used her free hand to unbuckle the gag strap, pulling the stuffed leather penis from between his lips.

'Whose is this horrible thing, boy?' she whispered, and felt him shiver.

'Yours, mistress,' he replied, his voice catching. 'Only yours.'

'Is that so?' Moxie said sourly. 'So why do I hear that you've been using it on that foul animal in the dungeons, eh?'

'Mistress Agana ordered me,' Pester whined. 'I had no choice.'

'Perhaps I should ask her ladyship to have the rest of your tackle cut off,' Moxie suggested. What she could see of Pester's cheeks, beneath the slave mask, blanched immediately.

'No, mistress Moxie, please!' he squealed. 'Not that!' They both knew, with a degree of certainty, that Moxie would never make such a request of Dorothea, and that, even if she did, the likelihood of their overall mistress acceding to such a suggestion was remote, but Pester's position was such that he could never be entirely sure. Besides, there was also Agana to consider, and the giant black woman was far less predictable.

'But this is such an unsightly and unruly little beast,' Moxie laughed, squeezing his organ the harder. 'It spoils such a pretty thing as you are, and without it, why, you could wear a pretty dress and curl your hair and be the fairest of all the palace

81

maids.' She chuckled again, seeing his cheeks turn from white to red, for he would never forget that day when Moxie had indeed dressed him as a maid, the slave helmet hiding his true gender, his remaining manhood strapped tightly to his stomach beneath the flimsy white tunic.

Attired thus, Moxie had walked him to and through the nearest village and, although the few inhabitants who had not been in the fields at such an early hour had taken him as nothing more than a youthful, flat-chested little maid slave, he spent two hours expecting the truth to be discovered at any and every moment. Rather a sound thrashing than such public humiliation.

'Perhaps, without this cocky thing,' Moxie continued, still keeping a firm grasp on him, 'we might sell you to the priestess at Mar Semlar. You'd make the perfect temple virgin.'

Tears began to well up in Pester's eyes, sliding down his cheeks and darkening the leather of the mask beneath the eye slits. Moxie shook her head and pulled the slender page to her huge bosom.

'Poor Pester,' she crooned, her gloved hand stroking the base of his neck beneath the stiff collar. 'You really should have been a girl, I think, but then you would not have this little toy to offer me, would you?' She squeezed his throbbing penis again and he gave out a little moan. The potion she had forced upon him back at the palace, combined with the strictures of the sheath and its harness, were combining so that his burgeoning flesh could not help but try to split the seams of the soft leather that embraced it. And the scent of her, as she pressed his nose deep into her cleavage, did nothing to alleviate this condition.

'Of course,' she sighed, 'you realise that I must whip you for your sinful thoughts and then do something about this wicked cock of yours?'

Pester withdrew his face an inch or so. 'Yes, mistress,' he

whimpered. 'I think you should whip me without delay.'

'I'll wager you do,' Moxie sniggered, scornfully, 'and then all the sooner to sheath that devilish dagger in my warm little scabbard, no doubt.' She released her grip on his shaft, took hold of his shoulders and held him back at arms' length.

'Look at me, you silly little girlie boy,' she said softly. Reluctantly, Pester raised his eyes. Moxie smiled, drawing the crop from her belt. 'Tell me that you love me,' she said, 'and then put yourself up against yonder tree.'

The soldiers who had earlier burst into her bedchamber seemed reluctant to actually lay hands on Dorothea, but if she harboured any hopes as to her future treatment at those hands, the sight of Fulgrim, seated in her own high-backed chair in the reception room off the main hall, quickly dispelled them.

The man, though his features betrayed the evidence of his long ordeal at Agana's merciless hands, looked alarmingly fit. And the anger that burned in his sunken eyes was unmistakable. His thin lips twisted evilly as Dorothea was escorted into his presence.

'So pleasant to see you again, dear lady,' he hissed. 'I cannot tell you how disappointed I have been that you have failed to visit me during all these months I've been your guest here. But then,' he continued, even the pretence of a smile vanishing, 'you knew only too well that your assistant was more than capable of ministering to my needs, eh?'

'Evidently, Lord Fulgrim,' Dorothea retorted, her chin jutting defiantly, despite the sickening feeling growing in the pit of her stomach, 'my assistant, as you call her, did not minister to you thoroughly enough. I knew we should have executed you a year ago.'

'Executed?' Fulgrim sneered. 'You make it all sound so legal. If I should have been executed, then I think the same sentence should have been extended to you. At least I was not preparing to betray my own country.'

'My reasons for doing what I did,' Dorothea replied coolly, 'were justifiable in my mind. At the time, at least. But that is now in the past and I am sure you have not had these brigands drag me here for a discussion on morals and history.'

'Indeed not,' Fulgrim snapped. 'The past, as you say, is past. And certain things,' he went on, laying heavy emphasis on the last two words, 'certain things cannot be altered nor regained, and for that both you and the black bitch will pay dearly.'

'I'm surprised you aren't already running back to whatever bolt hole you originally crawled from!' Dorothea cried. 'You may have wormed sufficient of your bandits inside my palace to wrest control of it, but I doubt you have a force sufficient to hold the territory.'

'That is perfectly correct,' Fulgrim replied, 'but then holding this region is not a part of my plans – not yet, at least. In time, rest assured, I shall control not just this region, but a good deal more of Illeum. For the time being, however, I am confident there is no cause for haste on our part.

'Those men who killed and impersonated the last guard relief were careful to leave no telltale signs, and we know that the next relief will not now be due for several weeks. What there is of the local populace will not be immediately aware of the change of circumstances here and, if they should suspect, why there is but a single road leading back towards the heart of Illeum, and we have already posted a guard there to intercept any foolish enough to attempt to carry the news back.

'By the time the Protector and his court learn of events here we shall be well upon our way, but that still leaves ample time for me to mount a demonstration of the fate that will await any who attempt to resist us upon our eventual return.'

'Slaughtering the local peasantry will win you no friends, nor allies, Fulgrim,' Dorothea said. Fulgrim's twisted smile returned fleetingly.

'Whether you are right or wrong, my lady,' he said, 'I see little point in killing ignorant farmers anyway. Death, as we all know, holds none in its grip for any purpose save its own – even the fear of death tends to count little among people whose life is full of hardship.

'What will impress these simpletons, however, is to see the object of one of their greatest fears brought low by an even greater power.'

'You intend to kill me in front of them?' Dorothea felt her knees beginning to tremble, but Fulgrim shook his head.

'Kill you?' he mocked. 'Why should I even consider such a swift and painless revenge? No, your death will be a long time coming and you will pray for it for many years before you finally achieve release by its means.

'The black bitch, however, is a different matter, though her death will be no swift matter.' He rose slowly and paced across to the great empty hearth. 'That vicious harridan is more feared by your local people than ever you could be, in any case,' he continued. 'So when they see the fate I have in store for her, it will surely freeze the blood in what passes for their brains.'

'Agana acted only upon my orders,' Dorothea said bravely. 'You surely cannot punish her for that. If you wish to wreak your twisted revenge upon anyone, then let it be me.'

Fulgrim turned, leaning against the heavy mantle, and laughed harshly. 'Oh, fear not, dear Dorothea,' he mocked, 'I shall have my revenge on you and take it a hundred fold. Every time a fat soldier's cock fills your withering cunt you will know my revenge, and there are a lot of soldiers where we shall be going, believe me.

'But first, you shall witness the fate of the one whose knife actually cut into my very soul, but you shall witness it on your knees, like a common whore slave.' He straightened up and nodded to the men who stood behind Dorothea.

'Strip her!' he roared. 'Strip her and shave her head, then string her up in the main courtyard. I'll flog her myself, after we have dealt with the black devil!'

From an attitude that had originally seemed almost respectful, Fulgrim's men quickly changed their approach to Dorothea, understanding now that her noble rank was to be no protection to her in the eyes of their master.

Hustling her out into the courtyard, they set about stripping her with a relish that was frightening, cutting her garments away with knives, so great was their eagerness to see her naked. Then, binding her hands behind her back, they forced her to her knees and one of their number proceeded to lop off her thick hair with a pair of crude shears. A second man produced water and a razor to complete the job, shaving the stubble with such thoroughness that her skull was left pink and gleaming.

Worse still, at the instigation of the man they were all now referring to as Captain Ingrim – who had originally arrived at Varragol dressed as an ordinary trooper – the fellow finished by removing her eyebrows. And only the fact that Dorothea regularly depilated her pubis prevented him from turning his attention – and the wicked blade – to that lower and more intimate target.

Throughout this horror and indignity there was no sign of Fulgrim himself, but Dorothea realised he must have been watching from some vantage point she could not see, for he appeared through the doorway leading to the main palace building as soon as his brutish minions had finished carrying out his instructions.

'May I say how lovely you are looking, my lady?' he taunted, standing a few feet directly in front of her, feet planted firmly apart. He had changed into a pair of leather breeches and heavy boots, above which he wore a pale blue silken shirt, open almost to the wide belt that encircled his waist. Dorothea stared up at him, determined not to show the humiliation she felt.

'I'd hardly say I was looking my best, you Vorsan bastard,' she hissed, 'but then you're hardly the greatest judge of true beauty.'

'Ah, but beauty is in the eye of the beholder, dear Dorothea,' Fulgrim sneered, 'and I cannot begin to explain to you just how beautiful this picture is. You cannot imagine how many hours I have imagined this moment, nor the moments that are to follow.' He turned to Ingrim and nodded.

'Fetch the black bitch out now,' he ordered, 'and see if your men have finished cleaning up that cage. Your dungeons are a real treasure house of imaginative creativity,' he said, addressing Dorothea again. 'So many truly ingenious inventions down there and most of them neglected for so long, it seems a great shame to waste them all.'

Dorothea made no reply, for she could only imagine what Fulgrim was talking about. She knew there were several cells beneath the palace that had not been entered, let alone used, for perhaps half a century, maybe longer, used only as storerooms for equipment that had fallen into either repair or disfavour in the meantime. Agana, possibly, might be aware, at least to an extent, what those chambers contained, but Dorothea herself very seldom ventured below ground.

A babble of voices, among them Agana's, heralded the arrival of Fulgrim's other prisoner. She cursed and screamed in a mixture of her own native tongue and the language she had adopted and learned so well since her arrival in Illeum. But despite her struggles and attempts to lash out at her guards with her bare feet, she could not prevent them dragging her out to join Dorothea in the centre of the yard.

Like her mistress she had been stripped and her cropped

hair shaved similarly, so that her black pate gleamed dully beneath the bright sun. The men had locked a stout metal collar about her long neck, cuffing her wrists behind her back and drawing them up cruelly, so they were fastened to that collar by mere inches of chain, another chain fastened to the front of the iron band providing them with the means to haul her wherever they wished.

Her expression was fearsome, her lips drawn back in a feral snarl, the whites of her eyes rolling with rage, but Dorothea knew that even the black amazon must be terrified, her magnificent show of anger and resistance simply masking her true feelings from their captors.

'Get her to her knees!' Fulgrim roared, and the burly guards obeyed without ceremony, kicking Agana's feet from under her and thrusting her face down into the dust, from which position they pulled her up and back, so that she finished squatting on her calf muscles. Even so, she seemed more concerned with Dorothea's fate than her own.

'Mistress!' she shrieked. 'What have they done?'

Dorothea, blinking away tears, shook her head. 'They have not harmed me, Agana,' she replied, fighting to keep the tremor from her voice, 'nor, I think, will they just yet, but I fear they mean a dreadful ill to you.' Agana, her breasts heaving as she fought to draw more air into her lungs, set her powerful jaw squarely.

'Let them do their worst, my lady,' she challenged. 'I am ready to meet my gods, as I have ever been ready. Death holds no terrors for the N'Gazi, for there is a far better life beyond this.'

'Ha!' Fulgrim exclaimed. 'Bravely spoken and no less than I would have expected.' He stepped forward, seized Agana's jaw in one hand and bent her head back savagely, forcing her to look up into his face. 'Death, however,' he continued, his voice taking on a sinister, velvet quality, 'is the least of your possible fears and will be the last of them, mark my words.

'Truly, I would like to keep you in the sort of suffering you inflicted upon me and for just as long, if not longer.' He released his grip on her and took a half pace back again. 'Time, however, does us no favours in that respect, but still you will not die quickly. It may take a few hours, it may take a few days, but it will seem longer even than the year through which I suffered at your hands.'

He turned away, looking back towards the entrance into the palace, and then addressed one of the nearby guards.

'You!' he roared. 'Get down below and see if Captain Ingrim needs any help. I want this bitch to see the fate that awaits her and get her started on the first stage of her long voyage to the seven hells.'

The bailiff quickly summoned two muscular young village men, who lifted Corinna from her horse, not without a few coarse comments when they saw the nature of the saddle and the effect its protruding shaft had had upon her. Mindful of Savatch's instructions, they stood by, waiting until Melik Ar Fenook returned with the leather chastity belt and then watched, grinning, as Savatch inserted the fat dildo and fastened the leather straps to keep it in place.

Corinna grunted as the hard shaft entered her, her eyes bulging at its size, and Savatch lost no time in explaining the truth concerning this latest invader.

'This pizzle was once the pride and joy of a prize bull,' he said. 'The original owner had it cured and stuffed, but his new bull trampled him to death before he had chance to introduce his mistress to its pleasures.' Even had she not remained securely gagged, Corinna would not have asked him how the monstrous weapon had come into his possession – there were some things, she knew, that were best not known.

'Right then, lads,' Savatch said, stepping back and slapping

Corinna sharply across her naked rump. 'Put her up in the pillory and then join me in an ale. And make sure the mud buckets are nicely full.'

Her sex may have been locked beyond their reach, but the young village men took every advantage of Corinna's defencelessness to paw and mould her breasts, tugging at the slave tags hanging from her nipples and stroking the tips of her engorged teats with their rough fingers, so that she squirmed and wriggled, despite her most stoic efforts to remain unmoved.

On the stone dais they released her mitted arms from the belt cuffs and bent her forward, neck and wrists forced into the waiting half circles, closing the heavy timber top section to complete their entrapment. While one man inserted the rusting padlock, the other stooped in front of her lowered face, staring up into her eyes.

'Methinks you're a hot one,' he whispered, licking his lips, 'and I'm a-wondering just how much his lordship might take for you, that I am. My grandfather left me eight fine horses this winter past and I reckon Master Savatch would think any two of them a worthwhile trade for a slave reject such as you.

'A few days under my whip and with something not far short of that dead meat inside you and I reckon you might make something of a decent bargain, that I do. If nothing else, you've a fine pair of tits to keep a man's hands and mouth occupied!' He laughed good-naturedly, reached out to caress Corinna's hanging left breast one final time, and stood up again. His companion now seemed eager to be off.

'Leave the wench, Bal,' he said. 'Savatch doesn't want to sell her anyway, the way I heard it, so let's go drink at his expense, eh?' Bal seemed reluctant to leave Corinna, but eventually bowed to the inevitable and the two friends swaggered off together in the direction of the tavern, leaving Corinna to her own thoughts.

Her solitude was short-lived, however. Word of the slave girl in the pillory spread quickly throughout the small village and out into the surrounding fields, and very soon a small crowd was gathering, forming a half circle before her. Approaching the dais directly, let alone mounting the steps, seemed to be forbidden, but the two wooden tubs filled with the wet sticky mud were clearly public domain and very soon the villagers, young and old alike, were enjoying their sport amidst a chorus of laughter and jeers.

Even the smallest children joined in, scooping handfuls of the sticky mess and pressing them into rough balls, before hurling them at their helpless victim, and it was not long before Corinna was covered in the gooey mass from head to toe. Fortunately, the thick leather of the slave helmet offered some protection, and it also seemed that those missiles which did strike her about that part of her body were mostly badly aimed.

To attack the head, it appeared, was considered un-sporting, whereas the sight of a pair of hanging breasts instantly evoked a spirit of keen competition. Time after time the sticky mud pats slapped into Corinna's tender flesh and her skin was tingling by the time Savatch reappeared to call a halt to the proceedings.

'Fetch water and sluice her down,' he ordered two more of the youths. 'And give her a drink, but put the gag back in her heathen mouth again afterwards. I hear tales that some of these pagan wenches are really witches and their curses have great potency.'

Once again, Savatch walked away, apparently disinterested in Corinna's fate. The designated young men eventually reappeared with buckets of water slopping from either hand, dashing the cold contents over Corinna's shivering body and mopping away the diluted mud with sacking rags. Eventually, having cleaned her as best they could, one unfastened the gag strap, drew the gag from her mouth and offered a small earthenware gourd of water to her lips.

Because of her position in the pillory, drinking by normal means was impossible and Corinna was forced to slurp the water like an animal, dribbling much of it. However, the youths had carried out their instructions and Savatch had not specified exactly how much the slave girl should actually drink and, mindful of his warnings about witches and spells, they seemed only too eager to gag her again and beat a retreat.

Corinna was finally left alone, her aching back dulled by the fire in her loins and the kaleidoscope of thoughts and emotions that now filled her head. This was truly unbelievable, she told herself, that she could ever have thought this was what she wanted, yet the evidence – the treachery displayed by her unruly reflexes – was undeniable.

Perhaps, she thought, closing her eyes, perhaps she was, in reality, some devil's spawn, some animal throwback. Perhaps she was diseased, possessed of some plague that attacked not the body, but the very mind, distorting, twisting and corrupting as it went, turning perfectly respectable young women into wanton whores. Wanton whores who gained vicarious thrills from having their most intimate secrets displayed before a baying public and then having the evil whipped out of them.

Except that the whip, Corinna knew, would serve only to whip more evil into her, if evil indeed it was.

The guard Fulgrim had addressed turned to carry out his instructions, but before he had covered even half the distance to the palace entrance, Ingrim appeared through the doorway, closely followed by two more of the Vorsans, dragging between them a curious contraption of black iron bands.

For a few seconds Dorothea was confused, but as they manoeuvred the rust spattered object out into the sunlight she suddenly recognised it, and a gasp of sheer horror became a desperate scream of protest.

'No!' she shrieked. 'No, Fulgrim, not that monstrous device. Its use was abandoned fifty years since and it should have been destroyed then!'

'Yes,' Fulgrim mused as the two men struggled to bring their burden between the two prisoners, 'I'm afraid its condition does rather reflect its age, but the rust is only on the surface and my men have oiled it where necessary, so I am confident it will still work as intended.'

'But even you cannot mean to use that?' Dorothea wailed. 'It is surely the most inhuman torture machine ever devised!' Fulgrim made no reply, beyond a low chuckle, but words were unnecessary and Dorothea could see, from Agana's eyes, that the black woman also knew the cage's purpose.

Made from an assortment of iron bands, it was constructed in a human shape, hinged at the side so it could be locked about the unfortunate subject, whose arms and legs, as well as torso neck and head, would then all be held in a metallic exoskeleton, legs apart, arms held out parallel to the ground.

At various points on the cage small iron rings had been fixed, by which chains or ropes could be attached to raise the cage once the wearer was inside. Its original designer had intended it be used to dangle miscreants, either from a high gibbet or from the battlements of the castle wall that surrounded the palace.

Unable to move more than fingers and toes, the prisoner would be held rigidly, exposed to the elements and to the eyes of the local population, a suitable warning as to the sort of fate that could await any others foolish enough to consider challenging the legitimacy of the steward's authority. In itself, a day or two in the embrace of the humanoid cage was a terrible enough punishment and few who survived it would wish to experience its horrors a second time.

However, the original designer had included features that ensured that the simple hanging could be made worse and that, in extreme cases, the terrible thing could be used as a means of eventual execution.

There had been, originally, two of these awful machines, similar in their basic design, but differing in order to accommodate the different sexes. That intended for male victims had incorporated a metal band that could be fastened around the base of the victim's genitalia, a screw mechanism allowing it to be inexorably tightened. The final effect of such treatment, Dorothea knew, though only by legend, was that the unfortunate man's equipment gradually turned black and finally tended to drop off, though that was only if he were fortunate. The less fortunate sufferers ended up with the flesh rotting disease, which gradually spread to the rest of their body, bringing with it the most dreadful and agonising death.

For female victims, apart from the dimensions of the cage being slightly modified to the differing size and shape of their bodies, there was a different attachment by which the torturer could inflict similar horrors. This was in the form of a long metal phallus, a curious and indeed ingenious piece of engineering. Once inserted within the woman's vagina, separate screw mechanisms allowed it to be lengthened and broadened, stretching her unbelievably and eventually, if her tormentor decided, puncturing vital organs that would mean a lingering death no less terrible, in its way, than that inflicted upon the male victims.

In both cases, however, the fiendish mind of the cage's creator had gone further still. Among the various metal bands were some, at strategic points, that could be slowly tightened: about the waist and chest, about the thighs and elbows, about the forehead and, if the torturer decided to finally end the suffering by a relatively humane means, about the neck, a wicked spike being available that could be driven into the top of the spine by degrees dependent upon the whim of the operator.

Grotesque as this garrotting feature was, it was preferable to the alternatives – crushed joints, burst muscles and the slow driving of the air from lungs that would gradually become punctured by the splintering of crushed ribs.

Fully aware that she could expect not even the slightest show of humanity from the man she had tortured so long, Agana now renewed her struggles, striving to rise to her feet with one final, superhuman effort. But the guards were too many for her and were not disposed to waste time on any niceties. A swift blow to the side of her head, delivered with the handle of one fellow's sword, sent her eyes rolling and she fell back again, stunned and disoriented. By the time she was even halfway returned to her senses it was too late, for the final locks and screws were clicking into place and she stood in what she knew would be her final, obscene pose.

'Get her up to the rampart and hang her over the top,' Fulgrim ordered. 'Tighten everything, but not too much just yet. We have three days before we needs move on and I want her to enjoy every last hour of that time.' He turned, grinning maliciously at Dorothea, who could now barely see through her tears.

'And you, too, milady,' he said. 'You will be taken outside every two hours, where you can watch your black whore as you are whipped. With luck, she'll take the sound of your screams to her heathen gods.'

The sun was now directly overhead, its heat burning into Corinna's unprotected back and shoulders, but still there was no sign of Savatch returning. Gnawing against her gag, Corinna was beginning to wish she had never suggested this misadventure, when suddenly she was stirred from her daze by the sound of approaching footsteps and voices. Raising her head as best she could, Corinna found herself looking down once again at the young man, Bal, and beside him, a homely female of about his own age.

'You see how a real master treats a worthless female, Erin?' Bal said, smirking. The girl's plain features registered horror at the way in which he spoke, but she said nothing. Bal gave a short laugh and pointed a finger directly into Corinna's face.

'And do you know why masters make such use of the slave hoods?' he went on. 'I'll tell you why. If he has a pretty slave, then he doesn't want her face to be admired, rather that men look upon her tits and arse, so that she might be just any other piece of woman flesh.' The look of horror on Erin's face deepened.

'And,' Bal said, relishing her discomfort, 'if he has a plain slave, then no one need know that's all he can afford. Men can look upon a featureless wench like this one and imagine what they will. Beneath that mask she could be the most beautiful woman in the world, or she could be the most repulsive. Either way, she is treated the same, as it should be.'

'But even a slave girl is a person,' Erin protested, though not loudly. 'Even this poor creature surely deserves to be treated for herself, as an individual.'

'But why?' he countered. 'She is bought, owned and has no rights, save that her master may not kill her without showing just cause.'

'Not much different to being a wife, then,' Erin replied, pensively. Bal seemed to ignore her observation.

'This creature,' he said, waving a hand at Corinna, 'is almost certainly a barbarian, without knowledge of her letters, without any civilising influence, save the collar and lash. Such as she are little better than the wild animals and worse than the pigs, sheep and cattle, for they are domesticated by nature and accept their station easily.'

'Yet so-called civilised men take so-called barbarians such as this to their beds,' Erin pointed out. 'So who, then, is the animal?'

'I said she was no better than an animal, not that she was one,' Bal answered. 'And in her hood and collar she can be made to perform like a civilised woman – maybe better,' he added, with a snicker. He turned to the girl and grinned down at her.

'Perhaps,' he said, 'it is the collar and lash that have the most beneficial effect on all women.' He met her indignant stare without a flicker. 'And perhaps,' he continued after a lengthy pause, 'we should explore that possibility at some later stage.'

Moxie's keen young eyes spotted the gruesome spectacle hanging from the battlements as she and Pester were emerging from the woods. For several seconds, as her horse continued walking, she could do nothing but sit in the saddle and stare in horrified disbelief, but self-preservation is an even stronger instinct than horror. Hardly able to speak, she reined her mount to a halt and wheeled it about, leaning across to seize the bridle of Pester's pony.

'Quickly!' she gasped. 'Back into the trees!' The young page, whose attention had been anywhere but on what lay ahead of them, almost toppled from his saddle, only the ropes about his ankles preventing such a painful disaster, and he cried out in alarm as he lurched in the saddle. Moxie, however, realised that every second was crucial and did not waste even one in explanations until they were back deep inside the cover of the trees.

'No, I don't know what's happening, you stupid little oaf!' she snapped, helping Pester to dismount from his precarious perch. 'All I know is what I saw – and you'd have seen it too, if your mind had been anywhere but below your middle!' Briefly, she repeated to Pester what she had seen and the youth stared at her, slack-jawed.

'But why?' was all he managed. Moxie barely managed to control her exasperation.

'I don't damned well know!' she stormed. 'All I do know is that Lady Dorothea would never be a party to Agana being treated like that, not in a million years.'

'You're sure it *was* Agana?' Pester persisted. Moxie wanted to slap him, but realised it would do no good.

'Of course I'm sure,' she said slowly. 'You tell me what other woman could ever be mistaken for that black bitch, eh?' She turned away, looking back down the trail along which they had fled. 'No, that was Agana all right, and I can think of only one reason for what I saw.

'Fulgrim,' she said, looking over her shoulder to where Pester stood, still bound in his slave garb and still apparently unable to grasp what was happening. 'That evil bastard is behind this,' she continued, 'which means he must somehow have escaped. But then surely the guards...' Her voice tailed off, her forehead furrowing in concentration.

'The relief guard detail,' she said at last, her words barely audible. 'That has to be it. Somehow, I don't know how, they must have been Fulgrim's men, though the gods know how.'

'I think I might know, miss,' Pester ventured. Moxie rounded on him, her eyes narrowing. Pester wilted visibly, but continued, his words tumbling out on top of each other.

'He asked me, miss,' he said, 'about – well, months ago, it must have been, when I was duty to take his meals down there. He offered me money – all the gold I could ever dream of, he said – if I'd get someone to take a message for him. He said there was a man in Illeum City and that this man would take care of everything, including me.'

'Yes, I'll wager he'd have taken care of you, my pretty boy,' Moxie growled. 'But you refused, of course?'

'Of course!' Pester replied indignantly. 'I wasn't going to help a monster like him, not for all the gold in the world.'

'Not to mention what Agana would do to you if she discovered you trying to sneak out and make it to Illeum City,' Moxie added sourly. 'But someone was tempted, or I'm a smithy's labourer. Have any of the pages gone missing of late?' she added. 'I haven't heard anything myself, but then that would be Agana's territory and half of you look the same to me anyway.'

'Pages and maids go missing every few weeks anyway,' Pester said. 'Some are caught and returned, but I don't think Agana is ever that worried. She just picks new ones from whatever the slavers have on offer.'

'And pages and maids taken from across borders and mountains are less likely to run off than those of you with families and friends in Illeum,' Moxie muttered. 'So, if someone was lured by dreams of Vorsan gold, no one would have been suspicious at the time?'

'No, miss,' Pester said miserably. 'I wish now I'd said something at the time.'

'So do I,' Moxie agreed, her usually full lips drawn into a thin line, 'though not half as much as I suspect Agana does right now!'

The girl, Erin, had refused to rise to Bal's bait. It was obvious, to Corinna, that there was supposed to be something between them – they were probably betrothed under the sort of arrangement that was common among the rural families – but that something was most definitely not love.

From what she had seen of the female half of the village population, Erin, Corinna thought, was a fair average in appearance. Country life and presumably generations of inbreeding did no favours to a woman's appeal, and most Corinna had seen were much the same. Sturdy of build, strong of back, but few would turn a man's head in the streets of Illeum City. The former tavern wench, Moxie, now Lady

Dorothea's favourite, had been a remarkable exception, but then, from what Corinna had gathered from the girl the previous year, her mother had been some sort of dancer, with roots originally in one of the warmer southern countries south of the Sea of Vorsan.

Bal, it seemed, was well aware of his intended's shortcomings on the beauty front and excited, without doubt, by Corinna's appearance, even though the slave hood concealed her features. And, unless the unfortunate Erin was careful, there was little doubt he would eventually have her reduced to the role of playing his personal slave maid.

Reduced? Corinna sighed, ignoring the trickle of saliva that dribbled from one corner of her gagged lips. Yes, it was reduced, but she had been only too willing to enter the role. But then, she told herself, unlike Erin, she did not have a life of toil and hardship ahead of her – behind her as well, in all probability – so it was hardly the same.

Was it?

She wondered what the plain peasant girl would say if she knew the true identity of the poor helpless creature she had looked upon so pityingly? She would be shocked and shocked beyond anything that Bal could say or do to her, but understand?

Never.

No, Corinna thought, someone like Erin would never understand, nor could she ever be expected to even sympathise. Rather, she would despise her, hate her, show nothing but contempt for someone who had chosen to allow herself to be abused and displayed so shamelessly.

Only minutes after Bal and Erin had finally left, the sound of voices from the general direction of the tavern heralded the appearance of Melik Ar Fenook, followed by a growing phalanx of village people, with Savatch walking slightly to one side and affecting an air of detachment. Peering sideways and watching his approach, Corinna wondered if he could really be as calm as he appeared. The whip Melik carried, coiled in his two hands, proved that Savatch clearly intended to go through with this, but how could he stand by and watch whilst another man whipped her?

Her eyes growing round behind the mask, Corinna felt herself beginning to sweat, her legs shaking as the crowd came up to her and began to fan out, jostling for the best vantage points. She saw Savatch approach Melik and bend to whisper something in his ear and, for a brief moment, believed that he must be about to call a halt, but such a vain hope was quickly dashed.

Slowly, Savatch himself mounted the steps to the dais, approached the pillory and removed the lock, swinging the top timber clear and grasping the back of Corinna's collar to haul her upright. The muscles in her back and legs screaming in protest, she barely heard his first words, but as she focused upon them she realised there was to be no reprieve.

'Is this what you wanted, princess?' he whispered, as he turned her towards the whipping post. 'Well, this is what you shall have, to understand the true status of slavery, where a master can order a slave thrashed by the hand of any he nominates.' He thrust her across the few paces between pillory and post, drawing down the thick hemp to bind her wrists before her.

'See now how they all gawp and wait?' he hissed, knotting the rope tightly a second time. 'Look at them, slavering like wolves, near to baying even and there's not one male among them who wouldn't gladly get himself between your pretty legs, or even take the whip from Melik and flay you himself.' He jerked on the bindings, checking they were secure and then hauled on the free end of the line, forcing Corinna's arms high above her head until she was standing, barely on tiptoe, her bare breasts thrust against the rough timber.

'And they'd gather for the spectacle, princess or pauper,' Savatch snorted, fastening off the rope and stepping back slightly. 'All are equal under the lash,' he added, his face twisted peculiarly. He reached out a hand, patted Corinna lightly on her right buttock and nodded.

'Enjoy your whipping, slave girl,' he muttered, and turned away for the steps, which Melik was now already ascending. The two men paused opposite each other and exchanged words that Corinna could not hear, and then Savatch climbed down to take up a position in the front row of the crowd, who suddenly fell silent as the bailiff began to address them.

'Friends!' he bellowed, raising the coiled leather braid in one hand. 'Friends, the good captain here has decreed, upon the orders of the Lady Corinna Oleanna herself, that this worthless, errant slave slut should be publicly punished for her ingratitude, insolence and disobedience. By the authority invested in me by that decree and by the authority of the office to which the State of Illeum has appointed me, I shall now execute that part of the sentence deemed to be carried out in our village.'

He stepped back, out of Corinna's line of vision, and she heard the sharp slap as he shook the whip out over the stone flags that formed the top of the scaffold dais. She closed her eyes, biting hard into her gag, as the first hiss of displaced air signalled the flight of the leather serpent he wielded.

The oiled braid snaked across her shoulders with a crack like splintering twigs and instantly the line of fire speared from shoulder to shoulder. Corinna squealed through the gag, her whole body bucking and writhing, her feet swinging clear of the ground so that she hung by her wrists momentarily, until her scrabbling toes found a new purchase.

Dimly, she registered the murmur of approval from the onlookers but, by the time the lash fell for a second time, their noise had merged with the roar that rose to fill her head.

The bushes at the edge of the woods finished more than a hundred paces from the foot of the castle wall and the small postern gate, and as she lay under their cover, at first Moxie did not recognise the sorry looking female being dragged out towards the heavy timber post that the first soldiers had set into the ground. Only when she heard the woman's defiant voice did she realise, with horrified disbelief, that the bald, naked female was none other than her mistress, Dorothea.

Hardly daring to breathe, Moxie studied the men. There were eight of them in all, ordinary looking troopers, all of whom, she presumed, had entered the castle as the supposed relief duty column a day or so earlier. Then they had been wearing the livery of Illeum, but now, she saw, their tabards bore a crest she had last seen upon the bestial Lord Fulgrim's attendants, a year since.

High above, trapped inside what appeared to be a human-shaped metal cage, dangled the helpless, outstretched figure of Agana, the big black woman silent but watching the proceedings below with an intensity that belied her own perilous position.

Gripping the handle of her switch so hard that her knuckles must surely have turned white inside her leather gloves, Moxie also bore silent frustrated witness, as the brutish fellows thrust Dorothea up against the post and tied her bound hands to it, high above her head.

One of the men was carrying a coiled whip, leaving little doubt in Moxie's mind as to what the ultimate intention of all this activity was, but there was nothing she could do to help her mistress, for she was outnumbered and the soldiers were all well armed. Round eyed with the sheer horror of the scene, Moxie remained transfixed, like a rabbit caught in the flare of a hunter's torch.

It seemed they were in no desperate hurry to begin, however;

instead, the small group formed a ring about their captive, jeering at her, making obscene gestures and taking it in turns to fondle her. For her part, from what little Moxie could see of her face, Dorothea was struggling to remain impassive, ignoring their crude jibes and steeling herself not to flinch at their rough handling.

At last, seeing that the noblewoman, despite what had been done to her, would not give them satisfaction in any other way, the rowdy group seemed to tire of their game. One of them, whom Moxie recognised vaguely as having been just another of the relief guard group, but who now wore some sort of officer's insignia on his shoulders, indicated the man with the whip.

'Give her ladyship three stripes,' he guffawed. 'Space them well and then Pengrom can try to lay another three between them.' His words brought a general round of laughter from his men as they stepped further back, making room for the whip man to take up a suitable position and stance. The officer, meantime, peered up at Agana.

'Look well, you black heathen whore!' he roared. 'Watch how your mistress dances for the common soldiery and then see how she squirms on the end of a few honest cocks!'

Hands spread upon Pecon's muscular chest, Demila slowly raised herself, until only the tip of his organ remained within her. Dreamily, she gazed down upon him, eyes hooded with passion behind the slave mask. Pecon sighed and reached up to take her breasts, one in each hand, fingers kneading the firm globes and sliding down to meet and grip about her elongated nipples.

With a strangled cry Demila let herself fall back again, every sinew in her straddled thighs stretched to its limit, as her pubic bone ground into his and his full length was once again embedded in her to its hilt. Her vaginal muscles contracted

104

fiercely and instantly he began to climax, his hot seed spurting high towards her womb like sharp arrows.

He bucked fiercely, but she held onto him with the strength of her contractions, her fingernails clawing his flesh as her own orgasm swept up and over her. Her eyes closed, opened again, yet she saw nothing, knowing only that she was falling into a yawning abyss and that if she never emerged from it again she was beyond caring.

'Money well spent.' His lazy drawl jerked her back to reality and she opened her eyes to see her latest master grinning up at her. He stroked her hanging breasts affectionately, as he might have petted a favourite dog, and Demila understood that he was reminding her of her true status.

'Thank you, master,' she murmured dutifully, but with no little genuine gratitude. She made to lift herself clear of him, but he grasped her hips and held her down, keeping himself sheathed within her. On a whim, she forced the walls of her tunnel to contract again and was rewarded by a widening of his smile.

'Keep that up,' he said, 'and I may just have to think about keeping you.'

'I would like that, master,' Demila whispered truthfully. After the obese Daskot, any man would surely have been an improvement, but Pecon was more than just that. He raised his eyebrows, mocking her.

'Should I worry whether my slave likes anything?' he asked, though his tone was gentle. Demila lowered her eyes.

'No, master,' she said, but could not resist demonstrating the power of her love muscles once again. Pecon's response was to laugh and slap her playfully across both breasts at once, drawing a small squeal from her lips.

'Enough, my little whore slave,' he said. 'Much as I could enjoy another performance like the last, the road ahead awaits and there are places I should be. Take your hot little scabbard to the stream and cool it down.' Demila lifted herself clear and then hesitated, hovering above his glistening shaft as it fell back across his stomach.

'Master?' she ventured.

'What?'

'Might I wash my hair and face?' she asked. Pecon looked up at her, considering this request.

'Are they dirty?' he demanded.

Demila shrugged. 'They are not as clean as my master deserves,' she replied carefully. 'And this mask makes everything so hot.'

'You wish to remove your slave mask, is that it?' he said. Slowly, avoiding his gaze, she nodded.

'And when your mask is unlocked, perhaps you might seek to slip away into the forest, no?'

'Oh no, master!' she squealed. 'I would not do that. But you could come with me, to watch that I do not.'

'I could,' Pecon agreed, 'but I shall not, I think.' He rolled onto his side, reaching for his breeches, and produced a small key, which he offered up to her. 'You may unlock the collar and remove the mask yourself,' he said, 'and after you have washed your face and rinsed the dust from your hair, you will replace the mask and secure the lock, before returning here. If you do try to escape, be sure I shall hunt you down, as I did before and, when we reach the next village, I'll have the tanner sew the damned mask to you permanently, understand?'

Smiling, but shaking at the same time, Demila took the key from his grasp and rose gracefully to her feet.

'I understand, master,' she whispered, 'but it will not be necessary. I am your obedient and dutiful slave, now and for as long as you wish it to be so.'

Jekka spurred her horse gently, urging it to increase its gait to a faster walk, and drew alongside Alanna, leaving Melina, still part asleep in the saddle, to follow on a length and a half behind them.

'We're being followed.' Jekka did not turn her head and spoke from the corner of her mouth, her lips barely moving. She did not need to warn Alanna against the instinctive reaction of looking back.

'How many are they?' Alanna continued to study the snow covered track immediately ahead of them. Jekka grinned, wryly.

'Just the one,' she replied, 'and, lest I'm very mistaken, 'tis the young oaf you wouldn't let me kill back there in the mountain. He's about two hundred paces to our rear and trying to make best use of what pitiful cover these scrawny trees and bushes offer.'

'He's probably seeking to retrieve his little hotpot from us,' Alanna smiled, the laughter evident in her voice. 'I doubt his male pride reacts well to a couple of women stealing his bed fodder from under his nose. I thought I detected something in his eyes back then and it seems I was not mistaken.'

'Probably his first decent fuck,' Jekka snarled. 'Well, let me deal with him now and have done with it. I can swing round and by the time he realises, I can ride him down close enough to put a bolt through his filthy neck.'

'I'm sure you could,' Alanna agreed, 'but why kill him for what's in his head.'

'In his bollocks, more like,' Jekka retorted. 'All men are the same, in my experience, though I wouldn't expect you to understand.'

'Except your experience isn't that great, my redheaded friend,' Alanna said. 'Our little refugee back there would be more to your taste, wouldn't she?'

'I can't say I've really taken much notice of her,' Jekka replied sullenly, 'but even if she were sow ugly, she'd be preferable to any man, though I wouldn't expect you to 'understand that, of course.'

'Of course,' Alanna said evenly. 'But men do have their uses, though *I* wouldn't expect *you* to understand that. Besides, he could be valuable to us.'

'Valuable?' Jekka snorted derisively.

'What say we maybe educate our simple young oaf?' Alanna said. 'Maybe teach him a view of life from the other side of the river, as it were? In the packs on the other horse there are several slave hoods and harnesses – I didn't want to leave them behind, as any trader worth his salt would pay a couple of krones for that little haul.

'Most are intended for females,' she continued, 'but I saw a couple of larger sizes there and I'm sure we could find something to fit our shadow, wouldn't you agree? A little bit of basic training and I'm sure he'd fetch a decent price at one of the markets we're bound to encounter on our journey back.'

Jekka's eyes lit up and her lips curled into a voracious grin. 'You *knew* he'd try to follow us,' she accused.

Alanna shrugged, affecting innocence. 'Who can predict human nature?'

'You, usually,' Jekka chuckled.

Swinging gently to and fro, Agana looked down helplessly as the awful spectacle continued below her. The metal bands that held her captive were tight, but not yet excruciatingly so – even the deadly metal phallus inside her was only mildly uncomfortable. But she knew, only too well, that soon Fulgrim would order his men to begin the process of adjusting the reducing screws and she could only imagine the agonies that would ensue from that.

For the moment, however, her biggest pain was in having to watch her mistress's ordeal and in her total inability to intervene.

Dorothea had managed to endure the first two lashes in

stoic silence, her features contorted as she fought against the desire to cry out, but the third lash wrenched a high-pitched screech from her lips and from then on, as the second man, and then a third, stepped up to take their turns with the deadly rawhide whip, she writhed and screamed continuously.

It seemed to Agana that the soldiers were intent on killing her mistress then and there, but just when she was convinced that the entire group would join in the torture, the officer leading them called a halt. For several minutes they stood about, taunting the hanging figure at the post, until one of their number passed back through the postern and re-emerged, carrying a bucket of water, which he threw over Dorothea with malicious glee.

Even so high above her, Agana could hear her mistress spluttering and choking back to something approximating consciousness, and her instincts told her what was coming next. She was not wrong.

Another of the guards stepped forward and cut Dorothea down, catching her as she slumped to the grass and hauling her back to her feet. Others eagerly took her by the arms, but she did not remain upright for very long.

Yet another man crouched down on all fours and she was thrown along his back, her bound arms over his head and about his neck, where he seized them, preventing her from rising again, though in truth it was evident that she could not possibly have stood unaided.

Clearly unconcerned at their victim's lack of animation, the men proceeded to take it in turns to violate her, their officer apparently exercising the privilege of rank, unfastening his breeches and dropping them about his ankles to reveal a ferocious erection. Unceremoniously, he dropped to his knees behind Dorothea and pressed the swollen head of his shaft against her unresisting nether lips, entering her with an ease that was in part belied by his grunt of satisfaction.

Agana wanted to close her eyes, to blot out the awful scene, but found she was totally unable to wrench her gaze away from Dorothea's suffering. In her mind, there was no doubt at all that she herself was going to die, and die most horribly, yet her concern was entirely for her mistress, as the first man pistoned himself to a convulsive climax and another was already shucking off his breeches to take his place.

Corinna hung limply from the whipping post, her back, shoulders and buttocks burning, tears misting her eyes, yet she knew that Melik's whip had not broken the skin, despite the agony it had inflicted. Savatch, she thought, would be very approving of that, for it required consummate skill with the lash in order not to draw blood.

Their most savage lusts sated, the villagers began to disperse, leaving the victim to her own thoughts and to the ebbing tide of pulsating shocks that were the final aftermath of her ordeal. Through the slowly abating haze of pain, Corinna could feel the warmth of her juices as they seeped around either side of the broad strap which still held the leather phallus deep within her, but she neither knew, nor cared, whether that evidence of her body's treachery was visible to anyone below the dais.

Despite the mind-numbing orgasms that the flailing braid and her own helplessness had triggered, Corinna knew still that she craved something even more. Desperately, she prayed for Savatch to return, release her and take her away from the danger of prying eyes, but Savatch had seemingly wandered away with the crowd and the only person now remaining to show any interest in her plight was the girl, Erin.

The plain village girl stood a few paces from the base of the dais, immediately in front of Corinna, who peered down at her around one side of the post from which she hung. The wench's face was impassive, but there was a deep trouble reflected in her eyes and she continued in her statue-like pose for several minutes, the only movement the occasional blinking of those haunted orbs.

At last, and without any warning, the spell was broken. With a shake of her head Erin spun on her heel and strode off, her crumpled peasant skirt billowing out behind her as she almost ran back across the green. Corinna watched her go, trying to imagine what thoughts kaleidoscoped inside that simple peasant skull...

Agana grimaced as Fulgrim continued tightening the various screws, compressing her body still further within the grip of the humanoid iron cage. Twice he had ordered the cage lowered from the makeshift derrick jutting from the battlements, each time adjusting the bands just enough to increase the pressure on her body, though still it was a long way from inflicting any permanent damage.

He was in no great hurry to kill her, as he had made plain enough, but thirst was beginning to play its part in her continued suffering, for her naked body had been exposed to the sun for several hours now. Grimly, she determined not to give away any sign that the lack of water was affecting her; with luck, dehydration might snatch her from his clutches and deprive him of much of his intended game.

Through half closed eyes she looked beyond Fulgrim and the two guards that flanked him, to where the whipping post now stood empty. How long, she wondered, before they would once again drag Dorothea out? How many more times would she have to endure the vicious kiss of the lash and the defilement at the hands of yet another crowd of these coarse soldiers?

Perhaps only until she, Agana, was finally dead, for part of Fulgrim's spiteful ploy was that each of the women should be witness to the degradation and torture of the other. Once Agana was dead there would be nothing to keep Fulgrim and his men at Varragol and they would surely be on their way without further delay. Once on the road, there would be less time for them to worry about Dorothea, whatever the ultimate fate Fulgrim had in store for her.

Whatever that was, Agana reasoned, it surely could be no worse than what they were doing to her here?

She grunted, gritting her teeth as the broad band about her waist closed in another inch, bending her lower ribs almost to breaking point. And as the rope and pulley creaked and the cage once again began its slow, swaying journey aloft, Agana closed her eyes and tried to will herself to die.

The wagon was primitive, but Savatch had piled several furs into the back, onto which he lifted Corinna. Still wearing her slave hood, her wrists once again cuffed at either side of the wide waist belt, she lay on her side, not daring to let her raw back come into contact, even with the soft pelts.

'I can ride… master,' she whispered defiantly.

'I dare say,' Savatch said, 'but a slave does as she is told and I am telling you that you will ride in this wagon – for now.' He crouched in the space between Corinna and the seat, studying her. 'Unless,' he said at last, 'you would prefer to end this now?' Corinna drew a deep breath and shook her head.

'No,' she replied. 'No, not until it is finished properly. We made a bargain and I shall honour my part. I expect you to do the same… master.'

'That I shall do, if it's still your wish,' he said. 'Meantime, I'll leave you securely plugged and trust you enjoy this next part of the journey.'

'I'd rather be plugged by something warmer,' Corinna retorted, smiling despite the pain from her burning flesh.

Savatch coughed and shook his head. 'Later, slave,' he said, 'unless you'd rather I took you back out there and invited the men of the village to take their turns with you? I reckon they'd pay a few copper coins each for the pleasure.'

Wriggling backwards on her stomach, Moxie made sure she was well into the cover of the woods before she finally stood up. Satisfied that the screen of thick bushes now hid her completely from any eyes looking out from the castle, she turned and trotted back to where she had left the bemused Pester holding their horses.

'They've got the mistress, as well,' she said, in answer to his unspoken question. 'I don't know whether they intend to kill her, but what they're doing to her is horrible enough.' The expression on her face was enough to warn Pester against pressing for further details.

She turned her back on him, trying to disguise the fear she knew would be showing in her eyes.

'I expect they will kill Agana,' she said, after a pause, 'whatever they decide to do with the mistress. Our lady may provide a good bargaining tool, so that could save her life yet, but Agana would have no value and Fulgrim is bound to want to repay her for the ways she's made him suffer these months.'

'What about the guards?' Pester demanded. 'Why have they turned traitor?'

'Because, you stupid boy,' Moxie retorted, 'all the real guards are most surely dead now! Those men, the ones who arrived as the last relief detachment, they're all out there now and all wearing what must be Vorsan livery. Fulgrim must have got his message out and his people have sent that company of men, disguised as Illeans.'

'And no one suspected a thing?' Pester said, incredulously.

'Why should they have?' Moxie stormed. 'No one expected any sort of rescue attempt, because *someone* didn't think it important enough to report that Fulgrim was trying to bribe someone to get help to him, did they?' She stood, hands on hips, glaring at the page, who cringed before her scorn.

'I'm sorry,' he whimpered, 'but I just didn't think.'

'No,' Moxie said sourly, 'you didn't think. But then you're a man, even if you don't have any balls, so why should anyone expect better of you? Now, shut up and let me think for a moment. We have to work out what to do… *I* have to work out what to do,' she corrected herself.

For several minutes she paced to and fro, her brow furrowed, muttering to herself under her breath. Eventually she stopped pacing and walked back to where Pester remained motionless between the two horses.

'We need to get help,' she told him, 'but it won't be that easy. There is only one road west towards Illeum City. And even to reach Garassotta, where the Lady Corinna now is, I believe, we would have to follow that road before turning northwards.

'Obviously, Fulgrim does not care who among the local people sees what he is up to, otherwise they would not have hung Agana up there for all to see, so he must have men watching the west route, and we don't know how many they are.

'Of course, we could try to go around them, but I don't know the countryside that well and I doubt you know it any better, so we could end up lost.'

'Then what are we to do?' Pester whined. 'Maybe we should just stay hidden until these swine leave, which they surely must do. There cannot be enough of them to hope to hold the castle for long.'

'No,' Moxie agreed, 'there aren't enough of them for that, though they could have more men on the way, for all we know.' She fell silent again, chewing her bottom lip. 'No,' she said at length, 'they don't intend to remain. The purpose of this plan was to free Fulgrim, I'm sure, and he will be eager to scuttle off back to the Vorsan territories.

'The trouble is,' she continued, 'if he doesn't kill Lady Dorothea, then he'll doubtless take her with him as hostage. He could easily disguise her as a slave girl and his men once again as Illean troopers, so no one would take much notice.

'I'm no expert on these things, but I have seen the large map in Lady Dorothea's private study, so I do know that they could make it back to their own country long before we could summon help from either Garassotta or Illeum. And once there, Illeum would be powerless to touch them.'

'Then our lady is surely lost?' Pester cried, tears moistening his large rounded eyes.

'Maybe so,' Moxie said pensively, 'but it all depends. If Fulgrim believes himself safe here for a few days at least, they may not set off immediately. In that case, we might get to Garassotta and Lord Savatch could perhaps ride south again and cut the swine off, even if he has to follow them across the border. I know he's no great respecter of such niceties, for I have heard her ladyship speak of him many times.'

'But you said we would not be able to reach this Garassotta,' Pester pointed out. 'You said they would be watching the road.'

'The road west, yes,' Moxie agreed, 'but probably not the way east.'

'But why would we go east?'

'Because,' Moxie explained patiently, 'that way lies the Vaal plains. There is a broad pass through the mountains, which are not that wide hereabouts, and then we could turn north. The land is mainly flat and easily travelled, with or without roads, and we may be able to hire a guide. If we go far enough north, we should then be able to head back west and find the way to Garassotta from that direction.'

'But how will we hire a guide?' Pester protested. 'We have

no money and if we sell one of the horses, how will we travel?'

'Leave that to me,' Moxie said grimly. 'There is coinage other than gold and, if the worst comes to the worst, I can always sell you.'

Jorkan laid his ale flagon carefully on the uneven tabletop and sank slowly onto the bench. Paulis, sitting opposite, raised his eyebrows, questioningly. His uncle looked about him, ensuring that none of the tavern's other patrons were within earshot, but the table they had chosen, set outside the door, was well away from the few drinkers that were using the inn at this time of the afternoon.

'It seems we could be in luck, lad,' Jorkan said. He took a swig of the warm brew and wiped froth from his beard with the back of his hand. 'Our friend passed this way around dawn today.'

'It was definitely him?' Paulis asked.

Jorkan nodded his shaggy head. 'Oh yes, most definitely. His face is well known in these parts, obviously, and the soldier I spoke to has just finished a week's duty up at the castle itself.'

'Was he alone?' Paulis demanded. 'Or does he ride with an escort?'

'An escort, no,' Jorkan replied carefully, 'but neither was he alone. It seems he had with him a slave wench, one apparently that the Lady Corinna found unfavourable and had ordered him to return from whence she was purchased.'

'Either too plain, or maybe too pretty,' Paulis suggested. 'Maybe her ladyship was growing a bit jealous.'

'Maybe,' the older man agreed, 'but my new friend couldn't say. Apparently she was hooded, as are most slave girls, of course. Supposed to stop young whelps like you getting ideas, among other things.'

'Be that as it may, uncle,' Paulis replied irritably, 'I don't see how this means we are in luck. I may be young, but even I am shrewd enough to realise that if we were to kill this Savatch fellow, the Lady Corinna would not then risk venturing beyond the safety of her castle walls. And meanwhile, as strangers in these parts, if we remained in the area suspicion would surely fall upon us.'

'That it would,' Jorkan said, 'though there are strangers enough to share that burden, believe me. However, shrewd as your assessment of the situation might be, it lacks one thing. It presumes that her ladyship is still within her sanctuary, does it not?'

'Well, yes,' Paulis nodded. 'But where else would she be, if not with this Savatch?'

'Ah, precisely.' Jorkan nodded sagely. 'A very good question. But let me answer that question with another. Tell me why, in your youthful opinion, the task of returning an unwanted slave girl should befall her ladyship's chief functionary, a man who, so rumour has it, is also her lover?'

'Well, perhaps she found him with the girl and decided to punish him by making him return her himself?' Paulis suggested.

Jorkan's eyes twinkled. 'I can see you are not the innocent I thought,' he bantered, 'and indeed, that could be as good a reason as any, save that surely her ladyship would not want to give him further rein for enjoying the girl's charms before being finally rid of her. Master Savatch, so gossip has it, has a liking for slave wenches.'

'Then tell me, uncle,' Paulis sighed, taking up his own flagon, 'what do you think the answer is? I'm sure you have one.'

'Maybe,' Jorkan conceded, 'though it might seem just a little far-fetched. My loose-lipped drinking companion had even more gossip that he was only too eager to share, not least the fact that the noble lady steward enjoys catering to her lover's tastes herself.'

'You've lost me,' Paulis confessed. 'What tastes are those?'

'Why, his taste for slave girls,' Jorkan grinned. 'Haven't I just told you?'

'But…?' Paulis' mouth hung open in mid-sentence as the light slowly dawned in his eyes. 'No!' he gasped, letting his flagon return to the tabletop with a thump. 'Surely you can't mean…?'

Jorkan nodded, grinning hugely. 'And why not?' he demanded. 'When you are a little older, you will come to understand that there are some curious notions find their way into the most unlikely heads.'

'But surely not that?' Paulis gasped. 'I mean, why would she? How could she? I've seen the way men drag these slave girls around and she's of noble birth.'

'So you think maybe that showing her tits off to all and sundry might not stir a few juices in her?' Jorkan laughed. 'Well, I've known stranger things, believe me. Besides, hooded like a common slave, who would know it was her tits they were looking at, eh?'

'Apart from the fact that it seems to be common knowledge,' Paulis pointed out.

Jorkan began to chuckle. 'Aye,' he said, 'and there's another valuable lesson. If our betters ever truly knew what we common people thought, it'd either make them rule us better, or else it would frighten them to death!'

Fulgrim's revenge was now extended towards the pages and maids with whom Agana had persecuted him during his incarceration, and Dorothea was brought out to watch, bound with her back to the whipping post and looking towards the castle wall, on top of which the Vorsan troopers had erected another timber construction.

Two heavy timbers, similar to the one from which Agana's

torture cage hung, were thrust out from the ramparts, a third timber lashed between them, parallel with the wall itself and jutting a few feet clear of the stonework. To this makeshift gibbet the men began to attach ropes, set an arm's breadth apart, a total of eight in all, with nooses fashioned at their free ends.

From her position, level with this mass gallows, Agana had a clear view as the first batch of young unfortunates, arms bound behind them, were brought up to stand on the inside of the ramparts and the nooses placed about their necks. Realising what was about to happen to them, they began to struggle and cry out, male and female alike, but there was no escape and, through her own agony, Agana prayed that the ropes would be long enough to snap their poor necks when they were thrown over the top and that they would not all be left dancing in mid-air, fighting for a last breath that would never come.

And, as that prayer was finally answered and the first eight corpses hung lifelessly in the late afternoon sun, Agana prayed too, that someone, somewhere would soon be in a position to do to Fulgrim that which she knew now she would never be able to do herself and that her spirit, when it finally departed this world, would be permitted to look down and watch it when his end finally came.

Demila was beginning to feel more at home in the saddle, though the use of unaccustomed muscles and the steady chafing against the insides of her thighs did not help her to feel more comfortable. However, even at walking pace, the sure-footed pony covered the ground quicker than if Pecon had insisted she remain on foot.

Despite their lovemaking of the previous evening, it seemed Pecon did not trust her not to try to escape, though Demila suspected that his precautions owed as much to his determination to reinforce their master-slave relationship as to any real ideas concerning security.

The hated mask remained locked in place and beneath it Demila perspired in the warm sunlight. Her wrists were no longer locked to her belt, but cuffed together in front of her and tied to the saddle pommel, enabling her to hold her mount's reins, but little else. In addition, leather thongs secured her ankles to the tops of the stirrup irons and a thin strap then connected these beneath the pony's belly, ensuring that she could neither dismount voluntarily, nor slip from the saddle accidentally.

They rode steadily throughout the day and the temperature began to drop slightly as they moved towards higher ground. From the position of the sun, Demila knew they were headed roughly eastwards, but as to their actual destination she had no idea. Pecon maintained a lead between them of one horse's length, a lead rein from his saddle running back to the pony's bridle, and did not once look back while they were actually travelling.

Indeed, except for the infrequent rest halts he called, it was as if he had forgotten that Demila was there at all and, even when they stopped he barely acknowledged her, other than to free her from saddle and stirrups and help her to dismount.

Late in the afternoon, as they watered the horses at a small, swift running stream, she could stand it no longer.

'Master?'

Pecon, squatting cross-legged in the soft grass, looked up, seemingly surprised at the sound of her voice.

'Master, has your slave displeased you?'

He shrugged his broad shoulders and turned his face away from her. 'Why do you ask, slave?'

'Because – because you have not once spoken to me since first light.'

He continued to look away, apparently concentrating on

some distant object. 'Should a master speak to a slave, except when he has instructions for her to carry out?' he asked.

'No, master,' she mumbled uncertainly.

Pecon looked back at her, over his shoulder. 'Then I don't understand the question,' he said blandly.

Suddenly, to her consternation, Demila found her vision blurred by tears and it was her turn to look away. She did not hear him rise, nor did she sense his approach, but his hands rested firmly upon her shoulders, fingers pressing into her tanned flesh.

'You wish to show your master your devotion?' he asked, his mouth close to her leather covered ear. Dumbly, Demila nodded. His right hand slipped down, his arm partly encircling her until his fingers found her nipple, taking the swollen teat gently but firmly, and slowly massaging it. She let out a deep breath and pressed herself back against him.

'You know of only one way to please a master?' he asked, teasingly. Again she nodded and squirmed her buttocks harder into his groin. He laughed, but now his other hand mirrored the actions of the first.

'Well, at least you are pleasing,' he said gruffly, spun her about, reached to her throat and pulled the slave hood from her head, exposing her flushed features fully. 'And you are quite pretty,' he smiled, dropping the damp leather at his feet, 'even if you do sweat too much.'

'Interesting,' Jorkan said when he and Paulis were once again mounted and heading back out of the village. 'You heard what that bailiff fellow had to say, didn't you?'

'I did,' Paulis said, 'but I still don't understand any of it. If that slave girl really was the Lady Corinna, why would she have permitted herself to be whipped at the public scaffold?'

'Why indeed?' Jorkan grunted. 'But then, who are we to question what goes on in the heads of our betters, eh lad? I'd say that her ladyship and this Savatch fellow are acting out some kind of game, though what she would ever hope to get out of it I wouldn't like to say. Mind you, nephew, I gave up trying to understand women even before you came into this world. That way lies madness, believe me.'

'But you're sure this was her?'

'You'll learn, lad, that it never pays to be sure of anything. But let's just say that I'd wager a day's ride on the outcome. Besides, why would he pay good money on a wagon and furs, just to ensure the comfort of a common slave girl he's just ordered whipped?

'No, maybe nothing's ever really sure, but this is sure enough for me. Sure enough that we put an arrow into him and take her afterwards. We'll know then, sure enough. And if I'm right, the sweet lady has saved us the trouble of finding a better guise in which to take her back to our paymaster.

'One extra slave girl, more or less – who's going to give her a second glance, eh? Except to leer at what she's showing. Her identity will be as safe with us as it is with this Savatch,' he added, laughing again, 'though I doubt she'll thank us half as much for protecting her secret!'

Fulgrim stood over the slumped figure of Dorothea and kicked her hard in the ribs. She moaned, shifted slightly and struggled to raise her head.

'The black bitch is strong,' he said. 'Though she won't last much beyond tomorrow noon. Already her ribs are cracking and her devil's cunt is stretched enough to take any five men.

'She tried to cheat me, the devious whore,' he continued, 'but I was wise to what she was thinking and we've forced water into her, so she'll stay alive a while yet.'

'In the name of mercy,' Dorothea begged, her voice cracking, 'kill us both, please!'

Fulgrim stepped backwards, aimed a kick at her legs and

guffawed.

'Mercy?' he taunted. 'What mercy was I shown? No, you'll both pay my price in full, believe me. The black bitch will die, eventually, but not you, my once proud lady. Tell me,' he continued, bending over her and grasping her jaw, 'how does it feel to have a belly full of common soldiers' seed, eh?

'You've seen the last of fine silks and soft female bed warmers, believe me. From now on, that cunt of yours is game to any man who needs a temporary scabbard for his aching sword, so you'd better get used to it.'

Dorothea groaned again, but her eyes burned defiance. 'Your soul will rot in eternity, Fulgrim,' she hissed, but Fulgrim simply laughed again.

'Maybe,' he agreed, 'but your body will rot in this life well before that time comes. You should have killed me while you had the chance.'

'Believe me,' Dorothea muttered, closing her eyes, her head falling back, 'I'd not make the same mistake again.'

Agana knew she was close to death, though she felt certain that Fulgrim did not fully realise this. He had continued to tighten the metal cage about her throughout the afternoon and early evening, but had taunted her that she would not die until the following day. Fortunately, she thought to herself, as the rope above her creaked in the stirring breeze, he understood little of the powers her people had long since accepted and learned, and soon she would be beyond his reach.

At least, she thought, not only was she now above the pain he could inflict, but so, soon, would Dorothea be, if only for a short while, and he also seemed to have stopped executing the maids and pages now. Presumably, having identified and murdered certain of their number, he had realised that they would fetch a not inconsiderable price if he sold the remainder, and doubtless his men would use them for fine sport meantime.

Such a shame, she sighed, opening her eyes for one last glimpse of the setting sun. Such a shame that she would not be the one who finally sent him back to face the retribution of his maker. Perhaps her own gods would forgive her spirit for her earthly sins, at least long enough to bear witness to his eternal damnation. Hers may not have been a blameless life, but at least she had served her mistress loyally. Such a shame she could not continue to serve her so further.

There was shame in many things, she thought vaguely. Shame and pity, pity and shame. And, as the sun finally dipped behind the distant hilltops, her spirit finally slipped away to join the gathering stars.

The cabin was set well back from the road and hidden from it by the dense combination of trees and undergrowth, so that only someone who knew of it, or perhaps someone stumbling upon it by chance, would know it was there.

Inside the floor was clean and the few items of furniture – a bed, table and two chairs – in good repair, though evidently made originally by a hand that was not entirely skilled in the art. The meagre, cramped dwelling had probably been originally built as a shelter for a hunter, Demila thought; perhaps he still used it, though there was no sign of recent occupation. The ashes in the small hearth looked old and there was no food on the single shelf in the alcove next to it, only a simple earthenware pitcher and two bowls.

Pecon unlocked her wrist fetters from her waist belt and nodded towards the fireplace.

'There should be wood already cut, stacked against the rear wall outside,' he said. 'You should also find plenty of dried twigs beneath the bushes. Gather some and start a fire, slave. Here.' He reached inside his jerkin and withdrew a tinderbox.

'When you have the fire well set, you will find a stream just a little deeper into the trees. Take the pitcher and fill it and wash yourself at the same time. You can wash my feet for me later – among other things,' he added, with a sly grin.

Demila took the tinderbox, laying it carefully on the table, and turned towards the door, trying to hide the smile that kept trying to force its way onto her face. The damned mask was uncomfortable, she thought, but without it she had to be wary not to betray her true feelings too blatantly.

When Agana's death was reported to him, Fulgrim flew into a terrible rage and, for several minutes, Dorothea believed he would kill her too. But he restricted his attentions to a few badly aimed kicks and a stream of insults that seemed to be aimed at the world in general. At last, he seemed to bring his anger under some control and ordered the guards to bring the surviving maids and pages out onto the grass beneath the walls and to set up several torches to illuminate the area.

Then, as the ten girls and seven boys stood in a shivering semicircle, he ordered Agana's corpse to be lowered and her rigid figure, still held within the iron bands of the torture device, lashed to the whipping post. Dorothea, too, was brought out, arms tightly bound behind her back, a heavy iron chain clipped between her nipples and dragging her once proud breasts into painfully elongated melons.

For several seconds an eerie silence descended upon the gathering, as they stood in the flickering light, all attention focused on the grim figure at their centre. Even in death Agana was an awesome sight, her eyes closed, her noble features now in repose, belying the nature of her end. And the soldiers, too, seemed affected by her appearance, but then Fulgrim spoke and the spell was broken.

'The black bitch can remain here, where the animals as well as the birds can pick at her carcass.' He turned to Ingrim, who was standing just behind him. 'Have your men bind the arms of all the slaves and stake them by the ankles. They can mount a final vigil for the corpse, and if any of them tries to sit or lie down before dawn, give them twenty lashes.

'And make sure, Ingrim,' he concluded, turning back towards the open postern, 'that the men do not try to make use of any of this young flesh – not this night, at least. Leave them to contemplate and make sure everyone is ready to move out one hour after first light.'

To Sprig it had seemed so very simple: wait until the women made camp, watch until they fell asleep, then move in and cut their throats before they knew what was happening. Foolishly, they had even left the weapons and most of the horses at the scene of the underground encounter and, when he had returned, he quickly armed himself with a sharp sword and two vicious daggers.

Riding back along the dried river, he had easily picked up their trail in the snow as soon as he emerged into the open air again, and it had taken no great skill to follow the prints left by the four horses. After an hour or two he had spotted them far ahead and simply dropped back out of sight, waiting for darkness to fall again.

However, as he now realised – much too late – they must have been expecting something, for as he fell upon the first huddled figure, plunging his sword into the general area of the head, something hard and heavy crashed into his skull and he had barely enough time to register that the sleeping 'figure' was nothing more than a fur thrown over a heap of snow, before the purple curtain rose up before his eyes. Then, amidst a background of roaring water, he slipped further down into the waiting, inky blackness.

He awoke eventually, head throbbing, body cold and shivering, and knew instantly he was in big trouble, though it took him several more seconds before his thoughts cleared sufficiently to recognise the nature of his plight. When he did he groaned, as much in humiliation as in pain, wishing they'd simply killed him outright.

'Aha, I see you're awake, slave.'

Sprig peered up through the slits in the slave hood and saw it was the blonde standing over him. He struggled to try to sit up, but his arms were pinioned to the broad leather belt about his waist and he could get no leverage. Breathing heavily, he fell back.

'I'm no slave!' he growled, trying to keep the fear from his voice, but it was impossible to retain any air of confidence, stripped of his clothing as he now was. How long he had lain uncovered he had no idea, but already his teeth were starting to chatter.

'Nor was the girl,' Alanna said softly. 'But she was given no choice in the matter, either. Not only that, but you and your murderous friends killed what family she had.'

'Then kill me too, and make an end of it,' Sprig snarled.

'That would be too easy,' Alanna said silkily. She bent over him, taking his flaccid organ in her hand. 'My impetuous young friend has suggested cutting this thing off, you know,' she continued. To his horror, Sprig felt his shaft beginning to stir at her caress. 'Of course,' she said, still smiling beatifically, 'that would be one way of ensuring you never again forced yourself upon helpless females, but then it would also detract from your value, when we come to sell you.'

'Sell me?' Sprig echoed, his eyes growing round. 'You cannot be serious. I'm a free man!'

'*Were* a free man,' Alanna said. 'As of now you are my property, you stupid boy, and perhaps you'll start to understand just how you and your people have brought so much suffering and misery into this world.'

Moxie did not sleep well, with only a few branches to cover her, and was wide awake well before the dawn's first fingers began creeping from the eastern horizon. Pester, however, had fallen into a deep sleep and remained in a huddle, the small saddle blanket over his shoulders.

The road leading towards South Erisvaal had, as Moxie had hoped, been clear. They had passed only a scattering of westward bound travellers throughout the previous afternoon and none had given much attention to what they assumed had to be some sort of warrior woman and her young slave. It was less usual to encounter a female with a slave, but not unknown, though the fact that Moxie was armed only with her whip and did not carry a sword did trouble her. Few generally ventured through the high passes without a proper weapon.

She had selected their overnight campsite carefully, leading the way up off the main track until they arrived at a small, fairly level clearing where the trees and bushes screened them completely from the road below. But now, leaving the slumbering pageboy, she slipped quietly through the undergrowth until she found a vantage point from which she could view that road clearly, and for a mile or more in each direction.

At this hour she did not expect to see much in the way of traffic, but after maybe fifteen minutes, a lone figure came into view from the direction in which they would be resuming their journey shortly. Keeping her head well down, Moxie studied the approaching horseman intently, her fingers wrapped tightly around the wide gold ring she had removed from her left hand earlier.

It had been given to her by Dorothea, a birthday present some weeks since and had to be worth at least three krones. Moxie hated the thought of parting with it, but it was either that, or the small ruby Dorothea had set in her navel, and the fiery red jewel meant even more to her.

Three krones. Three krones would buy twelve decent swords, or six swords, several blankets and food supplies sufficient for two weeks on the road. However, the chances of redeeming the ring for that sort of return were faint, out here on the verge of the wilderness, so Moxie knew she would have to accept a fraction of its true value – one sword, a couple of blankets and a handful of basic rations, if she were lucky.

Except that she would not get anything from the man below. As he drew closer still, Moxie could see he was no trader, but probably a hunter, or even a mercenary, for he rode light with just his sword, a crossbow slung across his back and a saddle pack too small to contain anything more than his own necessities. Sighing, Moxie sat back and waited.

Corinna traveled in the back of the wagon again next morning; her back and shoulders felt far less tender now, but she was exhausted, having had very little sleep during the night. Savatch had kept her tied to the wagon wheel for much of the time, facing it, her wrists spread wide and lashed to the junctures of spokes and rim, her ankles similarly treated, though not secured anywhere near so far apart.

He had come to her several times during the darkness, fondling her naked breasts, tormenting her aching sex, fingers sliding in and out of the helplessly sodden tunnel. Then suddenly, without warning and without speaking, he had entered her, thrusting deeply in and out while his fingers twisted her ringed nipples cruelly.

Four times he took her and four times they climaxed as one, yet each time he left her and returned to his furs without a word passing from his lips. If Corinna had ever truly wondered what it might be like to live the life of a slave, if her experiences at the hands of Fulgrim that previous summer had not already taught her, she was quickly beginning to understand now.

Although she knew that Savatch loved her as she did him, he was deliberately using her as a mere chattel, sating his lust on and in her quivering body and then leaving her to hang in her bondage, still masked, her waist cruelly compressed by the slave belt, the cold night air free to torment her naked flesh further.

Finally, with the first light of dawn, he had released her, added fresh wood to the spluttering embers of the fire and ordered her to prepare hot oatmeal for them both. Corinna had eaten it greedily, gulping also at the wine sack he passed her, but she had remained silent throughout, knowing that a true slave would be forbidden to speak without her master's direct instruction.

And she, Corinna, daughter of the Protector of Illeum, wanted to be his true slave.

The wagon lurched on, wheels bouncing over the sun-baked mud ruts, the metal springs squealing and protesting, though in truth they performed little function, so old were they. Behind the ancient vehicle, their two original steeds followed dutifully, their lead reins looped around a stanchion set in the tailboard and up front, crouched on the precarious driver's bench, Savatch maintained his silence as hooves and wheels slowly ate up the miles.

Savatch had replaced the leather dildo inside her before the day's journey started, but at least he had not plugged her rear, so Corinna was able to sit up against the inside of the wagon and look out through the front as they travelled on. She did not recognise the road at all now, for they had come many miles from Garassotta. Only the positions of the sun indicated they were now travelling south east and, as the narrowing road began to climb up into higher country, she guessed that Savatch might be heading towards one of the passes that led to North Erisvaal.

How far he intended to go she had no idea and had not dared, nor even wanted to ask, for a slave girl would not normally be privy to her master's travelling itinerary. She simply went wherever he took her and if he sold her on route, then she had to accept that fate, equally.

Not that Savatch would sell her, she knew; that was one fate, at least, she would be spared. He would beat her and use her, as she had chosen to be used, but ultimately he would always be there to protect her, as the castle at Garassotta and the palace in Illeum City would always be there whenever she elected to return to the life for which she had been born and raised.

She closed her eyes, smiling to herself.

The life for which she had been born and raised.

Maybe so, she thought, but maybe this was the life to which she was better suited; travelling as a naked possession, helpless, subdued, obedient, ready to spread her legs for her master's thrusting cock and without the necessity of being whipped into compliance. The whip, when Savatch used it, simply added further to fuel her lusts.

She was unnatural, a true whore. Fulgrim's evil touch had tainted her forever and maybe she would be as damned as he inevitably would be.

With an effort, Corinna opened her eyes, struggling to banish such thoughts, for memories of the Vorsan nobleman were not healthy for her. Deadly and murderous as he was, and perilous as her own position had been in his power, the things he had done to her stirred feelings aside from mere fear, feelings she did not want to admit to, but simply try to recreate in this sinful charade they were now acting out.

The sharp hissing sound, followed by Savatch's cry of pain, jerked Corinna immediately back into reality. For a second or so she had no idea what was happening, only that Savatch was hunched over even further on the bench seat and that he was flailing the reins desperately. Only as the two horses responded and broke into a fast trot did she see the shaft of the quarrel projecting from where the base of his neck met his left shoulder.

With a shout of alarm she struggled to get forward to him, but with her hands strapped so efficiently to her sides she knew she would be powerless to help even if she could manage to do so. And that also, without the use of her arms she was quite likely to find herself pitched headlong from the wagon, which was now lurching alarmingly in every direction as the horses broke into a canter and began to pick up even greater speed.

'Free me!' she screamed desperately. 'Try, for the sake of all that's holy – try to get my one hand free at least!'

With an almost superhuman effort Savatch managed to turn on the bench, whilst still maintaining a grip on the traces, but already the blood was spreading out across the front of his shirt and tunic and it was clear he was fighting a losing battle against unconsciousness.

Corinna crawled closer to him, twice banging her head painfully as the lurching wagon threw her off balance. Kneeling, she tried to turn, offering her right side towards him.

'Please!' she sobbed. 'Please try! I cannot help you as I am now. You must—' Her imploring words were cut short as the wagon gave one final leap and suddenly, as the terrified horses reared and screamed in terror, Corinna found herself looking down into nothingness – nothingness save for what appeared to be a river. And that river seemed to be so far below, so far that she could not believe it possible that the mêlée of tumbling horses, wheels and splintering wood were heading directly down towards it, taking with it her and the man for whom she would willingly have died and whom, it now seemed inevitable, she was going to die with.

'I think our new slave looks quite sweet, don't you Melina?' The rescued girl looked totally nonplussed, staring at the captive Sprig, who glared angrily back at the three women from behind the slave hood Alanna had secured about his head and upper face. She had also cinched the waist belt unnecessarily tight and added cuffs about his upper arms, just above the elbows, fastening them together with a length of chain that passed across his back, forcing him to stand with his chest thrust forward.

The final indignity had been the pouch. Jekka had discovered two of them in the saddle pack and hooted with laughter when she realised what they were for. Carefully shaped, the pouch slipped over the entire genitalia, covering, but not hiding anything of the anatomical shape, though once the restraining strap had been buckled behind the scrotum, the organ within was forced to remain in its flaccid state, regardless of stimulation and desire.

'He's certainly well formed,' Jekka mused, 'and quite fit looking. I think now you were right for me not to kill him. I wonder how much he'll fetch.'

'I wouldn't like to say,' Alanna said. She reached out and placed a reassuring hand on Melina's shoulder. 'No need to worry, girl,' she said. 'He'll not be able to harm you now, that's for sure. See, even as big as he is, he's quite powerless. How does it feel, boy?' she asked, addressing Sprig directly. 'How does it feel to be reduced to such a lowly status? Perhaps I should demonstrate to poor Melina just how useless a man can be made.' She stepped forward, reached down and cupped Sprig's leather sheathed testicles in one hand, gently pressing and manipulating with her thumb. The helpless barbarian groaned and tried to pull away, but Alanna's grip simply tightened further.

'You see, Melina?' she said. 'See how vulnerable a man can be? I tell you now, the gods who made us must indeed be female, for no male would fashion one of his own with his balls on the outside and at such a convenient height!'

Pecon spread the vellum sheet across the tabletop, using his knife and the two empty bowls to keep it flat. From her position on the bed, Demila could see that it appeared to be covered with a lot of scrawls and pictures, but none of it meant anything to her, for she had never learned to read nor write. Pecon, however, was not one to allow a simple fact like that to stand in his way.

'Come over here.' He beckoned to her without looking up. Demila slid to the floor and padded across the hard earth to stand beside him. 'Ever seen a map before?' She shook her head. 'Thought not,' he said, and jabbed a finger at a point near the centre of the vellum.

'This is how it works,' he explained. 'We're here, roughly, and the sun rises here…' his finger moved and jabbed down again, '…and sets over here. Now, if I'm right, this farm place you told me about must lie somewhere in this area, yes?' Again his finger moved, this time circling a small section of the map.

Demila looked blank. 'I don't know, master,' she said. 'If that is the Vaal country, then yes, I suppose so. I only know what they told me.'

Pecon nodded and stood upright again. 'Tell me,' he said, 'when they finally sold you, which way did you travel? Was the sun behind you in the morning, or in the afternoon?'

'In the morning, master,' Demila said. 'Definitely in the morning, for in the late day we were walking into it as it set and it was hard to see where we were walking.'

'Then they brought you from the east,' Pecon said, apparently satisfied, 'in which case you almost certainly came from the Vaal. Tell me, did you pass through the mountains?' This time Demila shook her head emphatically.

'No, master,' she said with conviction. 'We crossed some hills, but did not go into the mountains, though we could see peaks in the distance to both sides of us.'

'Then you came through from South Erisvaal,' Pecon said, studying the chart again. 'From North Erisvaal you would have come through one of several passes and further south, from Karli, it would have been the same. There is only one place such as you describe.

'But one final thing – how many days were you travelling before you reached those hills? Think carefully now.'

Demila wrinkled her nose and closed her eyes, trying to concentrate. 'Three or four,' she said, at length. 'At least, I think it was. Maybe it was five, but no more, I am sure of that.'

'Good.' Pecon nodded. 'Did you walk all the while, or did they carry you in the wagons for part of the journey?'

'We walked for the second part of each day,' Demila said. She looked at him as he stood bent over the table once more, apparently trying to make some calculations and measurements with his forefinger and thumb. 'May I ask why you need to know these things, master?' she ventured. It was a precocious risk, she knew, but her curiosity was getting the better of her. Fortunately, their night together seemed to have left Pecon in a good mood towards her.

'Well, my ignorant little slave girl,' he said, smiling at her, 'by working out how far a wagon would travel in half a day and then how far the entire caravan would travel with several slaves on foot for the remainder of the day, we can work out the distance between these hills here and the farm from where you were bought.

'My guess is that it would be somewhere about here, give or take a few miles.' He pointed at the map again, but it meant nothing to Demila. 'So, if we make for the general area, I'm certain we shall find someone who can give us directions to the farm itself.'

Demila shuddered and felt herself turning pale. 'You are going to sell me back?' she wailed. 'But they didn't want

135

me.'

'Sell you back?' Pecon echoed. 'I think not. As you say, you were too small for their peculiar needs, so there would be little point in trying. However, I am curious as to these pony slaves they train. Humans to do the work of horses – an interesting prospect for a businessman such as I.

'I think a visit to this farm, just to see what it is they buy and sell, and then I can decide if there might be a profit in it for me, too.'

Jorkan approached the edge of the ravine cautiously and stood, looking down at the swirling torrent far below and at the smashed wreckage and dead horses already being swept away by the furious current.

'Damnation!' he muttered, clenching his fist. Paulis, who remained on the road holding the bridles of their two horses, did not understand his uncle's apparent anger.

'What's the matter?' he asked. Jorkan continued to stare down at the river without speaking, but finally he managed to tear himself away from the scene of carnage and trudged back to rejoin his nephew.

'The matter, young Paulis,' he said, gritting his teeth, 'is that we have no immediate proof that Savatch is dead, and our paymaster won't part with any gold until the fellow fails to show up anywhere for some considerable time.'

'But he must be dead!' Paulis exclaimed. 'I saw your shot take him in the throat and anyway, how could any living thing survive such a fall?'

'Quite,' Jorkan said. 'But only we saw them fall, didn't we?' He sighed and reached out to take his horse from Paulis. 'And that's another thing,' he said, '*she's* gone over the edge as well and they wanted her alive, in case you've forgotten that.'

'It couldn't be helped,' Paulis protested. 'My mount shed a

shoe and stumbled, just as I was about to catch hold of their horses' bridles. I was lucky I didn't end up going over with them.'

'I know,' Jorkan conceded, 'but the sort of people I work for do not accept excuses and they'd as soon throw you down yonder gorge themselves, as they would accept your – our – failure.'

'Well, we could at least go down there and find the bodies. That way, at least we could take back their heads, to prove we did most of the job. Perhaps they'll pay half what they originally offered?'

Jorkan sighed and heaved himself up into the saddle. 'For a start, laddy-o,' he said, 'by the time we find a safe way down there, everything will be miles down river and we could spend days searching for wherever those bodies eventually wash up. Secondly, and far more important, if you fancy going back to these people and showing them the head of the woman they expected to use as their chief bargaining counter, then be my guest. They'll cut off your head and mount it on a pole, I shouldn't wonder.'

'Then what *are* we to do?'

Jorkan sighed again and indicated for Paulis to mount his horse. 'Firstly,' he said, 'we'll take a nice slow walk back to that village and get the smithy to take care of your horse's shoe. While he's doing that I intend to go into that apology of a tavern and get myself good and drunk on that swill they sell as ale.'

'And then?'

'And then,' Jorkan said, wheeling his horse back around to face the way they had come, 'I'm going to head south, down into Karli, or maybe Tamarinia, steal me a few slaves and sell them on and see if there are any others in need of my particular talents. You can come with me, if you want, or you can go your own way, but I suggest if you do, you put as many miles between yourself and Illeum as I intend to do – at least for the next year or so.'

A bolt of sickening pain seared through her head, but pain was good, Corinna realised: it meant she was still alive, though as she fought her way back to full consciousness it was a full half minute before she realised what had happened.

Immediately she tried to sit up again, gritting her teeth against another wave of nauseating agony, crying out as she saw the inert form of Savatch slumped across her legs and clawing desperately with her bound hands in an attempt to draw him to her. There seemed to be blood everywhere, his blood, splattered across her thighs and stomach as well as soaking through his clothing, and her breath caught in her throat, exploding as a helpless sob as she fought against the awful reality.

But no – no, he wasn't dead! His eyelids flickered, his chest rose and fell, albeit slowly and, when she finally managed to place her fingers against his neck, sliding them through the blood that still seeped out around the bolt that had pierced him there, she could feel a pulse, weak, erratic, but a pulse nonetheless.

All at once Corinna realised several things. They were lying in the midst of the pile of furs upon which Savatch had originally laid her. Somehow, as the wagon had plunged towards oblivion, he must have fallen back alongside her and the thick pelts acted to cushion their impact when they finally hit the sides or bottom of the ravine. Vaguely, she recalled the wagon's erratic and terrifying descent, tearing through bushes, ricocheting off trees, all of which must have contrived to slow the descent and the river had acted as their final salvation.

The wagon itself had suffered badly. Timbers were splintered, the canvas sagged from badly bent iron hoops and there was water lapping about their legs, but somehow it had remained afloat, the current rocking motion suggesting it was continuing downstream.

Easing herself from beneath his weight, she squirmed forward and, after an awkward struggle, managed to push her head out from beneath the enveloping canvas shroud. Sure enough, the wagon was in the middle of the river, bobbing and turning gently as it was borne along on the current. Quite why it had not yet sunk Corinna could not tell, but meanwhile, afloat or sinking, Savatch presented a more pressing problem.

Worming her way back to him she managed to turn, gripping his shoulder in one of her hands and shaking him, at the same time calling his name, while tears of fear and frustration coursed down her cheeks.

'Damn you!' she cried. 'You can't die – and I can't help you, not unless you help me get out of these manacles.' She shook her head, trying to clear her vision, hardly recognising the voice that berated him as her own. Desperation gave way to resignation and the strength seemed to drain from her body. With a groan she sank back onto her knees, cursing, praying, weeping, all at the same time.

'My belt…' He spoke so quietly, his voice so weak, Corinna hardly heard him, but when she opened her eyes again she saw he was looking up at her, his pain-wracked features testimony to the great effort that even to speak was costing him.

'Belt,' he repeated, his voice threatening to crack. 'Key… belt.'

The trader was elderly, travelling with a woman Moxie assumed to be his wife, who sat hunched beside him on the driver's seat of the rickety wagon. His white beard, straggly white hair and wizened features, however, disguised a shrewd bargaining brain and, by the time the vehicle lumbered off again, she counted herself lucky to have secured the rather blunt sword, two very cheap knives, two very coarse woven blankets and a few basic provisions that would not last her and Pester beyond the next evening.

The page eyed the meagre collection in a manner that betrayed his lack of enthusiasm, but Moxie was in no mood to argue.

'We'll scavenge, if we have to,' she told him. 'There will be farms and villages and it wouldn't be the first time I've raided an orchard, believe me. Now shut up, or I'll make you ride with the cock attachment on your saddle.'

'But this is all so pointless,' Pester whined. 'It must be days to this castle and neither of us really knows the route. And what if we meet any trouble on the road? You may have that sword now, but you're hardly an expert with it, are you?'

'The whole point about having a sword,' Moxie said, 'is that having it means you mostly won't have to use it. Whereas,' she continued sagely, 'if you haven't got a sword, that's when you get into situations where you wish you had one to use.'

'Yeah, well, if you say so,' Pester muttered. 'But you're still a girl.'

'I'm glad you noticed,' Moxie retorted, trying to hide the grin on her face. 'And so, hopefully, will everyone else.' She tapped one finger against her temple. 'Most things are won up here,' she said. 'Think about it – nearly all men carry swords, but half of them aren't competent swordsmen, so another man, say one who is better skilled, will always fancy his chances.

'But,' she added, tapping again, 'how many women wear swords, eh? Not many, as we both know, except the Yslanders and they all carry a bloody armoury anyway.'

'And know how to use it,' Pester pointed out.

'My point exactly, you soppy little boy,' she exclaimed triumphantly. 'Any woman who carries a sword openly is assumed to be more than just proficient with it, so a man would think twice before being tempted to find out otherwise. Besides, apart from the possibility of losing vital bits of his body, no man would ever willingly risk getting beaten by a woman, would he?' She looked at Pester's face and her grin widened still further.

'Well,' she corrected herself, 'not in a sword fight, anyway!'

The wrecked wagon finally ran aground among some small rocks on the southern bank of the river, but by this time Savatch had lapsed into unconsciousness again and showed no signs of reviving.

The effort of unlocking the cuff from Corinna's right wrist had very nearly proved beyond him, the tiny iron key repeatedly refusing to penetrate the buckle lock, the constant motion of the wagon doing nothing to help, and only her repeated urgings had kept him at the task. Finally, the lock had clicked open and, after a few more fumbled efforts, he had managed to free the buckle, allowing Corinna to deal with the left cuff herself.

Unfortunately the key had broken in her haste and although the lock actually turned as it happened, it meant she was unable to remove the slave hood and collar. Cursing under her breath, she had thrown the shaft of the key aside and turned her attention to Savatch's wound.

The iron quarrel had buried itself deep, but she realised it must have missed vital arteries and veins, or he would surely have been dead within seconds of being struck. However, he had still lost a lot of blood and was still losing more now, and would undoubtedly bleed to death eventually unless she could staunch the flow.

The arrow had to come out, that much was obvious, but Corinna knew also that removing it might allow the flow of blood to increase still further. First, she decided, she needed something with which to compress the wound. During her youth she had read stories where the heroines tore off strips, either from their dresses or their voluminous petticoats, but her current garb precluded that course of action.

Willing herself not to panic, she crawled over the tangle of furs towards the rear of the wagon and began searching for something suitable. There was not much: a piece of sacking, two strips of wide leather strapping and a coil of rope, plus the small chest from which she had seen Savatch take some of their dried provisions. She wrenched open the lid and offered up a brief prayer of thanks. He had used pieces of cloth to wrap cheese, beans and dried beef separately. They were not perfectly clean, but they were better than nothing. Quickly she unrolled the layers of thin muslin, dropped the cheese back into the box and ripped the cloth into two halves, wadding up the one half to make a pad.

Corinna scrambled back to Savatch's side. His eyes were closed, his face a milky white pallor and, for a brief moment, she feared he was already dead, but his chest still rose and fell slightly and she could see that a vein at his temple was pulsating gently.

For a long moment she knelt over him, the shaft of the quarrel gripped tightly in her right hand, hesitating, unsure that she could do what was necessary, terrified that her attempt to help might only hasten his end.

Do it!

It was as if she heard his voice inside her head and, if she had not been looking down at his unmoving lips at the time, she would have sworn that Savatch had actually spoken to her. She blinked away the returning tears, took a deep breath, and began to pull.

For an awful moment it seemed as if the shaft was not going to move and Corinna's blood-soaked fingers began to slide on the smooth metal. But then, just when she was beginning to fear the worst, she felt it give and in one horrible sucking movement, it slid free, eliciting a low moan from Savatch.

Blood did indeed begin to well up from the open wound, but it was not as bad as she had expected and quickly she thrust the wad of soft muslin over the gaping hole, pressing down on it. Briefly, she considered the spare strip of material, but the wound was so situated that there was no way in which she could utilise it as a bandage for holding the compress in place.

Instead she had to sit, keeping the pressure on with her fingers, willing the bleeding to stop, not daring to lift the temporary dressing to see if her silent pleas had been answered.

'You see, Melina,' Jekka said, taking the rescued girl's hands in her own, 'men have a great weakness.' She nodded towards where they had tied Sprig to a small tree. 'They mostly never think with anything situated above their waists,' she continued. 'This young beast is a prime example of that and look where it's got him.

'If he'd been using his head, he'd be back home in his own village by now, but no, he was determined to try to get you back, though no man in his right senses would ever consider taking on two Yslandic warriors on his own. Ye gods, but he'd already seen what we are capable of, yet still he came on.'

Melina, still very nervous, continued to stare at the near naked brigand, apparently fascinated by the way the leather sheath and its securing strap made Sprig's otherwise flaccid organ stand out from his groin.

'Will you really sell him?' she asked tremulously.

'Indeed, I think we shall,' Jekka said. 'Female slaves are more common in Illeum, but male slaves are nonetheless popular, and a young healthy specimen like this should command a good price. More than they'd have ever got for you, I'm afraid to say.'

'And they'll work him to death in the fields, I suppose?' Melina said.

'Maybe,' Jekka said, 'and if they do, well, it's no worse than his kind deserve. For centuries it's been accepted that men can abduct helpless women and sell them into a living hell, whereas few have the right to inflict the same fate on men. Usually, male slaves have to be convicted of some heinous crime and slavery is then used as an alternative to execution.'

'But surely,' Melina pointed out, 'this fellow hasn't even been tried?'

'Oh yes he has,' Jekka retorted. 'Tried and found wanting.'

'Yes, but not by any authority.'

Jekka released Melina's hands and took her gently by the shoulders. 'By Alanna's authority,' she said quietly. 'Alanna was vested with the authority to bring these outlaws to order, by whatever methods needed, including killing their chieftain and as many of them as the situation demanded. She could have let me kill this oaf on two occasions at least, but she has decided, instead, to commute his sentence.'

'But can she do that?' Melina asked incredulously.

'Yes,' she replied, 'she certainly can. And she has her own authority, an authority recognised by the state of Illeum for many generations and extended to a few very select individuals, even fewer of whom are not natives of the state.

'You see,' she continued, 'my friend Alanna, as well as being one of the finest swords women you're ever likely to meet, is also a princess – and a royal princess, at that.'

'But I thought—'

'You thought that all princesses lived in big castles, married princes and then had lots of other little princes and princesses and then maybe, some day, became queens, yes? Well, a lot may well do,' she said, 'but there are always some who make their own rules, and I doubt Alanna is the only one.'

To her great relief, Corinna saw that the bleeding had all but stopped, though Savatch showed no signs of coming to his senses again. Pressing the compressed muslin back against his wound, she crawled past him and wrestled her way through the tangle of canvas that hung over the front of the wagon, fearing that at any moment it might be swept out into the current once more.

Emerging from the cloying shroud, she blinked against the harsh sunlight and then pulled herself out to stand on the broken driver's bench, clinging to the forward iron hoop to maintain her balance. Looking around she saw there was no immediate danger of the wagon floating away again, for it was securely wedged between and against an outcrop of half submerged rocks, with one corner actually aground in the mud.

Of the four wheels there was no sign, and she realised they must have been torn off during the wagon's headlong descent. Quite how the wagon had even survived as well as it had, she could not imagine, but survive it had, even though it would never take to the road again.

Moving cautiously, she edged towards the side of the cart and then jumped across the few feet of water separating her from the bank, landing in the soft silt and sinking up to her ankles. Cursing quietly, she struggled the three paces to the embankment itself and pulled herself up onto more solid footing. Turning, she looked back at the beached wagon and shook her head.

Getting ashore herself was one thing – getting Savatch ashore presented an entirely different challenge and one which, she knew, she could never hope to meet unaided. She stood on the uneven grass, looking first left, then right, the river empty in both directions as far as her eye could see, torn between her instincts and common sense.

The former made the prospect of leaving her wounded lover, even temporarily, almost unimaginable, whilst the latter said that, even if he were to die while she was gone, without assistance he would have to remain where he was and, in all probability, die there anyway.

There really was no choice, but there was still a problem. Looking around, Corinna had no idea where they were, nor in which direction help might lie. The ground on either side of the river was uncultivated, semi-woodland and covered in clumps of dense undergrowth, which suggested that the soil hereabouts was totally unsuitable for farming.

Her best chance – her only chance – was in finding either a hunting lodge, or in finding her way back to the road again and hoping that she could find help from some passing travellers. There was more than an element of danger in this, for there was no way of knowing who might be on the road, but she realised, with a sigh of resignation, there was no other choice.

If she remained with Savatch his chances of surviving for more than a few hours looked grim, so danger or not, she would have to risk everything on the gamble.

Momentarily she hesitated, wanting to go back to him, if only for a final check on his wound, but an inner voice told her that she was only postponing the inevitable and that every minute she delayed might well prove to be fatal. Help might well arrive too late anyway, but the sooner Corinna set out to look for it, the better Savatch's chances were, even if that still meant they were slender.

Fulgrim surveyed the sorry looking coffle. The surviving maids and pages had been stripped, fitted with slave hoods and belts, their arms pinioned to their sides, a long chain linking their collars. At the head of the line stood Dorothea, her shaven skull now hidden beneath the leather of the hood that made her distinguishable from her former servants only by the maturity of her figure.

'Very fitting,' he smirked. 'You make as good a slave now as you did a year ago, and this time it will be for good. And you will lead your former charges still, but in a different form.' He turned to Ingrim, who was waiting patiently just behind him.

'When we make camp tonight,' he said, 'your men can make free with this bitch and as many of the rest as are not still virgin. There should be enough of them, but I don't want them ruining the value of any of the wenches that are still intact, understand? I take it you know how to tell the difference?'

'Sir,' Ingrim replied. 'I'll separate them out and fit belts to any that still are. We've loaded the necessary equipment in one of the wagons,' he added, grinning.

'Good,' Fulgrim said. 'Just make sure that every man has her ladyship before he moves on to more tender flesh, and that includes those who might prefer the boys. And, when they've all finished with her, bind her to a tree for the remainder of the night and I'll give her a sound whipping before breakfast.'

The sudden appearance of the hooded slave girl startled Pecon's horse and it reared and whinnied in fright, almost throwing him from the saddle.

'Whoah there!' he cried, pulling hard on the reins and wheeling the frightened beast around. 'Whoah, steady there!' The horse, usually such a placid animal, made one more half-hearted attempt to shy and then settled, responding to the sound of its rider's voice, whilst Demila's pony remained apparently unruffled, watching the proceedings with no more than a passing interest. Swinging himself out of the saddle, Pecon held out the bridle rein and called to her.

'Come, hold him!' he ordered. She nudged the pony forward and reached out to take the proffered rein. Pecon thrust it into her hand and rounded upon the newcomer.

'Bloody little fool!' he stormed. 'What in all the hells do you think you're playing at? Where is your master? Speak girl, or I'll have your hide!'

If he had expected the slave girl to cower before this tirade he was quickly disappointed, for she drew herself erect and addressed him in a manner he had certainly not anticipated.

'Sir,' she said, 'if I startled your horse, I am sorry, but I am in great need of your help and did not think.'

'My help?' Pecon echoed, striding towards her. 'A slave asks for my help?'

'I am not what I seem, sir,' she replied, standing her ground, 'but there is no time to explain. My – there is a man, a friend, badly injured and I need help to move him. I fear he is close to death, but if we could get him to a physician he might yet survive.'

'Indeed?' Pecon replied. 'And why should I trouble myself with the friend of a slave? I presume this is another slave and I dare say you are both running from your rightful master.'

'No sir, indeed we are not.' The girl's eyes flickered behind her mask. 'In fact,' she continued, 'the man is my master, in a manner of speaking.'

Pecon was not sure whether to laugh or shake the impudent girl. 'This man is your master, you say?' he said. 'And yet did you not just describe him as a friend?'

The girl threw up her arms in a gesture of supplication. 'Please!' she cried. 'Please sir, there is no time to explain. Later I can tell you everything, but for now, won't you please just come with me? It is not far, but I cannot bring him to the roadside unaided.'

'I think that perhaps you are feeling sorry for our new slave,' Jekka said. Melina, riding alongside her, felt herself beginning to blush and the redheaded Yslander did not miss this fact.

'Aha,' she said quietly, 'so I was right. Yet was he not responsible for killing members of your own family? How can you have any feelings for him but hatred?'

'I don't think he did any of the actual killing,' Melina replied. 'That was mainly their leader and one other man.'

'But he made no attempt to stop them, did he?' Jekka pointed out.

Melina shook her head. 'No, but then I think they might as easily have killed him, had he tried to interfere. They were evil men.'

'And he would have become just as evil in time,' Jekka said firmly, 'if he's not already so. He raped you the same as his friends did, I suppose?'

'Yes, but he was not so rough and he let me sleep under his furs, where the others just discarded me when they had finished,' Melina said. 'I heard him ask their leader if he could take me as his own slave.' Her bottom lip started to tremble. 'The brute then told him he had to whip me, to prove he was man enough.'

'Which, of course, he did,' Jekka said grimly. 'Some test of manhood.'

'It is probably the way with their people,' Melina said. 'Besides, in their eyes I was just a slave and men whip their slaves everywhere, so I understand.'

'So now,' Jekka smiled, 'let him learn how it feels to be on the receiving end, for it will be a long time before he has anything to do with a whip other than to suffer under it.

'Let you sleep under his furs indeed,' she growled. 'Probably just wanted a cock warmer on a cold night.'

Almost miraculously, there was a small hamlet less than a mile further down the road and, when Pecon inquired, to Corinna's relief he was told there was a physician. Though when they arrived at his cottage the sight of the old man, bent almost double, did little to inspire further confidence.

However, Pecon quickly organised a small wagon and two young men to assist in carrying Savatch up from the river, though the delay seemed interminable to Corinna and she feared they would return to find him already dead. Following Pecon back down to the beached wagon, she hardly dared hope and stood on the grass and waited while he clambered across the rocks to investigate.

'He's still breathing,' Pecon announced, jumping onto the river bank and stepping aside to make way for the two villagers. 'But lift him with care, or that wound will surely open up again.'

The climb from river to roadside had been far too precipitous for the old doctor, who had waited with Demila and the borrowed wagon. Now, as the men laid Savatch on the back of the vehicle, he leaned over him, fussing and muttering and probing with his gnarled fingers.

'It's not good,' he wheezed at last. 'He's lost much blood, as you can see for yourselves. By rights he should already be dead, though he looks as if he's strong and pretty fit.

'Fortunately the arrow that struck him missed all the really major vessels, but it's done damage enough, for all that, so we must get him back to my house, so that I can clean and dress the wound properly. If it's left, his blood will sour and he will die within hours.'

While the old man tended to his patient, Corinna sat on a fallen tree trunk a few paces from the back door of the cottage. Demila sat on the grass, cross-legged, some distance from her, staring down at the ground and making no attempt to communicate. Finally, as the sun was dipping low in the sky,

Pecon emerged, his features impassive. Corinna rose and rushed towards him.

'Is he…?' She could not bring herself to say the word, but Pecon shook his head.

'He still lives,' he replied, 'though the life spark is very weak. The old man cannot – or will not – say what his chances are, but his face tells an unpromising story.' He stretched his shoulders and let out a long, deep breath.

'Your master's fate now lies elsewhere than in mortal hands, I think,' he said, looking up at the sky. 'He must hope that some god sees fit to smile kindly upon him, for there is no more we can do.' He half turned and called out to Demila.

'Go take the horses to the trough,' he ordered. 'We must be on our way without further delay. It will be dark in two hours and it will take all of that to reach the place where we will be staying this night, especially as one of you will have to walk. That pony cannot carry two of you.'

Corinna stared at him, mouth agape. 'But I'm not coming with you!' she exclaimed.

'Since when has a slave had the right to decide where and when she does anything?' Pecon demanded icily. 'I have paid the old man to care for your master and to bury him if he dies. He seemed to have no money upon him, so therefore I am taking you as recompense.

'I have drawn up a document, which the old man has signed as well and he will give it to your *former* master, if and when he should recover. It is all done quite properly, so you now belong to me.'

Corinna gulped, thinking fast. His assumption as to her status was reasonable enough, given that she still wore the slave hood and belt, that her ringed breasts were on full display, and that her final modesty was covered only by the triangular leather strap that still held the leather dildo inside her.

'But my master had money on him,' she protested. 'There was a pouch at his belt.'

'Well, 'tis not there now,' Pecon snapped, 'and I have not taken it. I am many things, but not a thief, and certainly not one to steal from a man who cannot protect his own. Perhaps it was lost when the wagon fell into the river. You said it was a steep drop, did you not?'

'I did not mean to accuse you, sir,' Corinna said. 'If the pouch is gone, then it is lost, probably forever, but I can repay you your money and pay more, for your kindness and inconvenience.'

'Oh, you can, can you?' Pecon threw back his head and roared with laughter. 'Such fine talk, coming from a slave.'

'But I am not really a slave, sir,' Corinna said. It was a risk, revealing her true identity, but it was her only choice. 'That man in there, my master, as I called him, is not really my master at all, except that we were acting out a little game. He is Lord Savatch, captain of the household at Garassotta.'

'And you're his wife, I suppose?' Pecon chuckled, with obvious disbelief.

'No sir, I am not,' Corinna replied evenly, 'though I would be if I were free to marry him, and I shall be so, in another year or two. My husband – my husband's interests have taken him elsewhere and our marriage was not a true marriage anyway.'

'Ah, a slave who makes a political marriage, maybe?' Pecon said, derision in his voice. 'What cackafanny nonsense is this you would have me believe?' He stepped forward and seized Corinna's left arm. 'Enough,' he snapped, 'or I shall thrash you soundly.' He turned her roughly about. 'And from these marks on your back, you are no stranger to a good whipping.'

'But you don't understand!' Corinna squealed, trying to twist free of his grip. 'If only you'd let me—'

Her attempts to reason with him were cut short as he thrust

the wadded leather gag forcefully into her mouth and the restraining strap was fastened before she had time to react. With practised skill he forced her left wrist into the strap at her side, pulling it tight, the lock clicking into place.

In desperation Corinna tried to kick out at him, but the soft-soled sandals had no effect and he soon had her other wrist similarly restrained.

'That's better,' he said, stepping back. Despite his efforts, she saw he was not even breathing heavily and his expression was now one of mockery. 'Yes,' he said, nodding slowly, 'a fine big-titted wench indeed, bigger boned, bigger built and a lot stronger than poor little Demila. I think I know just the place to get the best price for you, my girl, and I may even show a profit on the deal.'

Three

The journey through the hills into South Erisvaal took two days, which passed uneventfully. As Moxie had predicted, the few travellers they encountered assumed that the sword she wore entitled her to a healthy degree of respect. And although a few of the males made no attempt to disguise their interest in her well-developed bosom, they offered no comments and did nothing to hinder the progress of what they clearly supposed was a warrior woman and her slave page.

Pester, despite the fact that Moxie had removed the leather slave hood from his head, maintained a sulky silence, except when she addressed him directly. He was not a brave soul at the best of times and the events at Varragol had frightened him badly, so he could not understand why Moxie was persisting in riding towards what he plainly considered as further potential peril.

'So,' she said, late on the afternoon of the second day, 'what would you have us do then, eh?' Pester pouted morosely and avoided meeting her gaze.

'At least ride somewhere there's civilised people,' he said. 'We know nothing of this country and I reckon we've been lucky, so far.'

'Civilised country?' Moxie raised her eyebrows. 'It depends what you call civilised, I suppose. In my experience, Illeum only thinks itself civilised. A truly civilised country would hardly permit men to beat women at will, nor would it permit the more fortunate to own the less fortunate as if they were no better than animals at times.

'Through accidents of birth, people like Dorothea and Fulgrim can set themselves apart and control the destiny and fate of people like us. Even if we were to turn around and ride back, what do you think awaits us there, eh?

'In case you've forgotten, Dorothea owns us both, legally, and the mere fact that she's been dragged off somewhere by Fulgrim and his bunch of cut-throats doesn't mean we're suddenly free. Any noble, or even any merchant who has the right seal, can seize us as his own, at least until they establish what has happened to the mistress.

'Worse still, if they choose not to believe our story, we could be taken as being runaways and the punishments meted out for that are worse than anything we would want to face. Our best chance is to find the Lady Corinna, for she'll vouch for us. I don't fancy standing up on a public block while some executioner or bailiff starts mutilating this body of mine, and you've still got a cock to lose, even though you were parted from your balls a long while back.

'And that would be a pity,' she smiled, in an attempt to lighten the mood between them. 'I've grown quite fond of that cock of yours and I'd hate to think of it being pickled or burned on some fire.'

'You know,' Pester muttered, 'you go on about the way people like Fulgrim and the mistress treat us, but you're just as bad. If you'd been born into a wealthy family, I reckon you might have been even worse.'

'Oh, poor baby,' Moxie cooed, teasingly. 'Doesn't he like having his poor little weasel in Moxie's nice warm burrow then?'

Pester sniffed and continued to stare straight ahead over his horse's head and they rode on in silence again, side by side, as their shadows lengthened on the road in front of them and the day gradually began to draw towards its end.

By the middle of the third day, Corinna was feeling more exhausted than she had ever thought it possible for a person to feel. Pecon set a demanding pace and schedule and she and Demila were forced to take turns walking. There were few signs of habitation on the road they now travelled, and in the two tiny hamlets they did pass through Pecon had no luck in trying to purchase another mount, though he was able to obtain a pair of stout knee boots for each of the girls, which offered better protection from the uneven road surface than did their flimsy sandals. And at least he did remove the phallus, which offered her some small crumb of comfort.

To her horror, however, he forced her to travel still gagged and when, on the first night, he removed the foul leather and she tried to reason with him again, he rewarded her by replacing it immediately, tying her against a tree and delivering several stinging blows across her bare rump with his riding whip. The tears that coursed down her face then were not completely tears of pain and, as the frustration welled up within her, she began to realise the sheer hopelessness of her position.

On the second night, when he had finished with Demila, he turned his attention to Corinna, something she had expected would have happened much earlier. He lifted her to her feet, holding her at arms' length, but showed no inclination to remove the hated gag. In fact, her mute state seemed to please him greatly.

'Women chatter far too much,' he grinned, 'and I have always thought that a gag lends a certain amount of appeal to a female face. Of course, I haven't seen your face yet, and I don't even know your name, but that is of little import. I'll not be keeping you long enough to worry about little details like that, but I think I should at least test the wares I'm offering.'

He forced her down to her knees and then onto her back,

and Corinna made no attempt to resist. With her arms still bound to her sides there would have been little point, and as he unbuckled the belt from between her thighs, she dutifully spread her legs for him, exposing the pinkness of her sex.

In other circumstances, she reflected later, she might even have enjoyed his taking of her, for after all, had she not craved to be treated so, but now, as he pistoned steadily in and out of her, although her warm tunnel gave him a well-lubricated welcome, her mind was with Savatch, hoping desperately that he was not dead, and praying fervently that he would recover and come for her.

Later however, as she lay alone under the fur Pecon had thrown over her, listening to the muffled sounds as he once again took his pleasure with Demila, the tears came again, for staring up at the stars in the cloudless night sky she realised the futility of such hopes. Even if Savatch did survive, even if he did recover enough strength to travel, it would be days yet, weeks maybe, and by then their trail would have grown very cold indeed.

Dorothea had long since ceased to react to the humiliations being heaped upon her. Each evening, when the caravan halted to make camp, Fulgrim's men erected a stout pole close by the fire, setting it deep into the ground and pounding the earth hard about its base, so that no single person could hope to move it.

To this stake Dorothea was then bound, arms high above her head, so that she was forced to stand only upon her toes and the balls of her feet, which were then stretched apart and tied to sturdy pegs which they hammered into the grass. Sometimes they left her hood and collar in place and she was grateful for the small degree of anonymity it afforded her, but other times they removed it, taunting her for her smooth pate and examining it for signs of re-growth, using vicious razors to scrape away even the smallest hair.

Then they took her, unhurriedly and awaiting their turns without argument, some of the guards amusing themselves with her maids and pages in the meantime. Most of the men seemed unworried which sex their victims were, and the only ones to escape their animal attentions were the three youngest among the surviving maids, whom Ingrim had earlier identified as still virgin.

These now wore leather chastity belts, thick triangular straps that were attached to the lower edge of their slave belts front and back.

Eventually, somewhere around midnight, the camp would begin to settle down. Drink and fatigue took their toll of even the most determined among the men and finally they slept, leaving their wretched victims to a few precious hours of peace and relief.

Only Fulgrim remained awake – it seemed he hardly ever slept at all – and then he came to Dorothea, taunting, prodding, twisting her nipples and ears and all the while speaking to her in a low whisper, so that the slumbering figures all about did not disturb.

'This is only the beginning, bitch,' he hissed. 'And this is but a small party of men, if we are honest. Imagine how it will be to service entire companies, hundreds of men each day and all through the night. I'll have you mounted on a block right in the middle of the barracks, available to any man who feels the fancy. Ye gods, but they'll fuck you to death, though not before I'm ready, believe me.

'No, I want you to live a good long while yet, so I can enjoy watching you suffer. You'll be fodder for whole armies before you get your release and you'll die a withered, dried up old hag.'

Moxie straddled Pester, hovering above him as he lay on his back in the soft grass. His penis was already stiff and he held it vertically, presenting it to her yawning sex lips. She lowered herself gently, allowing the purple knob to press gently against her silken labia, though denying it entry still. She looked down at his taut features and smiled.

'Do you love me, my little page?' she whispered. His eyes flickered and he nodded, swallowing hard.

'Yes,' he croaked, 'you know I do.'

'And would you die for me, my pretty little no balls?' He swallowed again, his eyes anxious.

'I – I don't know,' he confessed. 'I think so.' His tongue flickered out, moistening his lips. 'I just pray I never have to be put to that test. But I would certainly try to kill anyone who tried to harm you,' he finished defiantly.

'Me too,' Moxie said, and settled lower, drawing a sharp gasp from Pester as the first few inches of his length slid easily inside her. She smiled again, never ceasing to wonder at the size of his organ, especially when compared to his own unremarkable stature and the fact that he had no testicles. This latter absence never seemed to detract from his pleasure, though naturally his climaxes lacked one significant feature and he also appeared able to delay them for longer, which Moxie appreciated greatly.

She laid a hand on his hairless chest, stroking the smooth flesh and teasing one of his puckered nipples.

'You're just like a girl with a cock,' she sighed. 'So much better than being a hairy great ape like most men.' She let herself drop again, this time swallowing his entire weapon as he withdrew his supporting hand, and squirmed comfortably into his groin. He groaned and closed his eyes.

'All you're missing is a pair of titties and you'd make a fine girl,' she teased. 'Even your hair is long and soft.' With her other hand she took hold of a strand of his wavy hair,

159

using it to tickle his cheek. She felt him shiver and his rod pulsed inside her.

'I've sometimes wondered what it must be like to have a cock,' Moxie said dreamily. 'Not one of those pretend ones, like my mistress fits onto me, but a real cock, one I could feel with. Of course, you know about my pretend cocks, don't you?' she said. 'I wish we had one here now and then you could really play at being a girl again, couldn't you?'

Pester said nothing, but she could feel him trembling, remembering, no doubt, the numerous occasions when Moxie had smuggled one of the double-ended phalluses out of the palace, strapped it to herself with one end embedded deep within her and then used the rearing free end to take him as she bent him over any convenient tree stump or rock. She even made him dress in one of the maid's clothing, complete with the silver sandals that Dorothea insisted the girls wear around the palace, his hair tied back with a brightly coloured ribbon, the flimsy skirts swirling about his thighs. He had pretended to hate the charade, but made little protest when she repeated the game on several occasions since.

'Poor little Pester,' she crooned, rocking gently back and forth, her inner muscles contracting fiercely to grip him even harder. 'Neither one thing nor the other, are you? But I think I love you too.' She leaned forward, her nose touching his, and extended her tongue to touch his lips. Obediently he opened them and she plunged inside, finding his tongue and fencing with it as her mouth closed over his.

He was completely spineless, she thought, and would doubtless run a mile at the first sign of danger, but he was a beautiful creature and offered her, as much as that was possible, the best of both possible worlds when it came to pleasure.

The land they called the Vaal was largely comprised of flat plains country, featureless once the caravan had left the hill country behind. Dorothea recognised their route vaguely, for she had visited South Erisvaal twice in her younger days. Quite why Fulgrim had chosen to come this way, rather than head back for his home territory in the Vorsan states, which lay in completely the opposite direction, she had no idea. But she doubted it would make any real difference, either to her or to her maids and pages, where they were headed.

She also doubted that the purpose of the journey was primarily concerned with his desire to take revenge upon her, for that he could have done almost anywhere. His sadistic thirsts were slaked only as a by-product of whatever greater scheme he had, but what he hoped to achieve in the Vaal she could not begin to imagine.

If South Erisvaal was sparsely populated, its neighbour, North Erisvaal was even more so. The people were mostly nomadic, save for a few farmers who eked a sparse living from poor soil, and a few horse breeders.

Perhaps, she reflected, as she trudged wearily behind the lead wagon, perhaps he was intending to trade his captives for some of those horses, but she dismissed that theory as ridiculous. Horses – good horses – were worth more than most slaves, so he would hardly move himself and a half company of men such a distance just to collect maybe a dozen mounts at best.

No, whatever it was, Dorothea thought, it was much bigger than that. Fulgrim's original scheme to oust Lord Lundt, Corinna's father, and replace him with his half-brother Willum, the ill-fated plot to which Dorothea herself had originally been a party, that was the magnitude of Fulgrim's ambitions. If he had ever succeeded in his original plan, Willum would have ended up, at best, as a puppet in his hands. At worst he would have met with an unfortunate accident and Fulgrim himself would have found a way to take control of the most powerful state on the continent.

He had failed once, thanks to Savatch, his Yslandic friends and the unlikely assistance of her own maids and pages, but Dorothea doubted that a man as obsessed as the Vorsan lord would have let that one failure and his consequent year of suffering deflect him from such an ambition. No, she thought grimly, the likes of Fulgrim were not easily dissuaded and he'd had that entire year in which to think and plot.

She still had no idea what was so important about the Vaal, but Dorothea was now convinced that whatever it was, it would bode ill, not only for Illeum, but for every country in the civilised world.

The inn was not part of a village as such, but stood back from the river ford, a short distance from a large watermill and, to judge from its size, its position obviously brought it a fair trade from both travellers and local farmers alike. Apart from the main building, a two-storey structure of stone and timber, there were two sizeable barns and a cluster of smaller outhouses, including a stable block, in front of which four horses stood tethered to a timber rail.

However, what caught Corinna's eye was not so much the four-legged creatures, but the two-legged one tethered alongside them; a powerfully built male, his true age disguised by the leather slave hood that covered his head and most of his features, but probably young, to judge from his physique.

Like Corinna, he was bound with wrists buckled at either side of a broad waist belt and, apart from his boots, was naked save for the merest of concessions to his modesty – in his case a soft leather sheath that enshrouded his flaccid organ and bulging testicles. Despite her own predicament she would have smiled, had the mouth-distorting gag permitted, for the man's presentation betrayed a decidedly female hand.

Pecon guided his horse away from the stable building and dismounted at another rail, which was situated immediately outside the main tavern, hitching the rein deftly around the rough timber pole and then turning to release Demila from her saddle. Leaving the leather thongs coiled around the pommel, he lifted her to the ground, placed her hands back into the leather side straps and buckled them closed, before finally turning his attention to Corinna, who stood behind the pony, a leash from her collar to the back of its saddle.

'Come,' he said, taking up the free end of the cord. 'There is shade under those trees.' He nodded towards a group of four gnarled trees at the far end of the building, and guided both girls towards them, motioning for them to sit once they were beneath the overhanging branches. Demila he clearly trusted to remain where he told her, but not so Corinna, for he stooped and wound the end of her leash about a projecting root, knotting it firmly.

'I'll fetch you water later,' he said, straightening up. Corinna saw that his attention was now held by the male slave over by the stable, and that there was a curious glint in his eyes. Perhaps, she thought, it was not only powerless women that attracted him. With a sigh she wriggled herself backwards, leaned gingerly back against the tree trunk and closed her eyes, content, for the moment at least, to be off her aching feet.

Alanna stared coolly across the table at the tall stranger, while beside her Jekka continued to fiddle with the handle of her knife, making a great show of picking at the semiprecious pincel stone that was set into the polished bone.

'Fifty silver telts is not much for such a healthy young specimen,' Alanna said. 'The fellow is young, little more than a boy, and has many years in him.'

'How young?' the man, who had introduced himself as

Pecon, asked. 'Those damned hoods can hide so much.'

'As I say,' Alanna replied, 'little more than a boy. He probably still yet has more growth in him. He must be worth at least a krone – double that if he were fully trained. I've been honest enough with you on that score.'

'Perfectly honest,' Pecon nodded, 'but a gold krone is a lot of investment and I'll need to take him and feed him over several days, before I can hope to get my return on it.'

'Your return will justify it,' Jekka muttered. She laid the knife flat on the table before her. The traveller appeared genuine enough, but it paid to keep a weapon close at hand, and she had seen moods change dramatically too many times in the past to want to take anything for granted.

'I'll raise my offer to seventy-five,' Pecon said.

'Ninety. Anything less and we might as well take him with us and train him as we go. There are traders around Illeum City who would willingly pay three or four krones for such a specimen, once he's been broken in a little.'

'Illeum prices have always been inflated,' Pecon smiled, 'but I am not travelling in that direction. I'll tell you what,' he said, pushing his seat back a little and stretching out his legs, 'I'll pay you two gold krones if you include a horse, saddle, and a couple of blankets. I am travelling fairly light myself and I already have one girl on foot all the time.'

'Then we may be able to help you even further,' Alanna said. 'We have a horse for him, plus we have another, and its cargo should be of interest to you, especially as you seem to be a shrewd business judge. Where you are heading, I am sure you will find a ready market for it and make as much profit as you will do from our young slave.'

Corinna could scarcely believe her eyes when she saw the two females following Pecon out of the tavern. But her joy at seeing Alanna and Jekka quickly turned to desperation, for the gag prevented her calling out and the leash held her where she was, several paces away from them and too far to attract any serious attention.

A gagged slave girl squealing and jumping up and down would give little cause for suspicion. The mere fact that her master was keeping her gagged and bound would suggest she was either untrained, rebellious, or simply being punished, and not even an Yslandic warrior woman would consider interfering with a master's legitimate rights.

Desperately she wriggled her buttocks sideways, trying to bring her left hand close enough to the knotted leash, but the way her wrists were strapped made it all but impossible for her to bring her fingers down to the root level in the right plane. Frantically she scrabbled at the knot, but knew, almost before she started, that it was futile. Pecon clearly knew his business, and even with two unhampered hands it would have taken several seconds to loosen the tether.

Corinna howled into the gag, kicking at the earth with her booted heels. Alongside her Demila looked startled, but stayed silent and did not make any attempt to move. With her eyes Corinna tried to convey that she wanted to attract the attention of the two women, but it was useless to expect the slave girl to help. Even if she could be made to understand, it was extremely unlikely that she would dare risk her master's wrath by what would be seen as an act of serious rebelliousness.

With a final howl of anguish Corinna let her muscles relax again and turned to watch as the trio approached the stable block. Immediately their purpose became clear, for it was plain that Alanna and Jekka were responsible for the male slave and that Pecon was trying to make some sort of deal to purchase him. Perhaps, Corinna thought, they might come closer when they returned to the tavern, but deep inside she knew that was a forlorn hope.

Unless some divine power intervened, she was beginning

to realise, it looked very much as if she was going to get what she had only ever really thought about in her most intimate dreams – a life of slavery, sold and traded like any other commodity in this desperately unfair and unfeeling world. And the reality was a far less enticing prospect than the images she had until so recently cherished.

The girl was very young, still in her teens, with straw-coloured hair and a fresh rosy complexion, from which her green eyes shone like twin beacons. Her forehead was wrinkled in an expression of concern and, for several seconds, Savatch was confused, not understanding that her concern was for him.

Then, as if a veil had been lifted, everything came back to him: the arrow, the horses bolting, the sudden bend in the mountain road and the feeling of falling, the ground becoming sky, then trees, the rending of breaking timbers, the terrified screaming, and then…

And then what? With a groan he tried to sit up, but the girl laid a soft hand on his shoulder and pressed him back against the pillows.

'No,' she said firmly. 'You are very weak and you may yet tear your wound open again. You lost much blood and are lucky not to be dead.'

'Where am I?' His throat felt raw.

The girl perched carefully on the edge of the bed. 'You are in my grandfather's house,' she said. 'His name is Dagnar and he is a physician. You were brought here several days ago, near to death, as I said. My grandfather tended to your wound as best he could, but you should thank whatever gods you worship for the fact that you have survived, for there was little any mortal hand could do, save keep you warm and comfortable.'

'What's your name?' Savatch blinked, trying to control his vision, which kept going in and out of focus.

'My name is Mirit,' she said. 'What is yours? We were told you are known as Savatch, but your former slave girl said many curious and ridiculous things, so it was difficult to know whether she spoke the truth about you.'

'She spoke the truth,' Savatch groaned, though his spirits were instantly lifted at this mention of Corinna. Mirit had spoken of his survival as being a miracle; that both of them should have lived after such a terrible plunge was something else again.

'Where is she now?' he asked. 'Is she hurt?' Even as he voiced the question more memories began to creep back, flashes of Corinna holding him to her, of her crying, talking, pleading. But the images were distorted and made little sense.

'She was not hurt, apart from a few bruises,' Mirit said, 'or so I am told. I never actually saw her, for she was already gone when I returned from the goats.'

'Gone?' Savatch echoed, trying hopelessly to rise again. 'Gone where? Someone should have stopped her travelling these roads, though I cannot believe she would have left me here alone, not without a good reason.'

'There was a man,' Mirit began, 'a traveller. Your slave girl found him on the road and sought his help. He came here for my grandfather and paid for two of the village lads to help get you back here in a wagon. He also paid my grandfather to tend you, or to bury your corpse as necessary, and took your slave girl in exchange.

'My grandfather has the document all properly signed, and will return to you any money left over as and when you recover your strength enough to leave again. Ow!' She squeaked in pain and alarm as Savatch's hand closed fiercely about her wrist, the strength of his grip, for a man who had so recently been at death's door, astonishing and frightening her.

'This man!' he gasped. 'Who is he? Where was he travelling to?'

'Sir!' Mirit protested. 'You are hurting me.' She made to pull her arm away, but Savatch refused to release his hold on her.

'Tell me!' he snapped. 'Tell me about this man, or so help me I'll break your arm.'

'There is not much to tell,' Mirit wailed. 'I told you, they were all gone by the time I got back here, so I know only what my grandfather knew, which indeed was little enough. The fellow's name was Pecon – that much is on the document of sale – but beyond that he said only that he was a traveller and that he had some dealings with buying and selling slaves. There was a girl already with him, so I am told, for he wanted to buy a horse for your girl to ride, though horses are scarce in these parts so there was none available for him.'

'Damnation!' Savatch released his grip on the girl's wrist and fell back, exhausted again. 'Where is your grandfather? I must speak directly with him.'

'My grandfather is away in the next village until tonight,' Mirit said, withdrawing out of his reach. 'I doubt he will return much before nightfall, for it is a fair distance and he is no longer a young man.'

'The girl,' Savatch said, trying to think quickly. 'You said she spoke of many curious and ridiculous things. What sort of things?'

'Only that my grandfather overheard her telling her new master that she was not your slave and that she offered him gold if he would wait until you recovered and helped you back to some castle… the castle at Garassotta, I believe.'

'And he didn't believe her, obviously,' Savatch retorted sourly.

'He said he had no time for such stories, nor time to wait around for a man who would probably be dead soon enough anyway, let alone time to travel to Garassotta, which is hardly the next village.'

Savatch closed his eyes, breathing deeply.

'Mirit,' he said at last, 'the girl, the one who travelled as my slave, she spoke the truth. She is no real slave – no legal slave, at least. I could try to explain, but I doubt you would understand anyway. I must get word to this Pecon fellow. I'll pay him more than he could ever hope to earn in a year of slave trading, so long as she is returned unhurt.

'You must get someone to ride after him, for I certainly cannot sit a horse myself as yet. But then, wait! I had money, so why was there this need for him to pay your grandfather?'

'Apparently there was no money where you were found,' Mirit replied. She had backed away until she was standing against the wall by the doorway, but now she ventured a step or two closer again. 'We think your purse must have been lost in the river.'

'Then someone must lend me enough for this and I will repay them double, just as soon as I can get word to Garassotta. Who is the swiftest horseman around here?'

'It would do no good,' Mirit said sadly. 'There is little money in this village and none who had the sum you need would admit to it anyway. Besides, there is no horseman here who could hope to catch this Pecon. As I said, you have been here for several days now, so they will surely be many miles from here. He may well have already sold the girl on.'

'I hope not,' Savatch muttered. 'I hope not, for I swear I'll kill any man that touches her.' He forced his eyes open again.

'Mirit,' he groaned, 'you must do something further for me… please? I owe my life to you – you and your grandfather, and even, it seems, to this Pecon fellow, for all that he has exacted a terrible price, but I will reward you all handsomely as soon as I am able. Meantime, you must find someone to ride to the castle at Garassotta and take a message. It will mean yet more delay, but there is nothing else for it. We must bring help here – and as quickly as possible.'

Corinna was beginning to find the developing relationship between Pecon and his latest slave quite fascinating. The young man had obviously been captured by Alanna and Jekka, though in what circumstances she had no idea, and was finding his new status more than a little difficult to accept.

From his build, and what she could see of his features, he appeared to be, or have been, a young warrior of sorts, possibly from the far north, the region generally referred to as the Snow Kingdoms. From what Corinna knew of the men in those parts, slavery would come to him as anything but easy and his general attitude and demeanour did nothing but confirm this.

Meanwhile, the extra horses did little to help their progress. The pack on the fourth horse clearly contained something that Pecon valued, and was too bulky to permit even Demila to ride upon its back. And whilst the other horse was unquestionably more sturdy than the pony that Corinna and Demila had taken turns to ride previously, the pony itself was not big enough to carry Sprig for any distance and allow the two girls to ride the more powerful steed together.

The only advantage, from Corinna's point of view, was that now she had to walk for only one third of each day, rather than for half of it, though Pecon seemed eager to take advantage of this fact by setting a slightly stiffer pace. Two days on from the village where he had purchased the luckless young man, Corinna's feet and legs felt no less painful and the blisters beneath her toes were worse than ever.

It came as a great relief to her when, on that second evening, their small party encountered a trader who was prepared to sell Pecon one of the three mules he was leading behind his own horse. And when Pecon had transferred the burden from the packhorse to his latest acquisition, she hauled herself onto the larger animal's back and spent the final hour of the day's journey slumped across its neck in a state of semi-consciousness.

Once they had stopped to make camp, however, Corinna quickly realised that Pecon had plans for her that precluded any chance of her sleeping just yet. So far, he had paid her little attention, save for ensuring that she travelled securely gagged throughout the day, but now it seemed a thought had occurred to him.

'He looks fine enough,' Pecon said, indicating Sprig, 'but we none of us know whether he functions properly, so I thought we might test him this evening and see whether my coin was well spent.

'I think,' Alanna mused, as the two women rode slowly towards the brow of yet another hill, 'I think we could allow ourselves a day or so of rest and relaxation.'

'We've certainly earned that,' Jekka replied. 'This trip has been more profitable than we expected, after all. Perhaps we should have brought away more of their horses. I hadn't realised just how much a good mount fetched in these parts. Absolutely scandalous, especially when you're expected to pay more for a horse than you would a slave.'

'Unusual for you to be so concerned about money matters,' Alanna quipped, 'or are you still griping that I wouldn't let you make the fellow an offer for one of his females?'

'I can't see what you had against the idea,' Jekka said sulkily. 'After all, she'd have had a better life with us than wherever it is she'll end up now.'

'Until something happens to us, that is,' Alanna pointed out, 'or until some fellow takes a fancy to her and she to him and you end up slitting both their throats. Besides, I thought you hated the concept of slavery?'

'I do,' Jekka said, 'but she wouldn't have been like a normal slave, more a personal servant.'

'Yes, and we both know *how* personal,' Alanna laughed. 'But what if she balked at the idea of putting her sweet little tongue around your bud? What then? Would you beat her, whip her, leave her tied over a saddle until she saw the error of her ways?'

'No, well… well, it needn't have been like that. Besides, she'd probably have been very grateful to me for rescuing her.' The horses walked on a few more paces.

'Look, it's all right for you,' Jekka said at length. 'You never seem to need anyone in your bed and you assume, just because I can concentrate on my professional skills, you assume that I'm the same. But a girl gets lonely, and well, once I thought…'

She looked sideways at Alanna, who smiled consoling back at her.

'Well, it would have been more like incest,' Alanna said. 'I've always looked upon you as a sort of younger sister.'

'Half these villagers around these parts wouldn't be here if it weren't for incest.'

'Yes, but *we* are not peasants,' Alanna said. 'We are supposed to have genuine breeding, not inbreeding.'

'Which is probably why they all seem to have a lot more fun than we do,' Jekka retorted. She lifted the voluminous sleeve on her right arm and fingered the mechanism of the miniature crossbow, which was as ever strapped to her arm there. 'This needs oil again,' she muttered. 'You'd think they'd use a metal for the catch that wouldn't rust at the first sign of damp in the air.'

'Then why not see if we can't find a metalworker to replace the necessary parts?' Alanna suggested. 'They'll have one at Garassotta, for sure.'

'Garassotta?'

'Well, there's bound to be an armoury in the castle and I'm sure the Lady Corinna wouldn't mind you borrowing the skills of one of her artisans. And who knows, maybe she's even got a pretty little maid whose skills you could also borrow.'

'Ah, I see.' Jekka smiled knowingly. 'And I don't suppose

we might find Master Savatch at Garassotta also, by any chance? You wouldn't be thinking of borrowing something yourself?'

'Certainly not,' Alanna snapped. 'What was between Savatch and myself was in the nature of a convenient thing. We both of us knew it would end sooner or later and now he has his lady and she is more disposed towards his... preferences,' she ended, choosing her words carefully.

'No, I suggest Garassotta because it is less than two days' ride from here and, though it's not exactly on our original return route, it will not take us far out of our way and it might be pleasant to visit old friends.'

Jekka pondered this for a moment. 'Do you think there might be a maid there?' she said thoughtfully.

'Hundreds, probably. It's a castle, after all, and even grander than Varragol, which was overrun with pretty little maids.'

'All of whom were specially reserved for Lady Dorothea,' Jekka said. 'But then Corinna is no Dorothea, so maybe I could purchase a servant from her. She would know which among her servants was most suitable for my, um, requirements. That would answer one of your objections, at least.'

'She'd also have to be able to ride a horse well and rough it for more than half the time. Your tender chick might soon turn into an old turkey.'

'We survive well enough on the life,' Jekka pointed out.

'Yes, but then we're different,' Alanna said.

They reached the top of the hill and the horses started down the empty trail.

'Well now,' Pecon smirked, 'everything seems to be in working order so far.' He had forced the still bound Sprig to lay flat on his back and then instructed Demila to remove the leather sheath from the helpless slave's genitals. Then, at her master's urging, the girl had begun to manipulate his flaccid organ, which soon began to react despite Sprig's attempts to control himself.

'Shall I make him come now, master?' Demila asked bluntly. 'I don't think it will take that long, for I think the restraint has been on him for a few days.'

'You can mount him and ride him to a finish, if you want girl,' Pecon laughed, 'but then maybe not. Maybe we should see how well our other new slave performs. You,' he said, rounding on Corinna, who had remained sitting against a rock during the activities so far. 'You, come over here. It's about time we took that gag off you and let you use your mouth for more than your persistent ramblings.'

There was no room for ambiguity in that statement and, as she rose awkwardly to her feet, Corinna was under no illusions as to what was expected of her. As a slave, she had no say whatsoever in her daily fate and, if a master ordered her to do something, she would be expected to do it, whether it was with a noble or the lowest of slaves.

'There now,' Pecon said, as he removed the gag from between her aching jaws, 'it really is quite a pretty mouth. Perhaps we should also have a proper look to see if the rest of the face matches that promise, but not yet, I think.' He prodded her towards the recumbent Sprig, whose erection still rose impressively in Demila's grip.

'Right,' he said, 'I think you know what to do.'

Corinna nodded, shrugging resignedly. 'Yes, master,' she said. She hesitated. 'May I have my hands free for this, as well?'

Pecon seemed to consider this, and for a moment Corinna thought he was about to accede to the request, but then he grinned again and shook his head.

'No, not yet,' he said. 'Your mouth and tongue should suffice for the moment and Demila will be your hands, if and when

174

you need them.'

Sighing quietly, Corinna carefully knelt between Sprig's widespread thighs. She saw his eyes flickering behind his mask and knew that the sight of her ample breasts, with their distended nipples so blatantly ringed, would be exciting him, as indeed they would excite any man with red blood in his veins.

She glanced at Demila, who smiled encouragingly, all the while keeping Sprig's straining shaft held in a vertical position. Slowly, Corinna leaned forward, parting her lips and gently pressing them against the burgeoning purple flesh, letting her tongue dart in and out, its rough surface abrading the sensitive tip, so that Sprig let out a low groan of barely suppressed desire. Unhurriedly, she opened her mouth wider, sliding down so that it engulfed the entire head and first inch or two of the length.

Immediately Corinna realised there was no chance of her taking the entire stalk into her mouth, for the young barbarian was even more endowed than had at first appeared. Not even Savatch could have matched this weapon for size and girth, but thoughts of Savatch immediately brought tears to her eyes and she furiously fought to banish them.

Instead, she concentrated on the immediate task, sliding her moist lips up and down in increased rhythm. Demila had withdrawn her hand, relying on Corinna to keep control of the throbbing shaft, but a sharp word from Pecon and the girl quickly intervened, grabbing the glistening organ with one hand and using the other to grasp the back of Corinna's collar and haul her head up once more.

'Wait,' Demila whispered. 'Our master does not want him to come too quickly.'

'And not down that hungry little throat, either,' Pecon laughed, coming up behind Corinna. 'We'll keep him on the edge for a while longer and then see how well you take that

175

impressive cock into your belly. Who knows, if his seed finds fertile ground, it might even add to your worth. The offspring of a well made girl like you and a strapping ox like him – well, the people I'm looking for would probably think that worth an extra krone or two.'

Reality for Corinna had now become more than three hours walking each day, plus another seven hours in the saddle, followed by extensive evening sessions coupling with the magnificently endowed Sprig, whose stamina seemed untouched by the daylight toil.

Once they had made camp for the night, the routine was the same as before. Demila would prepare the hapless young man using her practised fingers, Corinna would stimulate him further with her lips and tongue, and then she would mount him, shuddering as the walls of her tunnel stretched to accommodate his incredible girth and length.

Urged on by Pecon, she would ride her human mount to his first orgasm, which seldom took too long, but then she was expected to use both muscles and wiles to keep him erect inside her and then, eventually, produce a second climax, a process which was not so rapidly completed. During this phase, Pecon took Demila beneath his furs and soon their moaning and cries mingled with those of Sprig and Corinna.

Corinna quickly realised that she could take advantage of these interludes, both to conserve her energies and to communicate with her involuntary partner.

'Ek sooruk zee?' she whispered, asking his name, the first time she risked speaking directly to him. Behind the mask, she saw his eyes widen in surprise.

'You speak the old tongue?' he gasped, using the same language. 'You are from the Snow Lands?'

'No,' she said, 'but I learned many languages from my tutors.'

Sprig looked perplexed. 'Tutors?' he said. 'What manner of slave are you?'

Corinna hesitated as another small dart of pleasure winged its brief flight through her body.

'I am no true slave,' she sighed, as the spasm waned, 'but the story is too long to tell.' In truth, she was more interested to learn about Sprig and of how he had come to fall into Alanna and Jekka's hands and, over the next two nights, she gradually extracted the details. Not that any of this knowledge would prove useful, for it was clear that the two Yslander women would by now be many miles away, but at least it was something to be able to talk to her fellow slave and not just remain an inarticulate possession with but one purpose in her master's eyes.

And that purpose, she quickly realised, was to demonstrate her fertility, for Pecon seemed determined that Sprig's seed should bear fruit in her belly. Quite why he was so keen for this to happen, Corinna was not certain, but he made several references to it increasing her value. Clearly he intended to sell her on, and Sprig too, and the prospective buyer presumably placed great store in fertile slaves, male and female. But on the subject of their ultimate fate, Pecon remained silent.

At last, Pecon announced that they were less than half a day's journey from their destination, but the fact that they made camp early in the afternoon and that he led the small party well away from the trail first, was perplexing. To Corinna's surprise, as Demila tended the small cooking pot over the fire, Pecon became quite communicative.

'I intend that we should all rest here for a day or two,' he said, addressing Corinna and Sprig together. 'I am told that these people are very particular as to the stock they buy and I want you two at your very best when they inspect you. Besides,' he added, 'I am in no hurry and it would be worth delaying a little, so that we give your efforts time to show evidence of your fruitfulness.'

'But that could take weeks, master,' Corinna pointed out, respectfully. 'A woman's cycle is that of the moon, as you must surely know.'

'True,' Pecon agreed, 'but I will suggest to your new masters that whatever price we agree shall be subject to a bounty, once they confirm your belly's worth. I intend to break my journey anyway and it is of no great import to me where I take that rest. One place is much the same as another.'

He spoke so coolly, so disinterestedly, that even Corinna, with her experience of the attitudes shown by traders and masters alike, was quite shaken. She was to be sold like some brood mare, her price increasing from the moment it was confirmed that she was with her first foal. And Sprig's value, like that of some prize stallion, would doubtless be calculated by his ability to cover as many females to produce as many healthy offspring as possible.

'I hear your milk will be much valued, too,' Pecon added, grinning. 'Apparently it is considered a delicacy in these parts.'

So that was that, she told herself, as she once again rode upon Sprig's thrusting member. She was no better than the farm beasts, kept to increase her master's stock, even the yield from her breasts having a market price. Alanna had once referred to her as a stupid cow, she recalled, and wondered what the Yslander princess would think of her now.

It did not take Dorothea long to understand the significance of their latest surroundings, nor why Fulgrim had chosen to journey eastwards, away from his homelands.

The place, a sort of large farm, but with as many buildings as most large villages, was deep into South Erisvaal and, as far as Dorothea could work out, a day's ride from a town called Erisroth, one of the few major population centres in the country. There was a river, too small to be the Varras, but probably a tributary that supplied water to the establishment and, for the first time in several days of travelling, there were plenty of trees, too.

Fulgrim's men herded their captives into a small compound set at the edge of one coppice, the overhanging branches offering the exhausted slaves welcome relief from the midday sun. And after an hour or so three men, all young, strong and swarthy of complexion, brought buckets of water and a basket of oatmeal cakes, which they distributed and then stood guard while the prisoners, wrists temporarily freed, devoured eagerly.

Restraints were then replaced – in Dorothea's case she was also gagged once more – and the three men sauntered off towards the nearest cluster of buildings, leaving a lone Vorsan soldier to watch over the exhausted group. Sitting slightly away from her former servants, Dorothea leaned her back cautiously against one of the trees and began taking stock of their new surroundings.

There was a large open field to one side of the stockade in which they had been left, empty save for a handful of small two-wheeled carts and two larger wagons. Beyond this field lay another, in which Dorothea could make out several figures. But the distance was too great to make out any further details, save for the fact that they appeared to be standing around in more or less the same place all the time and that when one or other did move, it was only to take a few steps back and forth. The obvious reason for this, she realised, was that they were all, in some way or another, tethered, probably to stakes in the ground.

The men she saw entering, leaving and generally clustered around the nearer buildings were a mixed bunch, but mainly comprised of indigenous Vaaleans, judging from the accents that drifted across on the soft afternoon breeze. There were a couple Dorothea judged were probably Karlieans, darker skinned, more guttural, deep voices, and three more who were darker still, possibly Colrasians, which made perfect sense.

Karlieans and Colrasians featured heavily in the slave trade of the northern continent, roaming deep inside their own countries, as well as further eastwards in their constant quest for more raw material. The two races were chillingly similar in their outlook on life: their concern for humanity started and ended with only one person generally – everyone else was considered fair game, to be sold, or sold to, or even both, if the opportunity ever arose.

But it was not the slave traders that drew most of Dorothea's curiosity, for finding such a cosmopolitan and unsavoury bunch under these circumstances came as no surprise whatsoever. The men who came and went from the further group of buildings were much more intriguing and their mere presence far more sinister. To find so many Vorsans, and soldiers at that, so far from the gulf states that were their home, bode nothing but ill and, as the afternoon wore on, Dorothea was given plenty of time to consider the implications.

There were other activities providing further food for thought, not least the appearance of another column of Vorsan horsemen, nearly a hundred of them, all riding openly together with their livery and insignia on clear display. That they were completely new arrivals was evidenced by the way in which they were drawn up in inspection order and then detailed off towards different quarters, each party under the supervision of one of the existing Vorsan personnel.

From her position, Dorothea could only see a small part of the surrounding area, but it was enough for there to be no mistaking what she was witnessing. How long this had been going on, she had no idea, but one thing was for certain:

Fulgrim was assembling a considerable fighting force, apparently with the full co-operation of the locals.

Somehow he had managed to get a message back to his cohorts, probably the militarist council in Ernsdt, the most belligerent of the Vorsan states, and they had not only dispatched a rescue force to Varragol, they had been sending even larger numbers of men to rendezvous with him here. That such numbers of foreign troops could travel undetected was surprising in some ways, but by no means impossible, especially if they had taken a circuitous route through the mountains in the south and then moved north through Karli, large parts of which were so disorganised and lawless that anyone who encountered them would have wisely turned a blind eye, lest someone blind both his eyes for him.

So, Dorothea mused, this time Fulgrim was preparing to move in force, rather than employ extortion as had been his earlier plan. But if that were so, he had to be far from ready for that as yet. Unless there were far more men nearby than she had so far seen, he was far short of the strength he would need to take the field against Illeum, which had to be his ultimate objective.

Towards sunset, a small group of men, two Karlieans and two darker-skinned, entered the compound, separated out all the younger slaves and marched them away in two groups, the three belted virgins trudging dejectedly behind one fellow, the remainder following the other three. A few minutes later, Fulgrim himself appeared and sauntered across to Dorothea.

'A good price for the three virgins,' he leered, 'and the rest as diversion for my men. I assume the presence of my Vorsan troops has not escaped your eagle eye, bitch?' He stooped over her, unbuckled the gag harness and snatched the leather plug from Dorothea's mouth with jaw-jarring force.

'Unfortunately,' he said, 'most of your young fodder are not up to the physical requirements of my main ally here;

they are all far too slight of build. You, on the other hand, are ideal, apart from your lack of youth, which would badly affect any resale price.

'However, as we have no intention of offering you for sale, that matters naught and you will simply be earning your keep, so to speak. Unfortunately, I have to travel east again and will be gone a few days, but Mussef Akka and his fellows are expert in their field, so it will be interesting to see what they have made of you by my return.'

'I'm surprised you can bear to miss even a minute of my humiliation,' Dorothea muttered, 'let alone leave my further sufferings to the hands of others.'

'Indeed, it is a wrench,' Fulgrim grinned, 'but one has one's other responsibilities that cannot be left to others, and they are even more important than simply watching you writhe and squirm. But, fear not my treacherous bitch, I shall not leave you without something to remember me by.' He reached to his belt and unhooked the coil of braided leather that hung there.

'On your feet,' he ordered. Dorothea sighed and struggled to obey, for there was little point in any meaningless show of rebellion, which would only worsen whatever punishment he had in store for her, if that were possible.

Pecon, it now seemed, was not going to leave anything to chance, not if he could possibly do anything about it. Establishing the fertility of his two slaves was clearly to his great financial advantage and, whilst any problem concerning Corinna was beyond his power to resolve, he most certainly could do something to ensure against Sprig's virility being doubted.

'A little insurance, slave,' he chuckled, depositing a scrap of cloth at Corinna's feet. 'I cannot boast quite the same proportions as the lad, but I do know that what I have functions quite properly and I shall not be staying around long enough to see evidence of which of us is your brat's real sire.

'Indeed, once their physician has confirmed the necessary, I shan't even stay to see that belly start to swell.' He stooped over her, intending to release the collar of her slave hood, which she had worn for many days now, and cursed when his key would not turn in the small lock.

'Damn!' he snapped. 'What manner of device has your former master employed here?'

'A patent lock specially made for the ruling house of Illeum,' Corinna replied, 'but I think there must be some sort of fault in it. These locks at my wrists would not operate smoothly, as you would have found if you had seen fit to release me from them throughout these past days. The key broke in one of them, which was why I still wore this mask when first you happened upon me.'

'Well, no matter,' Pecon said, pocketing his own key and drawing a wicked looking knife from the scabbard at his belt. 'Those Yslander women sold me a good selection of honest wares, so we'll just have to cut this stuff off you and throw it away.'

Corinna sat motionless as he eased the knife between the collar and her soft neck, but his skill and precision offered no real risk of her being cut.

'It's about time I saw your face, anyway,' he smirked, as he sliced through the thick hide, 'and about time you washed it, too. Come to that, your entire body needs bathing – you are covered in dust and you smell rank.'

'That, sir,' Corinna replied stiffly, 'is through no choice of mine, though I agree with you, a little fresh water would be most welcome. I can smell *him* on me all the time,' she added, looking towards where Sprig sat bound and tethered to a small sapling.

'There is a small stream just yonder,' Pecon said, as the

blade finally severed the collar. 'Take the cloth and clean yourself thoroughly. The warm sun will dry you quickly enough.'

'And my hands?' Corinna demanded, as he began drawing the hood up over her head. 'Am I supposed to wash without their use?'

'Patience,' Pecon snapped, 'and watch your mouth, unless you want to feel my whip again. I'll attend to your hands in a moment, just as soon as I've seen what else my investment has bought me, apart from a firm arse and big tits. Ah!' he exclaimed, as the soft leather finally came away, revealing Corinna's flushed features to him for the first time.

'Yes, indeed,' he said, smiling approvingly. 'Very comely indeed, though what's this we have here?' He bent, probing at the crown of her head and Corinna's heart skipped a beat, as she realised what had caught his attention.

'I see,' he mused, straightening up. 'So tell me, why would a fair-haired wench cover such sunshine locks with a drab brown dye, eh?'

'I tried to tell you that first day, sir,' Corinna replied steadily. 'I am not at all what I seem, but you would have none of it and all I earned for my pains was a thrashing and many hours with my mouth plugged with that foul gag.'

'Well, whatever you are, you are still mine, though I think we should perhaps do something about those pale roots of yours. Demila will probably know what plants can be put to the necessary use, and we shall have to make sure we keep your little secret until after I am finally on my way. Now, stand up and I will see to the rest of this stuff. A fresh rig will await you when you return in a suitably clean state.'

The water in the stream was ice cold, for the current was swift, and Corinna gasped for breath as she submerged herself, first up to the waist and then, steeling herself, up to her chin. Despite the temperature it felt wonderful as the dust and sweat was rinsed from her aching limbs, and only the gradual numbness finally forced her to climb out onto the bank.

After a few minutes basking in the warming sun, she knelt and lowered her head into the stream, splaying out the matted tresses with her fingers, so that the water could flow through them the more easily. With no cleansing oils, nor even the most basic soap, it took a long while before her hair began to feel clean again, but she was in no hurry.

For a while, at least, she was free of the harness, hood and cuffs, free of any impediment to a possible escape, save that she was completely naked and many days, even on horseback, from possible refuge. Besides, she reasoned, it was unlikely that Pecon was not somewhere nearby, keeping an eye on her, just in case she was foolish enough to consider trying to make a run for it. The man was obviously no stranger to the handling of reluctant slaves and, despite the fact that he would be able to ride her down quickly enough, he was not the type to want to waste time and effort in a pursuit he could render unnecessary by the simple expedient of not letting her out of his site for more than a few seconds.

'Much better,' he said, as Corinna stood to use the damp cloth to remove the excess water from her now lank hair. He emerged from behind a tree, from where, Corinna presumed, he was watching her at her ablutions, holding out a metal comb, which she took from him.

'Demila will fit your new slave belt,' he said, 'while you tidy that mess up. She will leave your hands free for now, but ask her if you need her help, for her fingers are skilled.'

'And then you will fuck me, I suppose?' Corinna snorted. 'And I shall once again be dirty, sweaty and rank.'

'Tush!' Pecon admonished her, his teeth flashing. 'Such language from one who would have me believe she was a lady!'

Corinna met his amused stare defiantly. 'A fuck, sir, is a

fuck,' she said. 'Whatever you choose to call it, that's all it will be. After all, you intend only to sow a few extra seeds, just to ensure the harvest that will up the price you get for me, so what else would you call it? To you, one warm sheath is very much like another, so why should you expect me to think any differently.

'You'll thrust your cock in and out, spray me as a bull might spray a cow, then do the same over again, just to be sure. Yes, I dare say you may derive some enjoyment from it, for you are a man and all men are much the same when it comes down to the basics, but why pretend you're doing something that you're not?

'You, my so-called master, will fuck me and I, despite my best efforts, will be betrayed by something that is not within my conscious power to control. I shall doubtless wriggle and squirm and pant and gasp and I may even scream a little, for I, sir, am a woman, and that's what women do when they are fucked!'

She tossed her damp hair back with a contemptuous shrug, handed the now sodden cloth, which Pecon was too surprised not to accept from her, and stalked past him, head held high, hips deliberately swaying as she moved.

'Well, well,' she heard him mutter from behind her. 'Well, well, well!'

Whether Moxie was the more surprised to be confronted by Alanna and Jekka as she entered the gates of Garassotta castle, or they at the sight of her, it was difficult to say.

So relieved was she to see them, Moxie began to gabble out her story, even before she had thought of dismounting.

'Easy, my little red mop,' Alanna soothed, reaching up to help her from the saddle. 'Draw yourself a breath or two and calm yourself. Now,' she said, as Moxie stood beside her, suddenly feeling very small so close up against the towering princess, 'start again, and slower. Come, we'll walk across to the kitchens and find you something to eat and drink, for you most certainly look as though a square meal would not go amiss.'

Moxie swallowed and nodded, now feeling curiously weak.

'I see,' Alanna said, when the tale was finally told. She turned to Jekka, who was sitting at the end of the small table they had commandeered in the kitchen area. 'I thought all along that it would have been safer to kill that bastard Fulgrim, but it is of no use being so wise about that now.'

'You say you did not think they intended to remain at the castle?' Jekka interjected. 'Why so?'

'Because,' Moxie explained, between mouthfuls of warm ale, 'they must surely have known that news of their infamy would get out sooner or later and they were not enough to hold Varragol against any force that the Protector would be certain to send against them.'

'Indeed,' Alanna agreed, nodding thoughtfully, 'and as you say, they could travel with Lady Dorothea disguised as a simple slave easily enough. After all, they got to Varragol without arousing suspicion in the first place and there are plenty of little used roads if they keep to the east as far as Tamarinia.'

'And by now,' Jekka pointed out, 'they will be well beyond our reach, or even that of an Illeum army. From what you say, all this took place many days since.'

'I didn't think it would take us so long to reach here,' Moxie muttered apologetically, 'but there was nowhere else I could think to go. Travelling directly west would have been far too dangerous.'

'Quite so,' Alanna replied, reaching out a comforting hand to pat Moxie's arm. 'Don't chide yourself, little maid, for you have done well and shown great courage. Perhaps there is Yslandic blood in your family line.'

'My thoughts were also of a selfish nature,' Moxie said quietly, looking down at the now empty flagon in her hands. 'Apart from seeking help for my mistress, I knew also that, with her gone, Pester and I could have been seized as runaways and that none would believe my story, not unless I could reach the Lady Corinna.'

'Wisdom, as well as courage,' Alanna said. 'But there we have another problem. The Lady Corinna is not here, nor is Master Savatch.'

'But where are they? Surely not gone back to Illeum City?' Moxie's eyes widened in surprise.

'Indeed not,' Alanna confirmed. 'There has been some sort of accident. A rider arrived here not an hour since, just moments before us. He brought with him a message from Savatch, who is lying injured in a village some little distance from here. The details were somewhat unclear, but apparently there was an attempt on Savatch's life and someone has made off with Corinna. It is a bad business, by the sound of it.'

'You will go to him?' Moxie demanded, already knowing the answer, for she knew, also, that there had been something between the mercenary noble and this enigmatic woman.

'We are just waiting for the guard vice-captain to organise a small detail,' Alanna said, 'and then we ride out again. Another hour and you should have missed us.'

'I should like to come with you, if I may,' Moxie said.

Jekka raised her elegant eyebrows, but said nothing.

'Then we must find you a fresh mount,' Alanna replied, without a flicker, 'for yours looks all in.'

Corinna was completely surprised by Pecon's gentleness and wondered whether her scathing words had touched some inner male weakness. Where she had been resigned to simply being thrown on her back and taken without ceremony, he was completely unhurried and almost seemed to be courting her.

Having first secured Demila and Sprig, he picked up a fur, draped it over one shoulder and, taking Corinna by the wrist, led her away from the little clearing in which they were camped and back down towards the bank of the stream. She was still naked, apart from the new slave belt that Demila had locked about her middle, but the early evening air was still warm and the sun had not yet quite touched the horizon.

Pecon spread the fur on a patch of grass and motioned for her to sit. As she did so, he turned his back on her and stood looking down at the rushing water and remained staring at it, as if transfixed, for several minutes. At last he turned, his expression impassive, though his eyes looked somewhat troubled.

'I believe,' he said slowly, 'that you may well have told me some truth before, but events have taken us too far and I have neither the time, nor the inclination, not when I can get an assured price for you now. Besides, I should not want to risk retribution against myself, but I shall do one thing for you.'

'And what might that be?' Corinna asked. Momentarily his soft words had raised her hopes, but she realised, in the next instant, that nothing had really changed.

'What I shall do,' Pecon said, 'cannot be done for some while yet, but I shall be travelling north again towards the end of the summer and I shall see to it that a message reaches this castle of which you spoke, telling them where I last left you. It will then be up to whoever is concerned to act as they see fit.'

'By which time,' Corinna said, 'I may well be many more miles away. Slaves are bought, sold and transported regularly, and I could well end up on the far side of the continent.'

'That is quite possible,' Pecon agreed, 'but if you are as important as you seem to think you are, then your friends will no doubt trail you to the ends of the earth. Are you that important?' he added. 'You haven't even told me your name.'

'And you, my pigheaded master,' Corinna replied coolly, 'have never asked it.' Once more, her pulse began to hasten. Perhaps, after all, now was the time to come out with the whole truth; the fellow was motivated by greed and, if he realised the value of his prize, perhaps he would be tempted to try to capitalise on it. Even if he still sold her on, surely whoever bought her would consider the prospect of a ransom or reward as more rewarding than whatever she might fetch in a slave market.'

'My name is Corinna,' she said, when he made no further comment. 'Perhaps you have heard it before?'

'The name is familiar,' Pecon agreed, 'but then no name is the property of a single person.'

'Lady Corinna Oleanna,' she said, watching his eyes. They narrowed slightly and she could almost hear his brain working.

'That name certainly means something,' he said. 'Oleanna, you say. So your house is part of the ruling dynasty in Illeum. Lundt is Protector there, is he not?'

'Not only Protector of Illeum,' Corinna said, 'but probably the single most powerful man in the civilised world.'

'So I believe,' Pecon nodded, 'though I care little for politics. So, this Lundt, this Protector, he is related to you, or should I say, you to him?'

It was Corinna's turn to nod. 'My father,' she said, simply.

'The old man says you are not fit to ride,' Alanna said firmly. Savatch was sitting propped up in the bed, but his features looked skeletal and his pallor grey.

'The wagon you brought with you,' he said, 'that will serve for a few days, and my strength is beginning to return at last. I cannot just lie here, not when I don't know what's happening to her.'

'I understand,' Alanna said, 'but you will serve her no good purpose if you try to do too much too soon. That wound was deep, and many men would have died from it. You were very lucky.'

'So that damned old sorcerer keeps telling me,' Savatch grated, 'but I didn't die, luck or no, and now Corinna is gone, probably with the same man who tried to kill me.'

'That I doubt,' Alanna said. 'Whomever shot at you was not the man who took her. From the story I heard, he found Corinna wandering on the road, bound and quite helpless, yet he then took her, found you and came to this village for aid, paying the physician to care for you and even signing a deed of sale to say that he had taken Corinna in return.

'What was there to have stopped him just taking her in the first place and simply leaving you to die in the river? That doesn't sound to me like the actions of a bandit.'

'You're assuming he was a simple bandit,' Savatch said. 'What if he was a hired assassin?'

'The same would apply,' Alanna said. 'Why bring you here? Why not just take Corinna, instead of paying good money for your care? No, whoever fired that arrow was not the man who took Corinna.'

'Yes, you're right,' Savatch agreed, morosely. 'I've had these same thoughts while I've been lying here, but I needed to hear someone else voice them. All the same, Corinna has been taken by a man who believes her a slave. I cannot believe she did not say something to him.'

'She probably did,' Alanna sighed, 'but, being a man, he probably didn't believe her, or if he did, he's probably taken her off somewhere while he works out how to get the best price for her. Anyone with any sense would realise that ransom, or even reward money for returning her unharmed would be the most profitable, but then, as I say, he's a man.'

'Who's a man?' The door creaked open and Jekka glided in. She stood for a moment, studying Savatch. 'By the gods,'

191

she said, 'you've certainly looked better, Master Savatch!'

'Thank you, Jekka.' Savatch smiled, despite his anxiety. 'And you've never looked lovelier, my sweet assassin. The red hair certainly becomes you and I'm glad to see you've kept the colour.'

'It goes with her temper,' Alanna grinned.

'And my wonderful pale complexion,' Jekka quipped, but suddenly her expression became serious once more. 'However,' she said, 'while you two old *friends* have been sitting here holding hands, I've been using what's underneath this red hair and inside this pale complexion. I've spoken further with the old physician and with two of the villagers who saw this traveller fellow. They described him – and the slave girl who was originally travelling with him, though the old man's eyesight isn't that reliable.'

'One man and his slave girl, what's to describe?' Savatch demanded. 'I've asked the same questions myself. Tall, dark, riding a black, or maybe brown horse, the girl smaller – there's a surprise – and riding a pony.'

'Yes,' Jekka said. 'One man, dark, probably from very far south he was that dark, and the girl smaller, as one would expect. But how small? Young village men tend to see what they want to see, so it was the girl who took most of their attention.

'I hear she was very small, and very slight of build, much smaller than Corinna, for instance. And the pony, there was just the one, so when they left here Corinna was walking. The fellow tried to buy an extra mount for her, but there were none available in the village.' She looked meaningfully across at Alanna, who had already caught on to what she was saying.

'The fellow we sold our little prize to!' she exclaimed. 'He wanted to buy an extra horse!'

'And he was travelling with two slave girls,' Jekka confirmed. 'One of average size and build, the other much smaller, except, Master Savatch, neither were fair-haired. We did not approach them closely enough to tell anything further, except that the bigger female was definitely gagged.'

'Corinna dyed her hair to avoid recognition,' Savatch murmured. 'Don't ask.'

'I didn't intend to,' Jekka said. 'But nevertheless, it all fits. One dark male, probably Colrasian. Two female slaves, one pony between them, one gagged, probably to make sure she couldn't try to tell her story when his back was turned.'

'Damnation!' Alanna exclaimed. 'To think we were that close.'

'You weren't to know,' Savatch sighed. 'And it's as I feared. Corinna taken by an itinerant trader. He could sell her anywhere.'

'He could,' Jekka agreed, 'but I don't think he will. Something he mentioned to one of the village lads who helped bring you here. Apparently, the first girl had made mention of a particular slaving establishment in the Vaal – South Erisvaal, he thought – and the fellow asked if anyone here would have known of it. Of course, no one had; few of these people travel more than a day's ride from their homes.'

'It definitely fits,' Alanna mused. 'The easiest route into the Vaal from here, particularly the south, would be between the mountains, just north of Varragol.' Her eyes darkened at the mention of the name, for she had not told Savatch anything of Moxie's story as yet. 'Where we met with him would be on the route he would have taken from here.'

'Then please, prepare that wagon!' Savatch exclaimed. 'We must get after them.'

'That we must,' Alanna said, 'but all in good time. They are already several days ahead of us, so a few more hours will make little difference. Meantime, there is something else I think you should know of, though what any of us can do about this particular problem, I have no idea.'

Pecon was still taking his time. He stripped slowly and slipped into the icy stream, splashing the water over his face and shoulders and dipping his hair into the current several times, though never did he take his eye off Corinna for more than a few seconds at a time.

Eventually he pulled himself back up onto the grass and, despite the fact that the evening air was beginning to cool decidedly, sat naked, allowing the breeze to dry his wet skin.

'So,' he said at last, 'you say you're a princess?'

'No,' Corinna replied levelly, 'not a princess. A princess is the daughter of a king and Illeum has had no king as such for several centuries. My title is simply Lady.'

'Except here you have no title.' Pecon turned his head towards her and grinned. 'Here,' he said, 'you're just another slave and, to use your own words, you're about to be fucked.'

'Yes,' she said, 'I'm a slave, and you, my current master, are about to fuck me.' She turned to look away from him, pretending to study the flowing water. 'The problem is,' she said, after a few seconds, 'that I really don't have a problem with any of this.'

Pecon chuckled and leaned across, drawing her closer to him. Corinna made no attempt to resist, sliding her buttocks along the grass until their shoulders and upper arms were pressing together.

'You see,' she whispered. 'You have no need to tie me down.'

'*I* have no need, certainly. But what of your need?'

'I didn't think the needs of a slave were of any interest to her master,' Corinna countered.

Pecon chuckled again. 'Perhaps not.' Slowly he bent his head, craning his neck until he was able to draw her already stiffening nipple between his lips. Instantly, Corinna felt her spine stiffen and the familiar bolt of heat surged through her loins.

'Whatever my needs,' she sighed, 'I fear they must be wicked and that I am evil.' Her left hand crept across his right thigh, descending until it found his limp organ, fingers ensnaring it in a tender, encouraging grip. Her action was immediately rewarded, for the slack flesh began to respond from the first touch and soon she was holding a long thick pillar in her fist.

'Slowly, princess,' he whispered, transferring his attentions to her other breast and leaning her slightly back, so that she had to use her free arm to take some of her weight. It was not a comfortable position for her and she quickly laid flat, all the while maintaining her hold on him, as diligently as his mouth maintained its hold on her.

'Perhaps the bonds that hold me in slavery are within me,' she whispered, staring up into the cloudless sky, now turning from pale blue to silver. 'Perhaps my slavery is one from which I shall never escape, no matter where I go.'

Pecon raised his head and looked down into her eyes. 'Maybe,' he said slowly, 'your slavery is your freedom.' He rolled sideways, lifting his left leg over her and Corinna obligingly parted her thighs. She could feel the steady drumbeat pulse beginning to build within her.

'And maybe my freedom was a slavery of its own kind,' she said.

'Then perhaps I should simply fuck you and have done with it?' Pecon suggested, but there was no harshness in his voice. Corinna smiled, stroking his thrusting pole with three fingers, whilst keeping its head firmly between the fourth finger and thumb.

'Perhaps you should,' she agreed, 'but perhaps not this time.' She wriggled her hips, raising herself slightly to make it easier for him to enter her. 'This time, my master,' she said, 'I think you want to make love to a wanton slut of a princess, not simply fuck just another slave girl.'

Four

Dorothea stared down at her feet and at the hideously shaped boots that now enclosed them. For three days she had been forced to walk around the perimeter of the field the men called the training paddock, the heavy soles, to each of which was nailed an even heavier iron horseshoe, making the task difficult enough, even without the cruelly elevated position into which they forced her insteps.

It was, the young trainer took great delight in telling her, necessary to raise a 'pony's' heels, in order to display her legs to the best shape and advantage, and similar reasoning was behind the fact that the wide girth belt was kept drawn so tightly about her waist that she could scarcely breathe.

As an aristocratic lady of the courts, Dorothea was well accustomed to the heavily boned corsets decreed by upper class fashion, but this cruel leather contraption was designed to constrict even further. Worse still, as the swarthy handler seemed to delight in reminding her, eventually it would be cinched to smaller dimensions still.

'Think yourself lucky you're not being trained for show or racing,' he growled, when she staggered to a halt, red in the face and gasping to draw air past the hideous bit that filled her mouth. 'They have waists that a man's hands can easily encompass and after a year or two they can't even stand upright without the support of their girths.

'You're just going to be used as a working mare,' he continued, picking idly at his nose, 'so your measurements aren't that important to anyone, just so long as you're big enough and strong enough to pull a cart or wagon.'

If she had been able to speak, Dorothea would have felt compelled to point out to him that she would be more likely to be able to haul a cart without the restrictions being imposed upon her, but she knew that would have been a waste of breath. Individual efficiency was not the overriding concern here; appearance was everything and these men were following a tradition that dated back into prehistory in their native countries.

Dorothea had only ever read of such matters before, and such scrolls and books as she had seen that dealt with the subject seemed to her, at the time, to be somewhat fanciful and probably grossly over-exaggerated. But now, finding herself actually a part of it, she realised that, if anything, the accounts were understated.

No stranger to the daily cruelty of routine slavery, there was something about this place and the men who ran it; an aura that was not evil, but worse, for they did not appear to do anything out of spite or viciousness. Every single thing had a purpose and the purpose was everything. The women and men they trained were simply a commodity, and whilst ordinary slavers regarded their human stock in much the same way, here it went even beyond that.

Ordinary slaves were frequently kept gagged, either as a punishment in itself, as a means to deaden the cries that a whipping inevitably produced, or simply to prevent slaves from communicating with each other. But in between times, when instructed, they were expected to be able to speak, albeit in the approved formal fashion, and to communicate. These pony slaves, of which Dorothea was now one, were not only prevented from talking by their bits, it seemed their trainers expected that they would never be required to speak again.

Everything they would do for their future owners would be learned as a four-legged horse or pony would learn, responding to whip and reins, to shouted single word commands, and expected to do nothing more than simply obey. Obey, or face the consequences that would befall any rebellious beast.

What was even worse, this dehumanisation extended even to the way in which the handlers addressed their charges. They called them mares, fillies, ponies and, if they used any name at all, it was one they bestowed upon the unfortunate human equines, a name suitable for an animal, but usually not for a person.

'We'll call you Gol,' her trainer announced when she was bitted, hoofed and bridled on the first morning of her schooling. 'It'll remind you of where you came from.'

He threaded plain metal rings through the holes in Dorothea's nipples, adding tethers to extend her bridle rein down to them. 'That'll help you turn nice and sharp, Gol,' he laughed, slapping her sharply across her naked buttocks.

'And tomorrow,' he said, 'we'll take you to the smithy and get the rest of your rings fitted.

They had remained in the camp for a further four days, before Pecon suddenly announced that they would be starting the final leg of their journey. During this time he took Corinna back to the riverbank each afternoon and there made love to her until the darkness came and it was time to return for an evening meal. Then, during the night, Pecon took Demila to his furs, leaving Corinna with Sprig, once more bound and hooded as a simple slave pair.

On the final morning, Pecon patted Corinna's stomach and grinned.

'Loving or fucking, princess or slave,' he said, 'if it's ever going to be filled, the deed must surely be already done, though I suspect your new masters will want to keep putting you to young Sprig for a while yet.'

'I expect so,' Corinna replied dully. She realised that she

should have expected no more from Pecon, despite their daily trysts and the gentleness and consideration he had shown her. She was, after all, still an investment as far as he was concerned.

'I would keep you, princess,' he said, 'but to do so would be dangerous, whatever you say. If Lundt really is your father, he will scarcely look kindly upon me for taking you so far away from your homeland, and to plead ignorance of my actions would avail me naught. Safer to take my profit now and be gone, though I will honour my promise and get word to your castle at Garassotta, when I am able.'

'I think you have already taken your profit, sir,' Corinna retorted stiffly, 'but then I am helpless in the matter, so it is best left as it is.'

The sight of so many Vorsan uniforms, as they rode and walked towards the first collection of buildings, astonished Corinna, but not so much as the sudden appearance of the one man she hated above all others in the world.

At first she did not recognise Fulgrim, for his skull boasted only a short fuzz of hair that was now grey, and his features were far more etched than she last remembered them. But when he turned in his saddle to look curiously towards the latest arrivals there was no mistaking those evil eyes, and Corinna jerked her head away, forgetting that her slave hood would disguise her identity and that her dyed hair, the roots now almost black again, thanks to Demila, would further confuse anyone who knew her.

The problem was, she thought, as Pecon tethered the three of them to a convenient rail and strode towards the group of dark-skinned men standing by the door of the largest cabin, simply changing her hair colour would not fool anyone who knew her for very long, and if Fulgrim saw her unhooded...

Pecon stood deep in conversation with one of the men in front of the cabin and, from their gestures, Corinna guessed they were haggling over the details of the proposed sale. For a few minutes she began to entertain the hope that they would not come to an agreement and Pecon would take her on with him, but she knew in her heart this would not be so, and was not therefore too disappointed when she saw the two men shake hands.

He said little to her when he returned, simply unhitching the saddlebag he had bought from Alanna and Jekka, and dropping it between Corinna and Sprig. Then, unhitching Demila's collar from the rail, he hoisted her back onto the pony, mounted his own horse and, taking up the lead reins of pony and packhorse, started to turn away.

'Good fortune, princess,' he muttered, his face rigid. 'I shall keep my promise.'

'Then maybe we shall meet again,' Corinna said, fighting to steady her voice.

Pecon shook his head. 'I think not,' he said, 'for I feel sure that I should be soon dangling on the end of a rope if it were so.'

They had stopped at a fork in the trail, and Alanna dismounted and walked back to the wagon. The Illean troopers, all cavalrymen, sat astride their horses and waited, their faces betraying the stoic patience of fighting men all over the world.

'The road splits,' Alanna said, climbing up over the tailboard to squat beside the temporary pallet upon which Savatch lay propped. 'Either could run in the rough direction we want, but which one we cannot be sure.'

Savatch lifted himself into a sitting position, wincing slightly as the movement put pressure on his neck muscles. 'Draw the canvas aside and let me see,' he said.

Alanna squeezed past him and pulled the dirty sheeting away, leaning forward to nudge the wagoneer to one side. Savatch blinked at the sudden brightness and narrowed his eyes. After a few seconds he nodded and lay back again.

'The right fork,' he said with conviction. 'The left leads northwards again, eventually into North Erisvaal. The place our unknown friend sought lies much further south, not far from a town called Erisroth.'

'You know this for sure?' Alanna demanded. 'We could lose several days if we have to double back.'

'I know that,' Savatch snapped. 'Take the right fork, as I say.'

Pecon had given no clue as to the nature of this place to which she and Sprig had been sold, but as they were led across the open field towards a series of long low buildings, one look at the figures tethered to the various stakes and rails was enough to dispel any doubts.

Mostly female, they were all human, but only in as much as they had two legs and two arms and walked only on the former, rather than all fours. In all other respects it seemed they had been turned into awful parodies of horses, bridled, shod in what appeared to be cumbersome hooves, their hair shorn at either side to leave a sort of flowing mane that ran down their backs.

Their bodies and even their faces had been painted to give a variety of patterns, mostly black and white dappled and most even had lifelike tails sprouting from above their naked buttocks, although closer inspection showed that these were actually attached to a thin harness arrangement that descended from the broader straps that encircled their waists.

The incredible thing about them all, Corinna thought, apart from their bizarre appearances, was their general air of docility. They barely moved their heads as the two handlers led their latest charges through their midst and Corinna was reminded of cows, grazing peacefully in a field. She shuddered, for this was the fate that was clearly intended for her, too.

The one positive aspect, if anything positive could be drawn from all of this, was that almost all the bridles incorporated a broad strip of leather that covered the eyes, leaving just two holes for the wearer to peer through. Like blinkers on a real horse, this, Corinna realised, would tend to restrict their peripheral vision and keep their attention focused directly ahead. In her case, she thought with genuine relief, it would replace her current slave hood as a means of disguise and the heavy face paint would play a further role in keeping her real identity from Fulgrim, if he returned.

Fulgrim. As the first shock of seeing him and the subsequent shock of seeing the human pony creatures began to abate, Corinna began to think more clearly once again. They were, she was fairly certain, many days' journey from where she had presumed he still remained a prisoner at Varragol, and even further away from even the nearer borders of Vorsania. His presence here, therefore, was as much a mystery as a surprise, but it bode nothing but ill, especially for Dorothea, for surely something must have happened at Varragol in order for the fiendish Vorsan lord to be once again at large.

However, Corinna was given little time to reflect on such matters, for they quickly arrived at what she saw now was a stables complex, each long structure a series of stalls, accessed by doors that were split into lower and upper sections.

'By the gods,' she whispered to Sprig, as their two guards brought them to a halt a foot or so from each other, 'whatever have we been thrown into?' The taller handler whirled around, his features contorted with anger.

'No talking!' he roared. 'Ponies do not talk, even when able to, which is not often, as you will shortly discover. Disobedience is punishable by a minimum of twenty lashes and one day in the fields without food or water.'

Corinna swallowed hard, fighting back the urge to make

some sort of response. These men were barbarians of the lowest kind from the forests in the far south, where no civilised man would venture voluntarily. If any human beings deserved to be treated like animals, it was their kind, yet they dared to bring their savage customs into a land where even slaves were treated according to civilised rules.

Two more men appeared from inside the squarer building that stood at the end of the wide way that separated the first two long buildings. They took one look at Sprig, exchanged a few words in a guttural dialect, and one of them ducked out of site again, returning almost immediately with another three fellows, all with the same dusky, flat featured faces. Corinna could not suppress a smile, despite her own predicament, for it was clear that they were wary of her fellow slave's sheer size.

'Come!' said the first handler, the one who had warned Corinna. He jerked on her collar leash and dragged her towards one of the open stall doors, pushing her inside with unnecessary roughness.

'Now,' he said, backing her against the rear wall, 'I explain all this only once so you listen good, yes?' Corinna nodded. The fellow's expression relaxed somewhat, but the hardness in his eyes remained.

'I am Attak'u,' he said, 'and I am a senior trainer. Many years experience, unnerstand?' His accent and clumsy phrasing would have betrayed his foreign roots, even if his face had not. Corinna once more nodded.

'Attak'u very good trainer,' he said, puffing out his heavily muscled chest. 'Soon will be boss trainer, because Attak'u ponies always the very best. You will be best pony also, or my whip will know reason. You now pony, not girl. You stop thinking like girl and you be treated fine. Good food, warm stable, good fuck sometimes, keep you happy.'

Delirious, Corinna thought to herself.

'You give trouble, only thing fuck you will be this big.' He held his hands, palms inwards, about eighteen inches apart. 'We got wood cocks for bad pony girls, stretch like cave and then you walk and walk. You not like that, pony girl, you better believe.'

Corinna believed, trying not to wince at the thought.

'Now,' Attak'u continued, folding his arms across his chest, 'we gotta find name for you. What your old name?'

Corinna hesitated, but only for a moment. 'Rina, master,' she replied. Attak'u nodded, considering this.

'Not good name for pony especial,' he said. 'We call you Flix from now. That good name for pony.' The significance of this remark was lost on Corinna and only later would she discover that, in Attak'u's own language, flix meant breasts. She would also discover that she was not the only unfortunate female to be given that name, for the Colrasian grooms seemed to have little imagination, except when it came to inventing still more ways to inflict pain and humiliation on their charges.

'We prepare you now,' Attak'u said. He produced a key from the pouch on his belt and began unlocking Corinna's travelling harness and collar, removing them and placing everything in a neat pile in one corner, including her boots, which he instructed her to remove herself. He then stood in front of her once more, hooking one index finger through each of her nipple rings and lifting her breasts.

'Nice flix,' he murmured. Corinna, still in ignorance, assumed he was using her newly given name and smiled. Up close, his body gave off a musty odour and there was little pleasing in his appearance, but her experiences at Varragol had taught her that the best approach in such situations was to appear as docile and compliant as possible.

'Rings fine, too,' he said, letting them go again. He stooped, peering between her legs and pressing his hands against the insides of her thighs to indicate he wanted her to spread them further. Hiding her revulsion as best she could, Corinna obliged, but was horrified when his first touch against her labia produced that so familiar reaction.

'Had rings here before,' he muttered, probing with his forefingers. 'Not enough, though. Need five each side, otherwise stud stallions still try to force way in.' He stood up and jabbed a finger at her mouth. Recoiling instinctively, Corinna only understood when he spoke.

'Open, pony,' he said. Corinna obeyed, closing her eyes when he prised her top lip back to expose her teeth more fully. 'Good,' he said. 'Good teeth.' He peered closer, fingering her septum. 'Had ring here, too,' he said. He stepped back, glaring at her accusingly.

'You been pony before?' he demanded. Corinna shook her head, but he continued to stare at her for several seconds longer, apparently trying to decide if she was lying. Eventually he seemed satisfied.

'No,' he said, turning away from her. 'You not stand, not move like proper pony.' He shot her a vicious smile back over his shoulder, exposing canine teeth that had been filed to vicious points. 'Soon will, though,' he leered. 'Attak'u make you good pony and good ride. Attak'u teach you how pony girl fuck good!'

He began with the hoof boots, taking them from a rough hewn chest that stood against one of the side walls of the stall, selecting them without any apparent consideration as to whether they were the right size for her feet or not. Luckily, they fit quite snugly, though snug was not exactly the word Corinna would have chosen for such appalling creations.

Inside the bulky, hoof-shaped leather, the boots were sculpted so that she was forced almost onto tiptoe and only the support they provided around her ankles, once he had laced them tightly into place, made it at all possible for Corinna to walk in them. When she tried, at Attak'u's command, to take a pace or two forward, the weight was unbelievable and only when he told her to raise one foot, bending her leg back at the knee, did she see the heavy iron horseshoe nailed there.

'You soon learn, Flix,' he laughed, nodding for her to let the foot drop back again. 'Very heavy, but make muscles work – make legs strong. Hooves make legs look good, weight make them stronger.'

Indeed, as she stared down, Corinna had to agree that the elevation of her feet to such a seemingly impossible degree did make her legs look much longer, and shaped them as she had never really seen them shaped before. At court, ladies regularly wore shoes with heels to obtain such an effect, but not even the most daring courtesan would ever have attempted anything as extreme as this.

Satisfied that his latest novice was not about to topple over, Attak'u left the stable, closing the lower section of the door behind him, but not bothering to secure either it, or Corinna, in any way. She leaned back against the wall for support and sighed. He didn't have to secure her, she realised. In the hoof boots she was not going far and, even if she did manage to prise the laces loose and get the accursed things off, where would she run to?

He was not gone for long, returning with a dark-skinned female, probably of the same ethnic roots as himself. She carried a stone jar, from the top of which projected a wooden handle. Even before she removed the brush, Corinna understood what was coming next.

'Bokina make you very pretty pony now,' he said, as the little black woman knelt to begin her work, starting with Corinna's legs. 'She best pony painter in whole wide world. Painted all ponies you see here.' He leaned closer to Corinna, who wrinkled her nose as she caught the sickly sweet smell of his breath.

'Paint stay for days,' he said. 'Not wash off with rain, not wash off in river, just with old skin, and Bokina paint again before that.' Corinna sighed. So, she was to be a black and white pony forever, or until someone decided otherwise. At least that would help her to blend in with her fellow two-legged equines. It would have been scant comfort under most circumstances, but if Fulgrim was still about – and the presence of those Vorsan uniforms had done little to suggest he would not be – then the less about her to attract attention, the better Corinna would feel.

Much more, Dorothea was beginning to realise, and she would eventually lose her sanity, much as she had seen happen with Willum's wife, Benita. But these savage swine would not let her die, not for a long time yet.

Primitives that they were, they seemed to know just exactly how far any one individual could be driven without causing any lasting physical damage, taking her to the very limit of physical exhaustion several times each day and then leaving her just long enough to recover sufficient strength for another tortuous training session. She ran, walked and trotted between the shafts of the different carts and carriages, beginning at first light and only returning to her stall as darkness fell, any periods of respite in between spent standing in harness, or trying desperately to suck the proffered gruel past the ever present bit in her mouth.

Several times she saw Fulgrim watching her progress, but always from a distance, as if he were now trying to reinforce the difference in their status. Whilst he strutted or rode around the village, she was now beneath even his contempt, her fate delegated to a band of brown and black-skinned sub-humans. At least, she thought, as the whip once more cut across her shoulders, her young maids and pages had been spared this.

Vaguely, as she bent forward to struggle up the slope at the eastern end of the training paddock, her thoughts turned to Moxie. She had not seen her buxom little favourite since that fateful morning, but that meant little. Fulgrim's men could easily have slain her when they made their move against the real castle guard, though Dorothea still nurtured the hope that the redheaded maid might somehow have escaped that carnage.

The image of Moxie, as Dorothea had first seen her in her father's rundown tavern, brought tears to her eyes that even the whip could not. No, Dorothea could not bring herself to believe that Moxie was dead, yet death itself was far preferable to her own situation and she knew she would willingly slit Moxie's throat herself than let her fall into the same plight.

As she and Sprig had been led to the stables, Corinna had not the chance to see much other than the wide girth straps that constricted the waists of the pony people they had passed. But now she saw the harness close up and realised what a complicated piece it was. It was also, she discovered, as Attak'u guided her arms through the broad shoulder straps, passing the complex bands either side of her breasts, very heavy.

'This make Flix stand like real pony,' he grinned, wrapping the main belt about her waist and buckling the straps at the rear. 'You breathe now, suck belly in,' he instructed and, when Corinna complied, he worked his way down the line of five straps, tightening each of them one more notch. Even now, though, he was far from satisfied.

'Again,' he said, and repeated the procedure, making Corinna feel as though she was being cut in two. He stepped back, studying the effect he had created. 'More later,' he grunted. 'Harness first.'

The complex shoulder straps assembly included two circular bands of leather through which the wearer's breasts were placed, the girth of these then adjusted by means of buckles, so that they constricted the base of the soft globes, forcing them outwards into an even more prominent display. At the back there were further buckles and these, when tightened, pulled the shoulders back, so that Corinna was forced to stand in such a way that she was thrusting her bosom out even further.

Still he was not finished. Her arms were now slipped into long leather tubes, the outside of which were open and connected with criss-crossed thongs. When these were tightened it was impossible for Corinna to flex her elbows, and when these were then attached to either side of the main girth, her arms had been rendered completely useless. Stiff leather mitts, buckled over her clenched fists, completed the task, and she was as helpless as if her arms had been amputated.

'Very good,' he smirked. 'Starting to look like very proud pony. Good flix.'

Bokina, who had scuttled off once she had completed the task of painting Corinna's markings, now returned, carrying a water bucket and a small leather bag, both of which she set down on the straw strewn mud floor.

'Pony kneel,' Attak'u commanded. With great difficulty, Corinna managed to obey, but without the use of either hands or arms her knees struck the hard surface painfully. She bit her lip, determined not to let either of them see she was hurt, though she doubted whether it would have worried Attak'u anyway.

Bokina now went to work again. Taking a pair of shears from the bag, she proceeded to lop away great hanks of Corinna's long hair, cropping either side of her skull to leave the same central mane she had seen on the unfortunate creatures in the field outside. Then, having reduced the two sides to a stubble, she produced a small brush, soap, and a well-worn razor. In another two or three minutes the job was done.

If Corinna had thought the body harness complicated, the bridle was even more confusing, but Attak'u was more than equal to the challenge. He carefully disentangled the maze of straps and lifted it over her head, lowering it carefully, as Bokina gathered up her remaining hair and guided it between the appropriate leather bands.

The broadest band, which also formed the eye mask, passed across the forehead, and from this depended the rest of the straps. One passed over the crown, dividing on either side of the mane hair and descending as far as the bridge of the nose, where it once again split, descending each cheek and rejoining beneath the chin. To this strap, at either side of the mouth, another band was joined by means of a metal ring, running around from one side, then behind the nape of the neck and re-emerging to join the ring on the other side.

To the two rings was attached the bit, a thick tube of leather wrapped around a metal bar, projecting on the inner side to cover the tongue, so that if the mere presence of the bar itself was not enough to prevent intelligible speech, the leather plate certainly was. The final touch, and in many ways the cruellest, was the collar, a high band of stiff leather that encircled the throat and, at the front, rose to a shallow point immediately beneath the chin.

'Now you really look like proud pony,' Attak'u said, as he finished adjusting the rear buckles and walked back around to view the finished effect. 'Keep head up at all times now.' Corinna eyed him through the slits in the mask, almost having to peer downwards, such was the effect of the collar in forcing her to keep her chin so high. However she was expected to walk, let alone see where she was going, she could not imagine.

'Bokina now comb out your mane and put colours in,' he said. 'Mane already good, but one day reach past rump, maybe

210

even further. You make good pony girl, Flix. You filly now, but be mare soon, so we best start training straight away, before belly gets too big for harness.'

Savatch lowered the brass tube from his eye, slid the thinner section inside the thicker and passed it back to Jekka.

'Impressive little toy,' he said. 'Where did you find it?'

Jekka elongated the tube again and put it to her own eye. 'A Lostovian sailor,' she said. 'He challenged me to a shooting competition and that was his stake.'

'What was yours?'

Jekka put the telescope down again and grinned. 'Something I wasn't prepared to lose,' she said. 'But enough of that. What do you make of that column?' She nodded towards the far hillside, where the road meandered gently upwards before disappearing between a line of trees along the ridge.

'Well, they're definitely Vorsans,' Savatch confirmed. It was the first time he had sat a horse since the attempt on his life and, although his colour was much improved, he still moved stiffly. Alanna, her horse just behind the other two, was keeping a close watch on him.

'That wouldn't perhaps be Fulgrim's men?' she suggested, peering towards the distant cloud of dust.

'I don't think so,' Savatch replied. 'Moxie was quite clear that there were maybe thirty of them at Varragol, and that column numbers more than a hundred. Of course, Fulgrim's party may well have joined up with that lot, but even supposing they have come east, they would be many days ahead by now.'

'The goatherd yesterday,' Jekka mused, 'he told us of soldiers coming through the day before and the day before that, both times heading up from Karli.'

'Where they don't have an army as such,' Savatch said. 'So the likelihood is that they were also Vorsans. But why are they here in the Vaal? Unless they are swinging around and back to Varragol and Fulgrim is intending to try to hold the castle after all.'

'That would be too obvious a move for someone like him,' Alanna said. 'Besides, Vorsan strategy has never included fighting defensive actions. They are cavalry soldiers, mostly, and prefer to fight in the open and on the move.'

'I know,' Savatch said. 'So why is Fulgrim gathering soldiers together out here in this wilderness?'

'You think it's him behind it, then?' Alanna asked.

'It has to be,' he said. 'After all, apart from his authority in Ernsdt itself, he's number two in the Vorsan alliance and commander-in-chief of their military. No one could move hundreds of troops into a foreign state without his authority; no one would dare. No, this is his work. His orders must have gone out with the message that stupid lad was bribed to carry.'

'But why invade the Vaal?' Jekka retorted. 'There's nothing here worth fighting for, surely?'

Savatch eased his weight in the saddle and grimaced. 'I don't think it's the Vaal they're invading,' Savatch replied. 'That column is riding all wrong for that – no scouts, no rearguard – they're not expecting any trouble just yet, so whatever they're doing here, they're doing it with the full knowledge of whoever has the authority in this particular region.'

'Then if not the Vaal and not Varragol,' Alanna said, 'what is their objective?'

'Perhaps Garassotta,' Savatch suggested. 'Garassotta controls the entire north eastern sector of Illeum, including access to the great timber forests, most of the border with Sorabund and the most direct routes into the heart of the Snow Kingdoms.

'If Fulgrim were to take Garassotta, he would find plenty of allies among the warlords there, and there would be plenty throughout the Vaal who would flock to his standard with the promise of booty. He can reinforce his own troops using the same route as now and effectively cut Illeum off from everything east of the mountain line.

'Vorsania is then well situated to blockade the southern sea routes, so Illeum would be virtually powerless to intervene if the Vorsans wanted to cross the Straits of Tolereum and invade the western continent. Dasnia and Maravania are always at each other's throats anyway, so a convenient alliance with either state would give Fulgrim total control in a matter of weeks.

'Then the balance of power would lie with Vorsania, rather than Illeum,' he concluded grimly. 'It's a clever plan, if that's what is in his mind. Taking the field against Illeum directly would tie down the majority of their forces, whereas this way they can split the Illean army in two and do it with only a relatively small force of their own.'

'Could there be other reasons for this incursion?' Alanna asked.

'Who knows? In truth, there could be a dozen, but I think it'll be Garassotta, which means that column must be close to whatever rendezvous point was agreed. Much further east would be pointless, so if I'm right, we're likely to find a Vorsan nest no more than a day from here, from where they have a straightforward ride north, across the open plains, far from any regular trading traffic that might raise the alarm.

'Besides,' he added, touching the dressing on his neck gingerly, 'the attempt to kill me stinks of Fulgrim's sort of treachery. He would definitely want me out of the way before attacking Garassotta.'

'And Corinna?'

'Exactly,' he said bitterly. 'If he takes Garassotta, he has Lundt's daughter as hostage, as he planned to do before. On the other hand, if he takes Corinna first, he uses her to force the castle garrison to surrender.'

'But whoever tried to kill you couldn't have known that was Corinna with you, not from what you say.'

'Perhaps not,' Savatch said, 'though I suspect they may have. I remember a rider, as I was trying to keep the horses on the road. He came alongside and was trying to grab the traces, but I think his mount stumbled.'

'So,' Alanna said carefully, 'the plan was to kill you and capture Corinna, but now, presumably, they must think her dead, yes?' Savatch nodded. 'Only, if they assume she died in the river with you and died dressed as a common slave girl, even if anyone found the bodies, they would not identify her for who she really was.'

'That's about it,' Savatch grunted. 'But, with both of us missing, when Fulgrim sends an emissary to say he is holding Lady Corinna, the garrison commander is going to believe him. The Vorsans probably select a female of the same height and build, colour her hair suitably and, from a distance, nobody would notice. By the time they did, it would be too late.'

'Except that Corinna isn't dead,' Jekka pointed out, 'and our friend with an eye for a bargain in slaves has brought her straight into just about the worst place in the world he could have chosen. If he were to see and recognise her...'

'I know,' Savatch said wearily, 'and I don't even want to think about it. I'm just praying that Fulgrim has too many other things on his mind to bother with trivialities such as slave girls.'

If Fulgrim ever considered slaves to be mere trivialities, the men who ran the human pony establishment certainly took their profession seriously, and none more so than Attak'u, as Corinna was quickly discovering.

No sooner had Bokina completed the task of plaiting coloured ribbons into what remained of her hair than the groom was clipping reins to the rings on either side of her bit and leading her outside, tugging urgently to encourage her to move quicker whenever she hesitated, and apparently unconcerned that she was finding it difficult to walk in the heavy hoof boots.

'You learn,' he rasped, jerking the rein fiercely. 'You fall, you get up. Fall too often, get whipped.' He brandished the vicious looking crop, a beast of a weapon that was at least five feet in length, and Corinna, grinding her teeth into the leather bit, staggered onwards.

He led her across the uneven ground, along the side of the stable building and around behind the cabin that apparently served as quarters for the grooms, and ahead of them Corinna saw the forge, three powerfully muscled, dark-skinned men, stripped to the waist, waiting outside. They greeted the sight of the new arrival with little real interest; fresh stock, male or female, was clearly just part of their daily routine.

The ringing process was painful, as bad as when Fulgrim had performed a similar series of operations on Corinna the year before, but made worse, if that was possible, by the sheer indifference with which the entire procedure was carried out. Where the Vorsan had taken great delight in the agonies he was inflicting, these men did not, even swabbing the piercings with cold water as soon as they had been made.

Fulgrim had originally pierced her septum for his nose ring, but the hole had partially closed in the months since and this was attended to first. The thick metal hoop inserted, slim chains were used to join it to the bit rings, so that any pressure on either side would be transferred to one of the most tender parts of Corinna's anatomy. The chances of a girl refusing to turn when thus bridled were quite remote, she thought bitterly.

Her earrings were replaced by much heavier models, to which were attached small brass bells, the slightest head movement setting them to a merry tinkling, and then finally they came to her labia. Five rings each side, Attak'u had promised, and that was precisely what Corinna was given, a total of ten brazed loops that could not be removed without the aid of a file or very strong cutting pliers.

When the men had finished, Attak'u held up a curiously curved metal rod. One end had been fashioned into a short T-piece, whilst the other ended in a narrow oval shape. He flexed it between his fingers and grinned his canine grin.

'This keep pony safe from stallion fucking, 'cept when Attak'u say,' he said, with an air of triumph. 'Attak'u have lock and key, see!' He held up the small padlock in his other hand and immediately Corinna began to understand. Willum had fashioned something similar for his wife, Benita, but this was obviously a mass-produced item, for Corinna had seen several other similar rods lying on the bench among the small piles of loose rings.

Whilst he had been happy to leave the actual task of ringing to the blacksmiths, Attak'u, it seemed, preferred to keep this final display of his power over his charges as his own province. Stooping down, he eased Corinna's thighs slightly wider and began.

The pressure on the rings made her already throbbing flesh hurt even more and only the bit between her teeth prevented Corinna from crying out loud. As it was, she bit down hard and managed to stifle all but a few gasps. She closed her eyes and prayed he would finish quickly, but although he worked with practised precision, it seemed to take forever.

Finally though, it was done, the curved rod passing through each opposite pair of rings in turn, the short T-bar preventing it from sliding all the way through and the lock through the oval loop, which itself was barely able to pass through the rings, prevented it from being withdrawn again. As Attak'u had said, it would keep any stallion at bay, sealing Corinna's sex until he decided otherwise.

'Good,' he said, standing erect again. 'Now you all ready to start training, so we take you to get cart. Not dark yet for two hours, so time to get plenty good sweat up.'

The coppice on the ridge of the low hill, one of the few pieces of high ground in this area of rolling plains, offered an excellent vantage point and Jekka's brass telescope helped counter the disadvantage of distance. The red-haired Yslander sat astride her horse dressed from head to toe in black leather: breeches, boots, shirt, and a close-fitting cowl, so that only her face was left uncovered and, in the darkness of night, she could melt into the surroundings, a skill that had been the downfall of many in her brief past.

'See the woodlands away to the right there?' she said, extending her arm towards the rising sun. 'Beyond that is their main encampment. They must number more than a thousand already, and another company came in while I was looking around.'

'We heard them on the road,' Savatch said. 'Didn't want to get too close, but it sounded like a sizeable column.'

'More than a hundred,' Jekka confirmed. 'From what I managed to overhear of a few conversations, they're still building up strength. I saw one group putting up billet tents and erecting fencing, presumably making another paddock for horses.'

'Working through the night, eh?' Savatch said. 'Fulgrim must be keen. But what about the slave area?'

'Well, it seems to be completely separate, apart from a few mounted patrols riding through every now and then,' Jekka said. 'The men I saw there, those who seem to be in charge of it, they're certainly not Vorsans. A few Karlieans, who sound as if they're the real bosses, plus more than a score of others, mostly from Colrasia, judging by their skins.

'So, considering what I counted were counted in the middle

217

of the night, there could easily be three times as many more sleeping in those cabins over there.' She pointed directly at the main cluster of buildings and then swept her arm away to the left.

'They appear to be organised into a series of separate enclaves,' Alanna observed. 'See how there are four long buildings in parallel rows and then a squarer building at right angles to one end. Then there are what look like workshops, or forges, but not at every enclave.'

'No,' Jekka said, 'from what I could see those forges each serve four or five groups of buildings. The long buildings are set out as stables and the square structures are quarters for the handlers.'

'You call them stables?' Savatch said. 'So what we saw just before dusk last evening was not just an isolated case?'

'No,' Jekka replied. 'And I imagine we shall see a lot more of that very shortly. The story we heard in Erisroth was certainly not exaggerated. This place is a pony farm, with human ponies, at least twenty in each of those blocks.'

'And even from here,' Alanna said soberly, 'I can see thirteen, fourteen enclaves, each with four blocks. That's more than a thousand of these poor creatures. What on earth can they want with that many?'

'They send most of them east again, once they're trained,' Savatch said. 'I've only ever heard the stories, mind, as I've never wanted to journey that far east. Never needed to, in fact.'

'And all these human pony creatures, they'll be sent there?' Jekka asked.

'Probably,' Savatch nodded. 'Most of them, anyway. It's a vast land to the east, maybe five or six times larger than Illeum and all the Vorsan states put together.' He paused, considering for a moment. 'I wonder,' he said at length, 'if maybe the Vorsan presence here is more than just a convenient arrangement.'

'You mean he might be intending to use these slaves himself, to trade with these eastern barbarians?' Alanna said.

'Oh, they're no barbarians,' Savatch assured her. 'The fine silks and most of the spices we enjoy come originally from them.'

'Fulgrim wouldn't be interested in trading for delicacies,' Jekka said.

'No, though it would be a profitable trade to control,' Savatch replied, 'and he'd be doing that, once he sealed off the borders. But I think there is more to it than silks. I think he is looking for further allies. If he offers a few hundred human pony slaves to one of these eastern princes, or warlords, or whatever they call themselves, perhaps they will send men to fight with him.'

'A dangerous game,' Alanna muttered. 'From what I've heard, the less we have to do with those people, the better. If Fulgrim goes inviting them to send forces west, where will it all end?'

'Only time will answer that question,' Savatch said. 'But meantime, I'm more interested in Corinna. I don't suppose you saw any sign of her down there?'

'You suppose right,' Jekka snorted. 'It was hell black down there, don't forget, and most of them were in their stalls for the night. The one or two I did see out in the open, well, you saw last evening. Their faces are painted as well as their bodies, and the tops of their faces are masked behind a sort of band, with holes in to allow them to see forward. I could fall over Corinna and not know her, and that's going to be our biggest problem. Bad enough having to sift through a haystack, but when all the needles look like the same straws...'

'You have nearly a thousand girls here,' Fulgrim said, 'so there is a good chance that you can find one suitable for my purposes, I think.' Gorvan Sul studied the miniature portrait and grunted, noncommittally.

'It is possible, my lord,' he said, 'but she is fair and most of my stock comes from the south and east. The women there are much darker.'

'I've seen as much for myself,' Fulgrim retorted, turning his back on the slaver. 'However, I'm not asking you to find an identical twin, just a girl with the basic physical characteristics. If she happens to be darker, then one of your women can paint her face and the fair hair can be faked similarly. She won't have to stand up to close scrutiny, in any case.'

'I understood that you intended to use the woman herself,' Gorvan said. He lowered himself carefully onto the padded couch, which groaned beneath his great bulk. 'Has something gone wrong with your plan?'

'A slight hitch,' Fulgrim snapped. 'Nothing for you to worry about. One of my agents was supposed to attend to the matter, but the men he employed did not carry out their instructions as they were supposed to. Instead of capturing the girl, they sent her and her damned lover hurtling into a ravine.

'I've only just received word, as the men concerned tried to run for it and it was mere chance that my fellow stumbled across them. Even then they had the effrontery to try to fob him off with some cock and bull story that the pair had managed to escape them, but they confessed the truth before they died.'

'So nobody else is aware that the unfortunate lady is no more, eh?' Gorvan chuckled. 'And by the time they realise...'

'It will be too late, yes,' Fulgrim finished for him. 'By now the people at Garassotta will know they are long overdue, but not what has happened to them, so when I inform them that I have their mistress, they will doubtless agree to my terms without much argument. No Illean officer would want to be remembered as the man responsible for the death of the Protector's daughter, I think.'

'Nor to her prolonged suffering?' Gorvan added, smiling.

'Quite,' Fulgrim smirked. 'We'll mount our decoy girl in full view of the battlements and give her a sound whipping every hour until they surrender the castle. We shan't put her close enough to be recognised – or should I say, *not* recognised? – but they'll hear her screams clearly enough.

'Now,' he continued, holding out his hand to take back the little portrait, 'do you think you can find me something suitable from among your vast stables?'

The third day of Corinna's training was progressing exactly the same as the first two, except that now Attak'u drove her in company with other trainers and their novice girls, pitting them against each other to gauge relative merits and progress.

'You not bad,' Attak'u said with grudging admiration, during a rare halt for rest. 'You be first class pony soon. Got good legs, good flanks.' He ran one hand appreciatively down Corinna's hip and thigh, his fingers slipping on the sheen of perspiration. Breathing hard from her exertions, Corinna kept her gaze fixed immediately ahead, for she had early on learned the penalty for poor stance and deportment and her shoulders and buttocks were already stinging from Attak'u's efforts to encourage her to even greater efforts during her first two runs.

Worse even than the whip now were the jeers and crude remarks the pony girls drew from the growing number of Vorsan soldiers, who had taken to coming out of their encampments to watch the training sessions, and several tried to offer bribes to the trainers to change places with them.

To Corinna's immense relief, Attak'u was scornful of their actions, but only, she discovered, because he preferred not to share the favours of his charges.

For the first time outside her stall, he removed her bit and offered a water bottle to her lips. Corinna gulped the tepid liquid gratefully, oblivious to the way in which the spillage ran down her chin and splashed onto her sweat-glossed breasts.

'Easy, Flix,' Attak'u warned, pulling the bottle away from her. 'Drink slow, or you get stomach cramps. Not want pony hurting like that.' He held up the bottle once more and this time, her initial thirst slaked, Corinna sipped more conservatively.

'You going to be special pony soon,' he said, as she finished drinking and he re-corked the bottle. 'How you like being pony, Flix?' he asked, as companionably as if asking her how, perhaps, she might like a new dress. 'Go on, you speak now.'

'It is very tiring, master,' Corinna replied cautiously, wondering what on earth he expected her to say.

'You get stronger with training,' he assured her. Corinna shifted her weight in the heavy boots and was rewarded with the gentle tinkling symphony that now accompanied her every slightest move. 'You soon run all day, no worries.'

'And then will I be sold, master?' Corinna ventured tentatively.

Attak'u shrugged and pulled a curious face. 'Maybe,' he said. 'Maybe not. Chief maybe keep you. Fastest ponies always stay some. Chief likes to go east for races every season, win big prizes sometime, make him very happy. Make me very happy, too. Good for Attak'u when his girls win, so you work hard, yes?'

'I'll do my best,' Corinna said, 'but then I don't have much choice, do I?' he looked at her and she could see the genuine puzzlement in his eyes.

'Ponies not have choice!' he exclaimed. 'Ponies train, work, run, race. You pony girl now, Flix!'

'Yes,' she sighed. 'I'm a pony girl now and it would be hard for me to forget that, but what I'm suggesting is that I might just run a bit better if you weren't treating me so harshly.' Now his eyes were huge, the whites almost blinding against his black skin.

'Harshly?' he echoed. Too late, Corinna realised her mistake. 'You not seen harsh!' He flexed the long crop menacingly and swished it through the air, the tip passing less than an inch from Corinna's face, arcing down and out so that it all but brushed the tips of her nipples and making her jump backwards in the shafts, bells once again jangling, this time almost as an alarm.

'You stupid, Flix,' he said, shaking his head.

'I'm sorry, master.' Corinna closed her eyes, certain he was about to start thrashing her for daring to speak out of turn. However, just as suddenly his mood changed back again and he opened his mouth and roared with laughter.

'You learn,' he said eventually, wiping his eyes with the back of his hand. 'You very stupid, but you got nice big flix, so Attak'u not whip you this time. Got better things for you, anyway.' He clipped the whip onto his belt and began unfastening the buckles that held Corinna between the shafts of the buggy.

'You also very pretty,' he murmured. 'Not like most big girls from south and east lands. They got rough hides mostly and sound like nanny goats. You got music voice.' He smiled and moved around to deal with the second coupling. 'I ask chief if I keep you as my pony, at least for little while,' he said. 'Then Flix have warmest stable, best straw, extra food.'

'Thank you, master,' Corinna whispered, forcing the words out with great difficulty, but knowing that she had to do everything possible to humour this monster, who really thought a fellow human-being should be grateful for something that any civilised person would give to their four-legged creatures as a matter of course.

Beneath the shade of the trees, Attak'u produced the small

key and removed the padlock from the end of the curved bar between Corinna's legs and drew the rod back through the labial rings. Laying it carefully down on the grass, he tugged at the laces that held his rough breeches together and opened them to reveal a member that, even in its dormant state, looked fearsome. Even Sprig, Corinna thought, staring fixedly at the slowly swelling shaft, would be hard pressed to compete with such a weapon, and Attak'u's feral grin showed that he was only too well aware of how well nature had endowed him.

'This for special ponies only,' he growled, but somehow Corinna did not believe him. His sort, she knew, would settle for any conveniently warm sheath, potential champion or not. 'Now,' he said, stepping towards her, 'we better have bit back in. Proper pony always have bit in mouth, otherwise not sound right.'

In a way, Corinna felt relieved as he thrust the leather bar back between her teeth and reattached it to the ring at the other side of her mouth. At least, she told herself, she wouldn't now be expected to use her mouth for anything, but then perhaps Attak'u was only looking out for his own interests. After all, she reasoned, one snap of a set of sharp teeth and all the retributory whippings in the world would do him no good.

'Now,' he said, walking around behind her and grasping her hips, 'we do this pony style. You bend.' He raised one hand and pressed it between Corinna's shoulder blades, indicating what he expected of her. Shuffling her heavy shod feet, she leaned slightly forward from the waist, but this did not satisfy him.

'Head right over,' he commanded. 'Let flix hang good, so bells ring.' With a sigh of surrender, Corinna bent further still, her breasts swinging forward to the music of their accompanying bells, and immediately he slipped his thumb through the right nipple ring, hooking it so that she could not straighten herself again.

His other hand slipped around in front also, sliding down over her belly beneath the tight leather girth, slipping between her thighs and probing between the beringed lips. She heard his sharp intake of breath and felt the air warm on her back as he let it out again, two fingers prising her entrance apart and exploring the already moist tunnel, ensuring it was ready to receive him.

Corinna shut her eyes tightly and drove her teeth into the bit in desperation, knowing that yet again her body was betraying her, even at the prospect of this savage despoiling it. Yes, she thought, as she felt his hardness pressing against her, she really had to be the most sinfully wicked creature, for why else should her pulses be pounding in her temples and her heart beating a brazen tattoo against her ribs.

He slid easily into her and she pushed back instinctively, contracting her muscles to grip him tightly, her eyes opening again and sharply focused. All about her the colours seemed sharper, more intense, the sounds of the birds in the trees above joining with the music her captive body played as it surrendered to its innermost lusts.

Corinna groaned, but it was not from pain. She snorted and grimaced around her bit, conscious of the saliva that now dripped from her helpless lips.

What would the court of Illeum say if they could see her now, wriggling on the end of a black savage's cock and squealing like a bitch in heat?

And then her thoughts became lost in the maelstrom and all she could think of was the instant itself, as she ground her hips and bucked desperately to give herself the release that she knew was her only hope of a return to sanity.

'I think I've managed to identify Corinna,' Jekka announced, slumping down onto the grass. They had established a camp among the trees below the rise, well away from the slave farm and the area where the Vorsan soldiers were gathering. Four of the remaining ten Illean troops – two having been dispatched back to Illeum City with news of the impending Vorsan action – were acting as pickets, to give early warning of any unwanted approaches, but so far they had been totally undisturbed.

For three days and nights Alanna and Jekka had used all their skills to get as close to the slave farm as possible, watching, listening and noting everything. But as Alanna had earlier pointed out, by daylight it was too dangerous to venture too close and after dark all the pony slaves were locked away safely in their stalls.

On this evening, however, Jekka returned looking unusually pleased with herself and Savatch knew, even before she spoke, that she had something positive to tell.

'Even you would have trouble recognising her,' Jekka told him. 'Most of the women have dark hair, the same colour as she dyed hers, give or take a shade, and those damned blinker masks don't make it any easier. However, I'd recognise her voice anywhere.'

'You were close enough to hear her?' Savatch cried, leaning forward eagerly. 'How did she sound? Where was this?'

'Yes, I was close enough,' Jekka replied, 'and she certainly sounded healthy enough from where I was.' She managed not to smile, but it was an effort of willpower. 'I managed to circle around among the trees on the far slopes,' she continued. 'There were several of these pony girls being exercised just along the foot of the hill, and I guessed they were probably all fairly new arrivals, judging by the amount of work they were being put through.

'As I said, they all look so damnably alike, but there were two that were of the right build, so I remained hidden and kept watching. Then, while most of them were kept hard at it, one was driven up close to where I was. The driver unhitched her and led her out of the sun.'

'Don't tell me,' Savatch groaned, 'I can guess the rest.'

'Yes, well,' Jekka agreed, 'I'll spare you the details, but for a few minutes the fellow removed that bit thing from her mouth and I heard her speaking. It was Corinna all right, I'm certain of that.'

'Was there no way you could have freed her then?' Savatch demanded. Jekka gave him a look of total disdain.

'If there had been,' she said coldly, 'I should hardly have returned here without her, should I? They were still in full view of the people on the lower slopes, even if they probably weren't taking much notice of them, so I could hardly confront the fellow. My intention was to wait until the last possible moment and see if I could shoot him, then call Corinna to come over to me and stay hidden with her until after dark.

'Unfortunately,' she continued, 'just as he was preparing to leave and I had a clear shot at him, a squadron of damned Vorsans rode up and began taking a close interest in Corinna. They obviously had no intention of leaving before the fellow started back with her and I wasn't about to try to take on twenty of the swine single-handed.'

'No, of course not,' Savatch said. 'Forgive me, Jekka, you did everything you could under the circumstances. Far more, in fact.'

'At least,' Jekka said, 'we now know how to identify Corinna. She was drawing a cart with red painted trims and wheel spokes and I'd recognise the man again, ugly great brute that he is. Mind you,' she grimaced, 'none of them are exactly paintings, I can tell you.'

'But what if she has different drivers on different days?' Alanna pointed out. Jekka pulled a wry face, shaking her head.

'I don't think so,' she replied quietly. 'Maybe I could be wrong, but I formed the distinct impression that this particular driver is fairly senior and is quite prepared to exercise the privilege of his rank, among other things.' She looked meaningfully at Alanna and then turned away, trying to ignore the warning expression she received in return.

'So,' Savatch said levelly, 'you now know which of those poor creatures is Corinna, but how do we go about getting her out of there? Did you see which block she was taken back to?'

'I did,' Jekka said, 'but that won't help us at all. Too many people in too confined an area and we'd never get her clear without risking getting ourselves killed or captured. And I for one,' she added, 'don't fancy ending up between the shafts, nor any of the other things that seem to be part of the daily routine down there!'

'But we can't just keep sitting here,' Savatch protested. 'Apart from anything else, the longer we remain here, the more chance there is of someone blundering across us.'

'I know,' Jekka said, 'but we must be patient. From what I've seen these past days, once they think they have the girls suitably under control, they start exercising them even further afield, usually in groups of five or six at a time.

'There are trails beyond that far hillside, all of which are in daily use and eventually, I think, Corinna will be taken there. That is when we must be ready to strike, but we must prepare well, for we'll have but one chance and one chance only.' She drew the close-fitting cowl back from her head and shook her red tresses.

'We are but thirteen and you, my lord, are not yet anywhere near recovered, and they are many, even without the Vorsans to consider. Therefore, we must do everything we can to tip the odds in our favour.' She rose, without any apparent effort and stretched, catlike.

'I have an idea or two,' she said. 'While I was waiting for darkness, I had time to think of some possibilities. I have something in my saddle pack to show you and then you must despatch some men, out of uniform, to Erisroth. I will change into something suitable and they can pretend to be my retainers. The town is busy enough for no one to give us more than a passing glance, and hopefully I should be able to find somewhere to purchase the items I need.'

Attak'u seemed very pleased with Corinna's progress and, in particular, with his own part in it.

'Best trainer gets best ponies,' he said smugly, fingering one of her nipple rings as she stood looking out over the stall door. 'See chief and ask to keep you.' He grinned. 'Flix will be true champion one day, and now we go out for nice long drive.'

As usual, he led her towards the lightweight cart and guided her back between the shafts, coupling the links to her girth and laying the reins back towards the seat. This morning, however, instead of climbing aboard immediately, he turned back towards the buildings and disappeared inside the one the grooms used as their quarters, re-emerging after several minutes with a small bundle under his arm.

'Long day today, Flix,' he said, dropping his burden into the wooden box behind the driver's seat. 'Plenty good sights to see, far away from here. We maybe stay the night somewhere and come back tomorrow.'

Corinna stared at him, but would not have known what to say, even if the bit had allowed her the opportunity. She shook her head slightly, the bells on her ears tinkling. Amazing, she thought, he truly expected her to be pleased at his announcement. A day out and away from the slave farm, but who, she reflected ruefully, would be doing all the work?

And she knew exactly what *reward* would be coming at the end of the day.

'Everything will depend upon which route they use,' Jekka explained. Apart from the four sentries, the entire camp was gathered around in a circle, at the centre of which was a patch of bare, dusty earth. Drawing her short knife, Jekka drew an irregular line on the ground.

'That's the course of the river,' she said, and quickly added another two lines at slight angles to the first and to each other. She stabbed the point down and scratched a small cross. 'Up to this point is common,' she said. 'Once they've trained the girls initially, using the long field, this is the route they use, presumably to get them used to rough tracks and longer distances.

'However, this first part of the track is no good to us. There are stable buildings here and here, and the main Vorsan encampment starts here.' She added more symbols to her makeshift map and looked up. 'If we try to grab Corinna anywhere along here, we're bound to be seen and we'd also be cut off from three sides, probably four, as they could move men in behind us before we had time to retreat.

'The same applies to this branch of the track,' she added, indicating one half of the fork she had drawn. 'In fact, if anything, this is worse, as we'd be putting ourselves further away from any practical escape route. On the other hand,' she continued, tracing the second line again, 'this trail swings up and around and passes very close to the river.

'It actually runs along the bank at this stage,' she added, 'but just by there is a small Vorsan camp, so that's not much good to us. The best place is here, just further upstream.'

'You think the river is our best chance?' Savatch asked.

'It's our only chance,' Alanna interjected. 'I've been over the ground with Jekka and she's right. For about half a mile this trail is out of sight of everything and everybody, but to get clear from that section on horseback would take too long and also mean riding right through the thick of hundreds of soldiers.'

'Whereas the river,' Jekka said, 'swings away in a loop, here.' She emphasised the curve in her original line. 'The ground on the inside of the bend is also very marshy, impossible to ride over, so that puts a very useful natural obstacle between us and almost all the potential pursuers.

'About here,' she said, scraping at the earth again, 'about two miles before the river reaches Erisroth, is a trail leading almost directly due south for about a mile, at which point it enters some woodland and then splits into three.'

'Forcing any eventual pursuers to do the same,' Alanna said. 'The ground is very hard and horses aren't leaving any tracks at the moment, plus we can cover our trail for the first part.'

'In any case,' Jekka grinned, 'by that time we should have a head start of a few miles, as the two nearest practical crossing points on the river are fords here and here, both of which will require them to make detours. By the time they reach these woods, they'll have had to cover maybe six miles, all hard ridden, so their mounts will be pretty exhausted.

'Our horses will still have galloped two or three miles from where we leave the river,' she said, 'but a mile further along we'll have fresh mounts waiting. If we keep changing between the two sets of horses, they'll stay fresher for longer and we should be able to outrun any pursuit.'

'The only time we're likely to come close enough for any direct confrontation is back here.' Alanna leaned across and pointed to the river line. 'This is where the river passes close to that second Vorsan encampment, just before we reach the bend.'

'We have to assume that the alarm will have been raised by this time,' Jekka said. 'The Vorsans have sentries posted on every piece of high ground in the entire area, so someone is bound to see us when we first take Corinna. By the time we reach the camp they'll be alerted, but they won't be expecting the little surprise I'm cooking up for them.'

'The bottle of oil you showed us?' Savatch suggested.

Jekka smiled again. 'Not just one,' she said. 'By tomorrow the old man in Erisroth should have distilled sufficient oil spirit for at least ten, and we were able to buy that many glass flagons, which should break even easier, especially as the ground along the river bank could be a little soft.'

'But to throw these things as you described,' Savatch said, 'we would have to bring the boat in too close, surely? They'll have bows and spears and we'll be well within their range.'

'We'd be within bow range even if we kept to the far bank,' Jekka said, 'which is why there will be two boats. One with you, Corinna, Alanna and two of the men, the other with me and the rest of the men. Allowing that we need to have two men with each group of horses, that'll be five of us altogether.

'We'll go first and swing in towards whatever's on the bank waiting. Then, while we deliver our gifts, you'll come past behind us. With luck there should be a wall of smoke by this time. The old fellow was able to supply me with all the sulphur I needed and the leaves are commonly available hereabouts. I've had a quantity drying for the past few days.'

'The foul-smelling sack hanging in the trees over there?' Savatch said. He eased himself into a new position, stretching his right leg before him. 'Are you sure this will work, Jekka?' he asked, his right hand going unconsciously to the scar on his neck. Jekka raised her eyebrows and made a small moue with her lips.

'No,' she said, 'but it's the best I can do. Everything will be ready by tomorrow evening, after which we just have to wait until our black friend down there decides to take Corinna along the right path.'

'Which could be days yet,' Savatch complained.

Jekka regarded him steadily. 'I don't think so,' she said.

'That path is by far the quieter of the two and much better suited to the sort of training exercises he seems to favour.'

'They tell me you are now fully trained,' Fulgrim jeered, standing in front of Dorothea, his arms folded across his chest. Dorothea remained silent, the bit filling her mouth leaving her little other option apart from intelligible grunts. 'And your name is now Gol, I understand. I must say, these harnesses really do improve a woman's posture.'

He reached towards Dorothea's breasts and she willed herself not to flinch at his touch, determined not to give him that satisfaction. Besides, she reasoned, there was little more he could do to her that her handler had not done already. At first she had been relieved that her groom had been a Karliean, rather than one of the dusky Colrasians, but she quickly discovered there was little difference between them, apart from a few shades of brown.

The young Karliean – she did not know his name, but privately thought of him as 'Bastard' – had learned his trade well from the darker men and did not spare Dorothea the whip whenever he thought she was not trying hard enough. He also made it very clear that he was not prepared to make any concessions to the fact that she was several years older than the other novices, and assured her that she would either match their performances, or else suffer the consequences.

It had come as a great relief when Bastard finally told her that her training period was over, and even the news that Fulgrim had decided to take her as his personal mare did not totally dampen her lifted spirits. She could, after all, have been simply shipped off to the gods alone knew what fate, and some of the tales she had heard of what eastern masters inflicted upon their female slaves were enough to turn blood to ice.

The other alternative, that of being used as a working beast, was equally horrendous, for the girls she had seen in that role – usually the plainer ones, or those with heavier figures – received little respite from dawn till dusk. Fulgrim would doubtless treat her harshly, but at least she would find time to rest whenever he stopped to confer with his officers.

'I see they haven't bothered to lock your rings,' he said, as he led Dorothea towards the waiting trap. 'I assume that means you've been getting plenty of use, as I stipulated. Soon you'll have forgotten what it felt like to curl up with one of your little doxies. A good diet of cock is what you need.'

He backed her between the shafts and began fastening the connecting clips, fumbling slightly with the unfamiliar equipment.

'I wish now I hadn't ordered all you hair shaved off,' he said, stepping back at last. 'You would look far more striking with a proper mane, but then it'll grow back in time, as will my own. I see they've started shaving the sides and leaving the strip through the centre.' He reached out and ran a hand over the tufty re-growth, grinning all the while. 'It will go well with your face and this white blaze.'

He was referring to the white stripe down the centre of Dorothea's face, the only part of her that was not coloured dark brown with the long-lasting stain. They had not shown her what she now looked like, but she could well imagine, having seen enough of her fellow sufferers.

He walked back around in front of her and folded his arms once again, all the while grinning sadistically and chuckling.

'Let's see how well trained you actually are, shall we?' he said at last. 'Show me how you display yourself for your master.' Obediently, Dorothea shuffled her heavy feet apart and thrust her belly forward. Fulgrim made a low noise in the back of his throat and his hand went fleetingly to his groin, but he quickly regained his self-control.

'Hooves together, Gol,' he snapped. 'Your cunt will keep

for later, I'm sure. We're going to have plenty of time for that, you and I. Not to mention you and half my army!'

'We start right away,' Attak'u announced, walking alongside the shafts and vaulting easily into his seat. 'Good trot over the hill roads and then we have rest for nice fuck, eh? Good filly deserves good fuck.'

He shook out the reins and barked a command in his own tongue that Corinna had come to recognise, as she now recognised many of his curious sounding words. Obediently she leaned forward, raised her right leg and began to pull. Seconds later, Flix the pony girl was trotting smartly along the sun-baked mud track, bells at her breasts jingling as they bounced up and down to the rhythm of her stride.

The young soldier, whose name was Ceth, seemed very edgy, and Jekka guessed he had almost certainly never seen any real action. She had spent some time deciding which of the Illean troops to take with her, and finally decided that the least experienced of them would be the wisest choice, as they would probably be confronted with no more than two or three men, none of whom were likely to be Vorsans, and Jekka had more than enough faith in her own ability to deal with that.

Alanna, on the other hand, would need hardened fighters with her, as she would quite possibly be called upon to fight a delaying action against any early pursuers, and these would more than likely include trained soldiers from the nearest encampment. With luck, they would all be well on their way towards the waiting boats before the hue and cry started, but there was always the chance that they would be spotted sooner.

'You know what to do, don't you?' she asked quietly. They were crouching in the middle of a thicket, less than half a bow shot from the trail along which she had watched the black handler drive Corinna the previous afternoon. It had been a

235

temptation to try to take him out then, but there had been other vehicles up and down the track at regular intervals and two groups of Vorsans drilling within easy hailing distance.

Instead, Jekka had crept through the undergrowth and watched in silence as the fellow halted his sweating charge, jumped down, unhitched her from between the shafts and then mounted her from behind, violently humping until her moans and gasps grew to a ferocious climax. Shaking her head, Jekka had not waited to see if the performance would be repeated, quietly slipping away and making her roundabout way back to their own encampment.

On the way she had almost stumbled over two sleeping Vorsan troops, deep in the woods. By the time she left them again, she had ensured they would never wake again and nor would they, their corpses hidden under a pile of leaves and branches, be found without a properly organised search. Hopefully their officer would assume they had wandered off somewhere and drunk themselves insensible and, by next day, when someone started wondering why they had not yet returned, it would be too late to matter.

Meanwhile, she had two tabards with Vorsan crests emblazoned on them, one of which Ceth now wore over his jerkin. The other had been given to one of the soldiers with the change of horses, in order to alleviate the suspicions of any casual passers by who might be in that area.

'The black fellow is mine,' Jekka said. She lifted her crossbow slightly to emphasise the instruction. Ceth looked down at his own weapon and nodded. 'Once I've dealt with him, you cut the girl free and lead her back along the trail I've just shown you. If anyone gets in your way, shoot and shoot to kill, understand?'

'Yes, lady,' Ceth replied. 'I understand. I'm a pretty good shot with this, you know.'

'I don't doubt it,' Jekka said, 'but I don't suppose you've

ever killed anyone with it yet, have you? Don't worry, though,' she continued. 'We shouldn't run into any trouble and I'll be right behind you, just as soon as I've made sure that no one has got past Alanna's people.

'You'll have to keep a firm hold on the girl while you're running, as she won't have any arms to help her balance, right? There won't be time to free them, either, so don't even bother trying. As soon as you've cut her free from the traces, you run and keep on running. If you have to you pick her up, put her over your shoulder and carry her.'

'I'll not let you down, lady,' Ceth asserted, his young features set like granite. 'I'll die before I let anyone take her, my oath on it.'

'You'll be no good to any of us if you're dead,' Jekka said, 'so don't even think about it. Just get her to the boat in one piece – and yourself, too. There'll be plenty of time for heroics later, I'm sure.'

Corinna was beginning to understand what was meant by the expression 'champing at the bit', for the position of the sun told her it was already near to midday and still Attak'u had not returned for her. His continued absence was worrying, for their daily routine had become established for several days past, and the appearance of the gross Karliean male with him early that morning was in some sinister way to do with this interruption.

From Attak'u's subservient attitude, Corinna had guessed that the obese man was an important figure in the pony farm set-up, but quite what role he played she had no real idea. She was, however, grateful that she did not have the daily task of pulling his trap, for he was easily twice her own trainer's weight.

As the hours crawled by she began to get an uneasy feeling that perhaps that was it after all, that the grotesque fellow had decided to exercise his seniority and claim Corinna for his own use. The prospect made her shudder, and made her consider Attak'u in a totally different light.

She shook her head, setting her bell earrings jangling. They were finally getting to her, she realised, this regime dehumanising her to the point where she was almost ready to feel grateful to a man like the black Colrasian, a man who whipped her, drove her to exhaustion and then used her like a mindless animal.

Garassotta and its sumptuously furnished chambers, its soft carpets and heavy draperies, all seemed so far away now, dim memories of a world that once had been, but was no more. Now Corinna's world was this cramped stall, a floor strewn with straw, the heavy harness and bridle, and the boots that forced her to trot and prance on tiptoe, a show pony with no control over anything save her most base bodily functions and needs.

The sound of heavy boots on the gravelled earth outside brought Corinna out of her reverie and she looked up, astonished at how much she was looking forward to seeing the canine features of Attak'u again, and to be taken outside and hitched up to that damned little buggy.

Ceth had heard stories concerning the Yslander women: his father and two uncles and their father before them had all served long in the army of Illeum, and even soldiers who had not actually witnessed the prowess of the tall blonde women told their tales as if they had, embellishing fact with fiction, flavouring liberally with fantasy and stirring until the whole became legend. However, nothing the young trooper had been told quite prepared him for the actuality.

Crouching in the bushes, he watched with thumping heart as the girl came into view around the bend in the trail, the little buggy lurching along behind her, driver sitting upright,

238

flicking his whip across her shoulders. He tensed, waiting for Jekka to make the first move and then, when the pony girl and her driver were but fifty paces from them, from the opposite direction a part of four mounted Vorsans appeared.

Ceth relaxed again, convinced that Jekka would make no move in the face of such immediate odds.

But he could not have been more wrong.

With a blood-curdling yell the redheaded amazon leapt out into the centre of the track, firing on the run and sending the first Vorsan lurching out of his saddle, a crossbow bolt embedded precisely between his eyes.

The effect of this was that his horse reared up and the other horses, already startled by Jekka's shrill scream, shied likewise, one unwary rider thrown headlong. Before the remaining two had time to comprehend what was happening, let alone bring their spooked mounts back under control, Jekka had reloaded and fired again. At the same moment Ceth saw the black robed blonde figure of Alanna emerge from the undergrowth behind the Vorsans, and the last mounted man hit the ground a second or so later.

Leaving the one remaining live Vorsan, who had clearly been stunned by his fall, Jekka wheeled around and started running towards the pony girl and buggy. The black driver had reined her to a halt and was frantically trying to get her to turn, but the girl appeared to be transfixed and, though his whip rose and fell in a flurry of blows, she simply refused to move.

Seeing this, the man leapt to the ground, desperate to save his own skin, but Jekka, with a calmness that Ceth could only watch open-mouthed, dropped to one knee and raised the crossbow, which she had somehow contrived to reload on the run. Her aim was unerring, the bolt hitting the fleeing figure in the back of his neck and bursting through the front of his voice box in a shower of blood and gristle, travelling another twenty paces before it clattered to the ground, spent.

The man himself ran on for another three or four strides, his hands clawing upwards towards the gaping wound in his throat and then fell, silently, pink froth welling from between his lips, his eyes already glazing over in death.

'Go!' Jekka shouted, turning to Ceth, who had finally managed to get his legs moving. 'Cut the girl free and get her into the woods. Go on! I'll be right behind you.' She swung back again, to where the stunned Vorsan soldier was now finally staggering back to his feet, raising her right arm as she ran towards him. Ceth did not hear the twang of the hidden bow, but as he started towards the unmoving pony girl, he saw the man drop sideways, again clutching at his throat.

The flight through the woods and along the narrow back trail seemed to go on forever. The girl, as Jekka had warned, needed to be steadied at every step of the way, her arms pinioned to her sides in some sort of leather sleeve arrangements. Her feet, Ceth saw, were encased in oddly shaped boots, yet surprisingly these did not appear to hamper her progress.

Jekka quickly caught them up, her crossbow once again loaded and she ran on ahead, urging Ceth to get his charge moving quicker still.

'There were another six Vorsans just behind those four,' she cried, looking anxiously from left to right, eyes scanning the trees for any sign of movement. 'Alanna and her lads took care of most of them, but at least one got away. He was wounded but he was still in the saddle, so he'll be raising seven sorts of shit by now!'

'She can't run any faster, lady,' Ceth gasped, narrowly avoiding tripping over a projecting root himself. 'I'd carry her, but I wouldn't be able to move any faster than we are now. How much further is it, do you think?'

'Only a few minutes,' Jekka assured him. She came to a

halt and held up one hand, indicating that they should do likewise. 'Take a few moments,' she said quietly. 'Get your breath and just listen. We should be well clear for the moment, but it pays to take nothing for granted.'

To Ceth's relief they reached the riverbank without further incident and he lifted the bound girl into the larger of the two boats, alongside Savatch, who quickly pushed her down into the bottom of it. A moment later Alanna appeared from among the bushes to their right, immediately followed by the Illeans who had joined her in forming the rearguard party.

'Right,' Jekka called out, 'everyone knows which boat they're supposed to be in, so let's get moving. The sooner we get under way, the less chance they'll have to organise any proper reception for us downstream. And keep those lanterns closed against the breeze – we need those flames to be steady when the time comes.'

As if in a dream, Ceth found himself sitting towards the stern of Savatch's boat, paddle in hand and dipping almost maniacally into the water as it headed out into the midstream. Savatch himself had made his way to the stern post and had grasped the tiller oar in both hands.

'The current will do most of the work, lad,' he cried, leaning forward to tap Ceth on the shoulder. 'Save your strength and have your bow at the ready. The other boat will head between us and the Vorsan shore, but they'll still be in range, so feel free if you think you can hit anyone.'

The second boat, slightly smaller and narrower, slid past them after a few minutes, the unmistakable figure of Jekka standing in the stern, crossbow raised to her shoulder in readiness. Behind her one soldier held the tiller steady, while in front the remaining men crouched in a line, each already holding one of the glass bottles that Jekka had prepared the previous evening. The two lanterns, Ceth knew, stood in the bottom of the boat, out of sight, but ready to provide the flames to ignite the oil-soaked rags that stuffed each bottleneck.

For several minutes they continued downstream, no more than a length between the two craft, and then Jekka turned and raised an arm.

'Steer wider, Master Savatch,' she cried. 'The Vorsan camp is just around the next bend. Wait until we run abreast of them and then get past us as quickly as you can.'

If the alarm had reached as far as this particular Vorsan encampment, it had prompted little reaction, Ceth thought. Either that, or they had not expected the fugitives to use the river as an escape route, for only a handful of troops appeared to be taking much notice of them. Jekka, however, seemed determined to raise as much havoc and cause as much confusion as possible.

As Savatch steered the larger boat out towards the far bank, the lead craft bore in towards the shore. Ceth saw Jekka aim and fire and the first Vorsan toppled headlong into the water, a look of sheer astonishment on his face as he made a flailing grab at the bolt which had pierced his skull just in front of his ear.

At almost the same instant three of the bottles went spiralling skywards, hanging at the top of their arcs momentarily, the small flames flickering around the oiled wicks. Then, almost as one, they plummeted down onto the bank.

It seemed to Ceth that there was a short pause after they struck, and then a wall of flame erupted, followed almost immediately by a curious whooshing noise. The flash was almost blinding and he turned away instinctively, but even at such a range he felt the blast of hot air. When he looked back the wall of flame had become a wall of smoke, thick black clouds billowing out into the river, completely obscuring the Vorsans and their camp.

Jekka was still not finished though, and three more of the flaming missiles went curving through the air, adding their brilliant orange flashes and even more smoke to the chaos. Meantime, not a single shot had been fired in retaliation and suddenly they were past the danger and picking up speed as the river narrowed slightly and the current grew stronger.

In the smaller boat Jekka was jubilant. She punched the air, threw back her head and howled in triumph, her voice rising to such a high pitch that Ceth felt the hairs stand up on the back of his neck. Then, behind him he heard a deep chuckle and turned to see Savatch, leaning on the tiller oar, tears streaming down his cheeks. The older man shook his head, wiped his eyes with the back of one hand and let out a long deep breath.

'Amazing,' he said. 'Totally damned amazing. Give me a dozen more like her and I reckon I'd conquer the entire continent!' Further forward, Alanna turned and grinned back at him.

'A dozen Jekka's?' she cried. 'The gods spare us that. But fifty or so of those spirit bottles of hers and you'd rout an army, and that's for sure!'

Fulgrim studied the cowed figure for several seconds, before turning to Gorvan. The fat slave master seemed well pleased with himself.

'Well,' he demanded, 'does she not resemble the wench in the picture?'

Fulgrim frowned and rubbed his chin. 'There is a similarity,' he admitted, grudgingly, 'though it's hard to be sure with all that paint on her face, and the way the hair has been cut tends to give the features an entirely different aspect.'

'The hair can be covered with a fair wig,' Gorvan assured him, 'and the face stain will wear off in a few days or so. Luckily, Attak'u has not had his woman refresh it yet.'

Fulgrim took a couple of paces to his right, his eyes narrowing. 'Yes,' he said, 'I can see the resemblance now.

You and your people have done well.' He fumbled into the pouch at his belt and drew out two gold coins, which he proffered to Gorvan. 'Give this to the fellow – what was his name, Attak'u? He has earned it. Once we have done something with the hair and given her suitable clothing, from a distance no one would guess that this wasn't the real Lady Corinna.'

'What do you mean, she isn't Corinna?' The rescue expedition had finally halted, Jekka's plan having worked to perfection. The change horses, however, were now also beginning to tire and, picking two of the soldiers to drop back with her to form a rearguard, Jekka had instructed the rest of the party to ride on for a few more minutes and then rest before changing back again.

Savatch, although he would never have admitted it, was relieved to be able to spend a few minutes recovering. His wound and subsequent convalescence had taken more out of him than he cared to admit, and the headlong gallop had drained much of what strength he had regained since. Alanna's announcement, therefore, came as a hammer blow. He stared past her to where the girl had dismounted, her bit now hanging loose since Alanna had unclipped it. She seemed dazed and confused, but then that, Savatch reasoned, was only to be expected.

'Are you sure?' he said stupidly.

Alanna nodded grimly. 'Perfectly. She says her name is Mahari and she comes originally from Tamarinia.'

'But Jekka was so sure!' Savatch cried. 'How could she have made such a mistake?'

'She didn't,' Alanna said gravely. 'Not originally, anyway. Mahari tells me there was another girl – the groom named her Flix – and this other girl was brought to the farm just a matter of days ago.

244

'The groom – the driver Jekka killed – was indeed training her in the very cart from which we took Mahari, and would have been driving her again today, except that she was suddenly taken way on the instructions of the big chief.'

'Fulgrim?'

'I don't think so. Not unless he's put on a great deal of weight very quickly. She described this man as being enormously fat and the boss of the farm itself.'

'Does she know why Corinna was taken away?'

'Not exactly, but she overheard part of the conversation. Apparently Mahari's stall was next to Corinna's and she was listening when the fat man arrived this morning. Something to do with her looking something like the woman in a portrait the Vulcan general had.'

'Oh no,' Savatch looked at Alanna, completely aghast. 'No, tell me it can't be what I'm thinking. Oh, please the gods, not that.'

Alanna lowered her eyes. 'There cannot be another explanation for it,' she said quietly. 'You yourself mentioned the likelihood of Fulgrim finding himself a look-alike to fool the garrison at Garassotta. None of us, however, considered the possibility that he might find himself a look-alike who looked *that* much alike.'

'Then we have to go back for her,' Savatch cried, his face bright red. 'Fulgrim is no fool and he's bound to realise something before long. We can't leave her completely at that maniac's mercy.'

Alanna stepped forward and placed her hand on Savatch's arm. 'The fact that we tried what we tried will surely arouse his suspicions anyway,' she said. 'If he hasn't realised the truth already, it won't take him long, as you say. But even if he doesn't realise he's got the real Corinna, our raid will have put them all on their guard now. Going back would be sheer suicide, and we both know it.'

'Then what's to be done?' Savatch's shoulders slumped and his red face rapidly began turning grey.

Alanna maintained her grip on his arm. 'Whatever is to be done, if anything can be done,' she replied, 'it cannot be done here. We must continue as we originally intended and find somewhere safe to hide for a few days, somewhere to collect our thoughts and consider the possibilities. After that, who can tell? The road from here to Garassotta is quite long and there will be many days and many nights.

'Meantime, even if Fulgrim does realise the truth, Corinna will come to no real harm, nothing more than she has endured so far, anyway. That Vorsan pig may be vicious and vindictive, but he wouldn't be stupid enough to risk losing one of his major cards, would he? He obviously wanted the real Corinna alive in the first place, so he's hardly likely to kill her now. After all,' she smiled, in an effort to lighten the mood, 'he won't find a better Corinna look-alike than the one he now has, will he?'

'You understand simple Illean, I'm sure.'

Corinna stared at Fulgrim, struggling to keep her face as blank as possible. 'Everybody knows Illean, master,' she replied, adopting the thick Karliean accent she remembered from the old nurse who had once been her constant childhood companion. 'I have spoken Illean since I was very small.'

'Where were you born?'

Corinna remained unblinking. 'I don't remember.' It was a fair enough answer for a slave girl.

Fulgrim glared at her, and then a faint smile stole across his features. 'So, you don't know.'

Corinna smiled back at him, certain she would be violently sick at any moment. 'No, master,' she said. 'Was a long time ago now, when I was very small.'

'I dare say you were,' Fulgrim said. 'So, what is your name?'

'Flix, master,' Corinna replied dutifully.

Fulgrim shook his head. 'No, I meant your real name, the name you were called before you came here.'

'Demila, master.' Corinna had to think fast. She had told Attak'u that her name was Rina, but that was too close to the truth and Fulgrim might well draw the obvious conclusion from that. As far as she knew, Sprig had no idea of her real name, for she had never told it to him, but if they asked him he would certainly remember that one of Pecon's girls had been called Demila. With luck, he would be uncertain enough to confirm that it was her.

'Well, Demila,' Fulgrim said carefully, 'you look more like a Corinna to me.'

'Master?' Corinna looked up at him innocently, eyes wide.

'Corinna,' he said, 'is – or was – a very important lady.' He suddenly produced a gilt-framed miniature and thrust it under her nose. Corinna blinked and looked down at it, wondering how he had ever managed to obtain the little portrait. To the best of her knowledge, only four pictures of her had ever been painted.

'That me!' she cried, affecting a mixture of surprise and delight. 'Who painted picture of me, master?'

'If that's you, then you're Corinna,' he said.

She shook her head. 'No, master, I am Demila – Flix,' she added brightly.

Fulgrim tucked the miniature back into his belt pouch and placed his hands behind his back. He turned, walked a few paces, turned again and walked back.

'According to Gorvan's records, such as they are,' he said, 'you were bought from a travelling adventurer about fifteen days ago.'

'Master Pecon, master, yes,' Corinna agreed eagerly. 'Very good master.'

'I doubt that,' Fulgrim growled. 'So, how long were you

with this Pecon fellow?'

Corinna blinked and pretended to think. Eventually, she shook her head. 'Not sure, master,' she replied cautiously. 'Not long, but not short. Little while, I think.'

'And before that?'

How far could he check back?

'Cold country,' she said. 'Sorabund, very far in the north lands.'

'Well, little Demila, or Flix, or whatever,' Fulgrim said, 'either you really are as stupid as you sound, or else you're a good actress. Either way, it doesn't really matter, but I shall find the truth eventually.' he turned away, picked up the whip that lay coiled on the table and turned back to her, holding it up between them.

'This will get to the bottom of things,' he said. 'However, there is plenty of time and, as I say, it doesn't matter who you are, it's what you look like, and you look exactly right. The resemblance, even with your black and white face markings, is uncanny. So uncanny that it makes me think.

'And do you know what I think, little pony girl whore?'

'No, master, except maybe you want to fuck me. But then all masters do that.'

'Oh, I dare say I shall fuck you all right,' he leered. 'It would be a waste not to, especially as you look so fetching in your pony harness. But first I'll tell you what I think, shall I?

'I think that one coincidence – the fact that you look like someone who is important to a plan I have – one coincidence is fair enough. However, more than one coincidence... I'm not so certain.' He paused, examined the whip with exaggerated care and then looked at her again.

'Earlier today, the fellow who has been your trainer since you arrived here was killed. He was killed whilst driving one of your stable mates in the very same cart in which he has been driving you these past several days. The girl was abducted – a girl, I am told, who has been given markings almost identical to yours and with hair of the same colour.

'Now, given that this place is in the midst of a large military camp, this abduction was no opportunist affair. It was well planned and expertly executed, hardly the sort of operation to waste on a stupid slave girl who could probably be bought for a few krones.

'Reports tell of two women; one tall, almost white hair, an Yslander warrior woman, without a doubt. The other was similar in appearance, but with flame-red hair.

'Remind you of anyone, *pony* girl?' He uncoiled the whip, twisted it into a loop and suddenly snaked it around Corinna's right breast, pulling the braid tight again and snaring the soft mound at its base. Corinna was almost toppled off her towering boots and fell helplessly against him.

'For now,' he rasped, 'you can go on being a pony girl, if it amuses you. In fact, I have another pony you can work in harness with and the pair of you can pull me all the way to Garassotta.'

She could feel his hot breath against the shaven parts of her scalp, and was certain that he, in turn, must surely be able to feel her heart thundering against her ribs, even if he could not hear it.

'Princess or pony, it's all the same to me,' he sneered, stepping back and releasing his hold on her, though not before he had managed to stretch her breast painfully. 'It's a long road back to Garassotta,' he said.

'A long road to Garassotta, but after that there will be plenty more roads, too. And I think we both know what that means, don't we?' He turned to the Colrasian handler who had been standing quietly by the door all this time.

'Put her bit back in and get her harnessed up,' he ordered. 'And make sure from now on that everyone knows her name is *Princess* Flix.'

As the black fellow began to move, Fulgrim rounded on Corinna again.

'Princess Tits,' he chuckled. 'Very suitable. Very suitable indeed!'

Exciting titles available from Chimera

* * *

All **Chimera** titles are/will be available from your local bookshop or newsagent, or direct from our mail order department. Please send your order with a cheque or postal order (made payable to *Chimera Publishing Ltd*) to: **Chimera Publishing Ltd., PO Box 152, Waterlooville, Hants, PO8 9FS**. If you would prefer to pay by credit card, email us at: **chimera@fdn.co.uk** or call our **24 hour telephone/fax credit card hotline: +44 (0)23 92 783037** (Visa, Mastercard, Switch, JCB and Solo only).

To order, send: Title, author, ISBN number and price for each book ordered, your full name and address, cheque or postal order for the total amount, and include the following for postage and packing:
UK and BFPO: £1.00 for the first book, and 50p for each additional book to a maximum of £3.50.
Overseas and Eire: £2.00 for the first book, £1.00 for the second and 50p for each additional book.

*Titles £5.99. All others £4.99

For a copy of our free catalogue please write to:

Chimera Publishing Ltd
Readers' Services
PO Box 152
Waterlooville
Hants
PO8 9FS

Or visit our Website for details of all our superb titles and secure ordering
www.chimerabooks.co.uk